DODGE CITY PUBLIC LIBRARY
DODGE CITY, KANSAS

Y0-EIX-928

DATE DUE

71038

F (M) Russell, E S
The fortunate island
X38090

DODGE CITY PUBLIC LIBRARY
DODGE CITY, KANSAS

10001157
Dodge City Library

The
Fortunate Island

By E. S. Russell

THE FORTUNATE ISLAND
NICE ENOUGH TO MURDER
SHE SHOULD HAVE CRIED ON MONDAY

E. S. Russell

The
Fortunate Island

PUBLISHED FOR THE CRIME CLUB BY
DOUBLEDAY & COMPANY, INC., GARDEN CITY, NEW YORK
1973

71038

With the exception of Nolton H. Bigelow, M.D., who is only mentioned, all the characters in this story are fictitious, and so are the things that happened to them.

ISBN: 0-385-02838-5
Library of Congress Catalog Card Number 72–96255
Copyright © 1973 by Enid Russell
All Rights Reserved
Printed in the United States of America
First Edition

For Stan, of course.
And for Scamp and Frey and Capo,
who were my good companions.

AUTHOR'S NOTE

This book has a special meaning for me, and so I want to thank the good friends, generous advisers, and excellent teachers who helped me with it:
  William J. Adelson, M.D.
  Nolton H. Bigelow, M.D.
  Bernard F. Coffey, Detective Sergeant, Sharon, Massachusetts, Police
  Melvin C. Haddad, D.V.M.
  John L. Keeling, Funeral Director
  Willis A. Scott, M.S.W.
  M. Dale Giddings, B.S., Reg. Pharm., and best of brothers

Fortunate isle, the abode of the blest
—The *Aeneid,* Virgil

Chapter I

The Weidens would have been blessed beyond all other vacationers on the island if the only impediment to their peace of mind were the road to Graham Barstow's summer home. It was deeply rutted where it was not humped with surfacing stones, so overgrown as to resemble a path through a rain forest, and almost as steep as a wall. The old car quivered like an ancient stallion, then backed, snorted, and fought its way up, steam hissing out in front and black smoke billowing behind, while Kristin held her breath and John clung to his steering knob and swore steadily.

An omen, she thought. We shouldn't have come. We shouldn't be here. One of us shouldn't. It isn't going to work. It can't . . .

Halfway up the hill the road branched off to the right past a weathered illegible sign, but they continued to the top and emerged onto a circular area as flat as a dinner plate containing a mixed green salad. In the middle, confined by a ring of fragrant dust, was a creeping tangle of blackberry and honeysuckle and stiff little blueberry bushes covered with fruit, and pert black-eyed Susans and shy white daisies. Out of this rose a stunted black pine as unyielding as the salt wind that had deformed it, and tenanted by a furious blue jay. Beyond, clinging to the other side of the hill and facing the sparkling ocean, was a wide low house whose white cedar shingles were beginning to silver in required New England fashion.

"God!" he said, sweating and panting, as they came to a stop at the back door. "Barstow said to take the hill in low. What the hell else would you take it *in?*"

"A new car. That's what he must have meant. First get a new car. Then go up the hill." She laughed, to neutralize her now chronically acid humor.

He made an effort to respond lightly. "Tell you what. I'll be a sport and win the car raffle at the fair. How's that?" He wiped his face on his sleeve and grinned uncertainly.

"Very gallant. Thank you." She felt that someone else's smile—a reflection of his own, perhaps—was pasted awry on her face.

The foundation of their marriage had deteriorated steadily since that rainy night in Michigan three years ago on their way back from the Coast, when she had fallen asleep at the wheel, and never had any attempt to rebuild it been so circumscribed by fear. So they sat looking around, afraid to move, afraid to commit themselves to the unbroken privacy they would have to share for two weeks under the Barstow roof. For her it would be an extension, a costly futile relocation, of their misery. For him it would be a trap, which he himself had chosen although it was the kind he had always avoided so adroitly.

"Why are we sitting here when the house awaits?" he said a few moments later. "It looks great. All the comforts of home."

"I'm not so sure I wouldn't sit here if this wreck were an air-conditioned Rolls with hot and cold running scotch. Or doesn't that make sense?"

"No, it doesn't. And if you're getting one of your hot flashes again, keep it to yourself."

"What I meant was, the Barstows will be with us even though they aren't here. Their personalities must be stamped all over the place. And right now I just can't cope with anybody we know, even at one remove. If that consulting job in Africa came up right now and there were money for me to go too, I couldn't make that either—and Africa's about as far away as you can get from everything and everybody we're familiar with. I'm—wrung out. I don't have anything left inside. Now, anyway."

"Don't start analyzing things *now,* for godsake! I'm not in the mood. I'm a hell of a lot more tired than *you* are."

Yes, she thought. It's very hard driving one-handed, although driving is one of the few things you can still do—and remind me of constantly. But you won't let me drive you anywhere anymore. That's another way you have of twisting the knife. I do five times what I used to do, to fill in the gaps. Maybe I've done too much. Maybe it was wrong. . . .

2

The dog stirred behind them, standing to stretch and look out of the window, and she reached back to open the door for him. "Go on, Frey," she said worriedly. "A walk will do you good." But he dismissed the scenery with a grunt and flopped down again.

If they had pulled into a motel parking lot, he would have been off like a rocket to the shrubs and the kids and the pool, and they would have followed immediately, Kristin grateful to see strange faces and relax in a room that had accommodated too many people to retain even its own obtrusive personality, John impelled to seek the facile reassurance and admiration that strangers gave and forgot so readily. But a blue jay was a blue jay to Frey, who was accustomed to giving back as good as he got from the jays at home, and the prospect offered nothing new and intriguing, and the ocean's special lure was too distant for him to recognize. So he yawned and fell asleep again, and John yawned too, saying that it was catching, and they continued to sit and gaze about.

A luxuriant garden—a thrifty one, New Englanders would say—began at both sides of the door and stretched symmetrically along the back of the house and part of the turnaround in a welcoming arc. On either side of the step were little squares and circles of kitchen herbs identified by handmade weatherproof signs and separated, as in a formal garden, by tiny paths paved with pebbles and crushed shells. Then came masses of flowers skillfully chosen to blossom continuously, and grouped so that each kind enhanced the color and texture of its neighbors. Homely hollyhocks, shorter now in their second bloom, nodded over them like sleepy nursemaids, and all were guarded by towering sunflowers, their worshiping faces easily fourteen inches in diameter, that clustered at the ends of the arc. And it was apparent that the same hands that had fed the sandy soil and created such splendor had trimmed the brush on the crest of the hill, ensuring the flowers tempered ventilation and gentle screening from the ever-present wind.

"I can't believe it," she murmured. "Did you ever see such a garden? It's a work of genius, absolute genius. The best garden I ever had was a Boston schoolyard compared with this. What a horrible way to start a vacation—with an inferiority complex. If the inside's anything like the outside, I'd just as soon leave . . . John, what are the Barstows like?"

He had said nothing about them, and, for too long, little about anything else. Yesterday, deliberately to provoke her, he would have told her to stop prodding him. Today, now, he grasped the excuse to stay where he was, and talk. "I never met his wife. Barely met him, if it comes to that. He's always off somewhere, according to Nesmith."

"Nesmith?"

"Acting department chairman. Not as big a wig as Barstow but— Anyway, Barstow's a nice guy. Well liked. Friendly. Long lean mountain-climbing type—about fifty-five, I'd say. Bouncy as a mountain goat, though god knows how he manages that in this weather! I liked him and I'm sorry he's leaving just when I finally get there. Personally I think he's crazy to resign. I made it after teaching everyplace else for fifteen years—I'll never leave! What does he think he can find that could possibly equal the university, let alone surpass it!"

She wondered too. The Olympus of education, John had always called it. "Did he say?"

"Yeah. After twenty-five years there he wants a whole new bag, a new lease on life. I can see that, I suppose, but what a switch! He drops the chairmanship and national exposure for a lousy assistant superintendency in a town like Hollybrook! It isn't a question of money, although he told me he'll actually be making a little more now. He's loaded, what with all his books and guest lecturing and consulting. And he's got private means too—a Brahmin from way back. But I still think he's nuts."

"What is he renting for?"

"A gesture, I guess, what with me coming and him going. I happened to remark that we didn't have a reservation yet, and he said he'd appreciate us staying here while he winds up at the university and moves."

"At a hundred and fifty dollars a week it's hardly a gesture."

"We're damn lucky, Kris! The island's bulging at the seams with the fair about to start, and there isn't a thing to be had here for a piece of August. Certainly not for anything I can afford. And they

4

were willing for us to take Frey. Most people won't let you take a bird in a cage!"

For three months he had talked about making a reservation and delayed attending to it, but he had rejected her offer to do it. There were still some things he could do, he had said, even if he was a cripple.

"Do they have kids?"

"Suppose so. Plenty of snapshots in his office. Why?"

"Oh, just a thought."

He was beginning to get restless and bored. "How about it? Ready to go in?"

That too was a gesture. He was no more ready than she, or he would have gone in by himself.

"Oh—it's nice just to sit and do nothing—something we haven't done for a long time." An intricately scented breeze cooled her hot face and as she inhaled it deeply the taut strings of her thin body began to loosen. "Mmmmmm . . . honeysuckle and salt water and spicebush and fish—what a mixture! It just doesn't smell this good anywhere else in New England."

"Partly it's the altitude. This is the second highest point on the island—two hundred fifteen feet, Barstow said. He says that on a clear day you can see shipping in the Lisbon roads."

"I'd settle for that loft over the pier at West Harbor. It was for sale last summer. I've always wanted to live here."

"Oh sure. You had to be practically carried off Fish Pier a couple of weeks ago," he said nastily, and got out of the car and leaned against it.

That was very different, she thought sadly. Last summer she had been sketching on the village pier, happy and content for a few hours by herself while he was fishing with some college faculty friends he had invited over for the day. A few weeks ago they had given him a farewell party to celebrate his long-sought appointment to the university, and somehow they had wound up on Boston's Fish Pier after eating too much rich food and drinking too much liquor despite the heat. . . .

The broadening silence swelled with the cicadas' high-pitched hum, a continuous pervasive sound that seemed to acquire material presence so that it lay like a pulsating net across the air. Under it the daisies bowed to restless bumblebees, and monarchs and swallowtails stitched a jagged pattern of orange and black and yellow, plummeting to loop shepherd's-purse into a pink and white fringe. Shy chewinks safe among the scrub oaks commanded everyone to drink tea, and the jay, calm now, was sending flutelike messages from his pine branch. The sky was so deeply blue, so clear, so vast, that the infinity of space seemed to Kristin a demonstrable and achingly wondrous fact, and the fragment of life that was herself confirmed, accepted, by it, not lost somewhere under its unimaginable reaches. So for a little time she felt herself to be a part of the furnishings of the landscape, part of the long bright peace of this summer afternoon, part of the dream that life always became for her on this lovely speck of earth so similar to home in ways that could be quantified, yet so different simply because it was separated from the mainland by two hours' worth of salt water.

At length she sighed and grasped the door handle with the determination of one about to take an icy plunge. "Come on, babe," she said to the hundred-fifty-pound monster in the back. A liquid brown eye blinked at her languidly. Clucking with worry, she got out to see what was the matter with him. "Listen, Frey, if you don't get out of this wreck and *go,* you'll blow up and burst," she warned, putting a gentle hand on his forehead.

"Does he have a fever?" John said with concern. This at least, and his feeling for the kids, had remained constant.

"I don't think so. His eyes don't have that hot glitter. Come on, ol' sweetie, come on and get up. There. Attaway. Now."

Dusty ground might have been something Frey had never seen before, and he stepped down onto it as if it were a bed of hot coals. Instantly the blue jay aimed at him a barrage of obscenities like so many machine-gun bullets, but with the majesty of an aging lion he ignored it as he made a stately progress around its little kingdom. They watched worriedly, but when he began lumbering after the butterflies John unlocked the door and they went in.

And stopped short, blinking.

Chapter II

The long entrance hall was dark, since the curtains in the rooms giving onto it were closed, and there was hardly a glimmer of light at the other end. But all the hot musty air in the house appeared to have been funneled into it. An odor of damp potting soil and decaying matter was so concentrated that the atmosphere seemed opaque. The cause was benign enough, as they soon discovered, but Kristin recoiled and touched the door. All at once the bright afternoon on the other side of it was very far away.

John felt for the light switch. "Whew! Let's air this place out—quick! Barstow said his caretaker's supposed to do it every day."

They tiptoed down the hall and hurried from room to room pulling back curtains and opening windows.

"It's absurd but I feel we're—trespassing," she whispered, and jumped when he said, "What're you whispering for, for crissake! Let's unpack and get something to eat."

"Let's take a good look first. Who knows—maybe we'll decide not to stay." She gave a little shudder. "Garden or no garden, the Barstows will never make it, welcomewise, with that hall. Plants are supposed to freshen the air, but there are too many here, and they've been overwatered. It smells like open graves after a tropical storm to me."

They were in the large kitchen, which hung some two feet lower than the rest of the house on the slope of the hill. With its curtains closed it had seemed like a dark cave, but it was flooded now with light from three sides. Over the sink were two small windows; opposite them a Dutch door with six panes, leading to a railed sun deck. A picture window in the long wall overlooked the green hill that fell into the ocean: a glittering lavender-blue wash that faded to palest gray and then merged with the far horizon—or slid over it into Portugal, possibly, she thought.

"No wonder they let us take Frey," she said, pointing to an empty bird cage over the sink and several plastic bowls on the drainboard. "They must have a zoo. Oh, look at that washer and dryer! For once I won't have to hassle the laundromat and waste a lot of time." She smiled wryly. "So I'll be free to labor in the Barstow Botanical Garden, I guess. It's an evil plot, John. Someone in the Ironical Department is having sport with us."

Along all the window sills, and hanging from wall brackets, and standing on the table, and spilling down from cabinet tops, were dozens of thrifty begonias.

"My god, doesn't Mrs. Barstow do anything else but take care of them!" She regarded with an unfriendly eye the heaps of dead and dying blossoms that fall daily from this exuberant plant. "I never could stand begonias. Come on, let's see the rest of the place. I didn't notice, but maybe they've got philodendrons in the other rooms. I didn't notice much of anything, actually." She went hopefully up the steps into the living room, which was directly behind the sun deck.

A neat, independent philodendron hung from a bracket near the huge picture window that framed the glorious expanse of sky and ocean, but there were scores of other plants, most of them varieties of begonia. They stood in a long row under the window and on the mantel and on the coffee table and in odd spaces on the crowded bookshelves which covered the wall opposite the fireplace. Their containers were a handsome and imaginative collection garnered from all over the world, ranging from the hands of eager experimenters in island cellars to potter's wheels that had ceased to twirl five hundred years ago, half a world away.

The furniture was a pleasant mixture of rattan, iron, and antique cherry and maple, with bright cushions. The coffee table had been made from an enormous and very beautiful piece of driftwood that weighed at least three hundred pounds. A thick fiber rug covered the polished hardwood floor. On either side of the hearth was a basketwork bed, one large, one small. Everything was clean and orderly, and the bits and pieces here and there, memorabilia of a lifetime, gave the room a comfortable look.

"But not a warm look, not a friendly look," she murmured as John went to try out the couch, and she turned to examine the books as if they could tell her why. But she discovered only that the Barstows read everything from archaeology—through botany, law, pedagogy, psychology, and sexology—to zoology. And they grouped the books whimsically. *Lassie* was sandwiched between *The Naked Ape* and *The Human Zoo,* and three colorfully jacketed Ian Flemings and two Spillanes stood boldly among Ellis, Karpman, and Krafft-Ebing.

"Well, I can answer my own question now," she said thoughtfully. "Let's go on before I—" and stopped abruptly.

"Before you *what?* Oh, never mind!" he said impatiently. "I'd like to unpack and eat and take a nap. That's a pretty good couch. Not long enough, though."

"Too bad," she said crossly, going into the hall. "It still smells terrible in here. I guess it always does, although you'd think a house in full sun would never feel damp. Did he say anything about which bedroom to use?"

"Why would he? We'll use the master bedroom, of course. It must be this one, on the left."

"Obviously! It has its own bathroom."

"What's biting you?" he said angrily, but she did not answer because he did not really want to know. He functioned successfully on a professional level, not only because of his competence but because of his lifelong guardedness against invasion. You did not have to be deeply personal with colleagues, and if you were attractive your looks and manner masked your hollowness, and everybody liked you, even envied you, and you were safe. But at home it was harder to hide, and you fought desperately. . . .

Silently, separated by a virtually unbridgeable distance, they looked about the master bedroom and bath, and then she read the titles of a pile of books on a night table and wondered which of the Barstows was studying up on law, while he examined an ornately framed family tree that hung opposite the bed.

In its lower left-hand corner, in spidery old-fashioned handwriting done with a split nib, was the signature Jonathan Nathaniel Barstow, and the date December 25, 1912. The earliest date on the tree was 1674 (Aaron Barstow), the most recent, 1957 (John Barstow).

"Here's Graham," he said, pointing. "1916. Married Myra Sandison. That makes him young John's great-uncle. Hmmmm . . . funny . . ."

"What's so funny?" she said somewhat hysterically. "I've always hated the name Myra. It means death! And there are nine more sopping wet plants in here and three in the bathroom. On the toilet tank! Three!" She sat on the end of the bed, unwilling to continue exploring.

"Look at this. Someone must take this down periodically and add to it. The ink's different all through this part, starting with old Jonathan's issue, which includes Graham. Jonathan, Junior—1900 —was twelve when he made this—must've been a Christmas present for his parents. But his wife and kids and their spouses and kids have been added in different ink—blue—along with their birth years. Myra's birth year isn't on it, though."

Two weeks was all the time John was willing to devote to patching up the morass of charges and countercharges that their marriage had become. Unless she tried very hard to co-operate, there would be no chance to retrieve what they could during a vacation that had come too late and would end too soon. She got up to look.

"No birth year—and no issue. That's what I thought." Sadly she stared at the limb of the tree that had ceased to grow and bear fruit.

"Why? What're you thinking of *now?*" he sneered.

"If you were interested I'd tell you gladly." Oh god, why did I say that! she thought. "Come on, we might as well finish the tour."

Two doors faced each other across a short narrow hall at right angles to the entrance hall. The room at the back was furnished sparsely and contained no plants. "Probably it's the guest room," she said in relief and lifted the hem of the bedspread. "Yes, it must be a guest room. This is a trundle bed. What about the other one? Isn't it silly! We were in there just a few minutes ago and I can't remember what's in it."

"You were never known for your powers of observation."

The fact was that neither of them had been in it. Sandwiched between the kitchen, the bathroom at the end of the hall, and the back room, it had only one window and with its curtains closed was so dark that they had passed it the first time without noticing it.

It was a study, unmistakably masculine and having an intensely private air that seemed to meet them at the threshold and bar their entry. Kristin hesitated in the doorway, and then she marched to the window, reached across a shabby comfortable couch to draw back the curtains, and pushed up the sash with undue force, asserting her right—if not her wish—to be there.

"Thank god there aren't any plants in here either!" she said in angry gratitude.

The one noteworthy feature of the room was a pegboard that covered nearly all of one wall and displayed in attractive patterns a number of things that the Barstows had found all over the island. Stones, bits of minerals, dried plants, old artifacts of red man and white, shells, tiny sun-dried skeletons, butterflies and moths, and much more: they were not, with the possible exception of an ancient flint cutting tool, individually valuable. But the aggregate, a celebration of Earth's treasures, was priceless, because implicit in it was the love the Barstows bore for this island which provided it.

"That's some piece of work," he said. She stood like a statue. "I wonder if Barstow ever thought of showing it at the fair."

"'Deed he *does,* Dr. Weiden. Has every yee-yuh since they *ben* hee-yuh," said an upcountry voice in a leisurely, intimate tone. "Brung it down two weeks ago. Drives a hackney in the hoss show, too."

They turned, startled, to see a scrawny little wrynecked man in filthy clothes leaning against the door frame and chewing on a straw. A hard-working prosperous farmer, he looked like a wharf rat who had been washed ashore years ago in the same outfit.

"I'm Dr. Bah-stow's cay-uh-tak-uh. Perley Stokes from the vil-lij. Jes making' cer-tin you folks got hee-yuh all right. Open the winders'n cur-tins in the maw-nin, close 'em at night, but my mare dropped 'er foal at dawn so I couldn't come air out the place like I ben do-in'. Watered all them plants yesterday, though. Any-thin' yuh want, why you folks jes let out a holluh. May have a mite a trouble with the plumbin' in the hall bahth. Son Toby's a plummuh. Ben workin' on it but he ain't satisfied yet."

His busy eyes, the knowing tilt of his head, and an insolent tinge in his voice and stance belied his friendly greeting, as had his silent entry. He looked as if he had been watching them for a long time.

Kristin disliked him instantly. She had met this type before—the professional hayseed, the quaint character, whose contempt, mistrust, and envy of the tourist trade were surpassed only by his determination to milk it dry from Father's Day to Labor Day, and buy peace and insularity for the next nine months.

John said, "Thanks, Mr. Stokes, that's very nice of you. I guess we'll manage all right. Dr. Barstow gave me your number, of course. We've been opening the windows out and looking around."

"Oh, there's lots t'see in this house," the farmer agreed, and again Kristin caught that insinuating inflection in his voice. " 'Deed there is. Well, I'd best be go-in'." He gave them a nod and a little tug of his old hat and left as noiselessly as he had come.

"Now what did he mean by that?"

"How the hell do I know! For godsake, Kris, what's the matter with you! He was just being neighborly. It's a great house—"

"Is it? Did you hear what he said? That Barstow's going to show that pegboard at the fair—and drive in the horse show. John, are they going to be here—with *us*? Did you arrange that? Without even telling me? Is *this* your idea of going away to work things out?"

"It wasn't exactly definite. They may come tomorrow afternoon," he said evasively. "But what difference will it make? They'll only be here until Sunday afternoon or evening anyway. We could hardly expect them to stay somewhere else when we're only going to use one room. We're damn lucky—"

"Are we? How long the Barstows stay isn't the point and you know it!"

"Look, Kris, we'll have most of the two weeks alone, just like I promised. I don't understand. You ought to be glad—"

"About what? You *knew* I didn't want to come here. You knew

—you *know* what I hoped to do. I'm not springing anything on you. Frey hasn't been well, for one thing—"

"Jesus Christ! I need a vacation and so do you, but anyone would think you cared more about a dog than about us!"

"There you go again! When I suggested boarding him, you said you wouldn't consider it, but all of a sudden I care more about my dog than about my husband. All right! You want me to thank you? *Thank you.* Are you satisfied?"

"It's a start."

"What is? Thanking you? For pulling another of your little stunts? If those plants didn't get any water and light for a month they'd have a better chance of making it than we do."

"Oh, for godsake don't go symbolic on me. It's just too hot."

Red lights gleamed in her short curly hair, but her gray eyes, usually large and very clear, were dim with tears. "Yes, of course. And in January it was too cold. Or you've been too busy or too tired or too *some*thing the last three years to do anything but dodge and run. The trouble is, most of the things that take you away, that divert your attention from us, are valid enough. Suppose that consulting job in Africa finally came through? Or suppose they want you back in L.A. for another shot? You'd *'have'* to go! Only, what has more priority, your career or our marriage? The one thing that's hung us up ever since we met was your refusal to accept your share of responsibility for our fights. Everything wrong was always *my* fault! Always! All you choose to remember about the accident is that I was driving. But I begged you to stop somewhere because we were both exhausted and it was my turn to drive—and you refused to stop. Was I supposed to drag you out of the car singlehanded? Do you remember *that?* And do you think two weeks—less!—in someone's summer house can give us the help we need? We could buy a lot of therapy with the rent money for this place, and all the other money we'll spend here—"

"Forget it. We don't need a shrink." He unbuttoned his short-sleeved shirt and took it off, slipping it with exaggerated care over the stump of his left arm. He had had the left sleeve of almost all his dress shirts and jackets shortened, and tailored with buttons on the cuff, to show the pale mutilated skin. And to challenge her more than anyone else with the sight of it. Rarely did he wear his hook or the cosmetic arm and hand. "Whatever we have to do, we can do by ourselves."

"How? By paying to fight here? Or paying not to talk at all? We might as well have stayed home and used the money for a new car. We haven't talked in years. You don't talk, you indict! Everything's gotten worse, not better," she said hopelessly. "I've begged your forgiveness, I've done everything I know how to make it up to you—"

"You'd have to go pretty far to make up for this!" he shouted, thrusting the stump at her.

But he had used this melodramatic ploy too often. "How far?" she said quietly. "How far would I have to go? How far do you want me to go? Because I'm ready."

"What's gotten into you! Are you going to throw away twenty-three years of marriage and the kids because of a few fights?"

"Are you?"

"What are you talking about? Polly and Josh—"

"Polly and Josh are old enough to stand on their own feet. Either we get professional help—together—or I'll leave you. Is that clear enough?"

"Very. But don't start in on it again, not now. And don't tell me I'm ducking. Look, we're here, so let's enjoy ourselves. We could use the change—"

"Is that all you have to say?"

"Right now it is," he said coldly. But something new in her manner frightened him. "Look, Kris, let's make a deal. Forget everything for now, put it aside. This heat's making everything look worse than it is, that's all, and we're tired and depressed. The island will do you good, the way it always used to. You were always happy here. We'll have two weeks to work things out—"

"And then?"

"You'll see. It'll be better." He put his arm around her, crushing her to him, and whispered thickly, "You'll see, Kris."

She pushed him away, her face stiff with contempt. "I'm ashamed for all the times I fell for that gambit because it makes me just as much to blame as you are. We kiss, we make love, and things keep getting worse between us anyway, after a little while. Don't ever try that again. It's an insult to both of us. We're not animals."

His eyes were heavy-lidded, his fair skin flushed with desire which, except for anger, was all she aroused in him anymore, but he surprised her by stepping back instantly and putting his arm behind him. "Would you rather skip unpacking and go get something to eat? We could go to the beach and relax."

Suddenly he seemed so anxious, so childishly sincere in his wish to please, that she softened momentarily. "I'd like that. Oh, John, if we work together, maybe we can make it after all."

"Maybe. Do you love me, Kris?"

"I—don't know. I did. You know I did. Now . . . I feel too bruised—" He laughed ironically. "Go ahead and laugh. Do you think you're the only one who's suffered?"

"I've lost a hell of a lot more."

"I wonder. It always seemed to me, before the accident, that the most and worst anyone could lose was love. And the most and best they could gain was—love. Right now all we've got is old habits and anger. Hatred. I'm getting so desperate I can't hide it any longer. I've lost my balance, my sense of humor. I'm angry most of the time, which isn't fair to you. And I'm scared."

"You always had a lousy temper, Kris." His voice was tender now, but when he kissed her gently contempt flared in her again.

"The same thing all over again, isn't it! I admit some of *my* shortcomings, I criticize *my* behavior, and you kiss me and forgive me! Don't touch me again!"

"I'm going to unpack," he said furiously. "And on second thought, we'll use the guest room till the Barstows leave. I will anyway. They're entitled to their own room. You can do as you goddam please." He stamped out.

She stood there for a moment, too dejected and apprehensive to be angry, and then, because she had no choice, went out to the car to help.

Frey was lying on the cool step, panting in ragged whistling gusts, so they did not disturb him. But it was very hot, and after making several one-armed trips over his vast bulk with food cartons, suitcases, and loose items, John finally exploded at him.

"If you'd use your appliance for once!" she cried. "What's the matter with *you*? Can't you see he isn't feeling well? For someone with *your* great powers of observation—!" and she yanked out the drawers in the guest room dresser as he flung open the closet door.

"Now what are we supposed to do? These drawers are stuffed!"

"So's the closet." He took out an expensive suit tailored in the latest mode and held it up. "This must be Graham's—looks like his size and style. The rest of it too."

"It seems as if everything he owns is here. And the other closet was pretty full too. I don't like to move anything but I don't plan to live out of a suitcase for two weeks, either. We'll have to make space in their room after all."

The closet in the master bedroom was less crowded. "But there's a complete wardrobe here," she said. "Dresses, blouses, slacks—" She took a pair off the hanger and held them to her waist, shook her head as she hung them up, and examined a row of shoes on the floor. They were large and plain but all of them were clearly women's footwear. "Graham Barstow may be a clotheshorse, but I'm afraid his Myra is built like a mastodon."

"Then whose are these?" he demanded, holding up a scrap of sheer black lace and opening it out for her to see. "Underpants—from the Combat Zone Collection in Washington Street. Embroidered slit in the crotch, too. Very chic. There's a pile of them here. How do you explain that?"

All at once she felt unbearably melancholy. "Wishful thinking, I guess," she said slowly as he folded the little panties and put them back. "And it looks as if they sleep in separate rooms too. John, must we stay here? Can't we—"

"Are you out of your mind? What do I care if the Barstows don't see eye to eye? Let's just relax—"

"How *can* we? How *can* we work on our marriage in a place that has what looks like the same problem? After spending two days with them we'll be—we'll be so much more infected that we'll never be able to get anywhere! Can't you feel it? It's an unhappy house. I felt it the moment we walked in. And it's stronger now. There must be a deep division between them—all those plants except in his two rooms. There's something—"

"If you don't want to stay I'll take you back to the ferry and then you can get the bus home. It'd be small loss if you did. *I* am staying. I'm going to eat something and then I'm going to stretch out on the couch—"

Suddenly Frey began to bark wildly.

Another station wagon, a new Chrysler driven by a woman and containing a frantic collie and a Siamese cat, stopped behind the Weidens' Chevrolet. A moment later a bright yellow Porsche roared up the hill.

The Barstows had arrived, at John's invitation, a day too soon.

Or had John known all along that they would come today? She suspected that he had, and when he tried to hide his relief she knew that she was right.

Chapter III

Early on Saturday after Perley Stokes had driven off to the fair with Graham Barstow's pegboard on the back of his truck, Kristin said, "Frey's fagged out, John, so would you mind if I leave you at the fair for a while? I'd like to take him to a vet."

The question was a formality, part of the game of manners they had been playing since the Barstows' untimely arrival. If she could have cared less what he minded or didn't mind, she would have. Like something programed by a computer and manipulated by a puppeteer, she graciously helped carry Myra's floral babies to the new station wagon, wishing every moment that she could hurl them one by one into the ocean.

"Let's leave Frey here to rest, Kris," John said for the Barstows' benefit when they were ready to go. "Come take a look at that car I'm going to win for you. Then we'll come back together for him."

"Fine!" she said gaily, and as they followed Graham's bright Porsche down the hill she bit her lip to keep from crying. Since yesterday she had been subjected to an unremitting test of her control, and she was exhausted.

Myra had assumed that she was expecting them, that John had told her about their good fortune in getting the last two spaces on the extra boat. "Graham won't go anywhere without his car, so we were very lucky. But then, the ferry always runs extra boats for the fair. I'm so glad, aren't you?"

Graham had assumed that she and John were sleeping together. "You must take the master bedroom—after all, it's your vacation, and anyway I may do some work tonight. Myra and I don't share a room when I'm winding up another manuscript."

Both had assumed that she and John were dining *al fresco* with them on the sun deck, so all of them jostled each other preparing supper. "Isn't this fun!" Myra said. "Just like a picnic," Kristin said.

The Barstows and John had assumed that she would enjoy a dreary evening of university shop talk undisturbed by the coughing and moaning of Dandie the collie, who had a cold and was conspicuously in heat, and the grunts and snarls of Frey, who was unwilling to oblige the restless animal.

And John had assumed from her charming response to the Barstows that she was as glad of their presence as he. He had fallen asleep instantly, and she had spent an interminable night rigid and sleepless by his side in a bed too narrow to accommodate them and the chasm between them. When a light rain began to fall, the odor of soil and decay intensified throughout the house, and the atmosphere became so oppressive that it alone could have made her night the misery it was.

Her tension was obscured by the bustle attending breakfast, the removal of the pegboard, and Myra's last-minute selection of plants and containers to display at the fair. But the moment she and John were alone again and confined in their car, the feeling between them became intolerable and each spent the time honing and polishing the charges to be leveled against the other.

The day was fresh and clear, the fairground mobbed, and the narrow roads converging on it jammed with cars. The Barstows, having display space in the Grange Hall, were able to park next to the old building and leave their cars there, but she and John had to drive around for a quarter of an hour before finding a spot almost a mile away. It was impossible for them to talk to each other, and by the time they reached the admission booth they were seething. But once he had pushed through the turnstile his behavior changed predictably. Like a child he thrust off tension as though it were a cloak, and prepared to enjoy himself. He had even put on his cosmetic arm and a long-sleeved shirt so that his fun would not be spoiled by staring strangers.

Well, why not? she told herself, trying to be fair. You'd have to be a dedicated masochist who was also deaf, dumb, blind, and paralyzed to walk around *here* with a big chip on your shoulder. Only, what's our marriage worth to him? Doesn't he want to fight for it? For me?

She trailed behind him, stunned by the enormous weight of her anger and despair, and looked dully at the Chrysler New Yorker station wagon being raffled off. A splendid vehicle just like Myra's, it was festooned with miles of red, white, and blue bunting, as if supporting Chrysler Motors were a patriotic duty. In bursts of fealty, optimism, and pessimism people were taking out their money as they chattered excitedly about the car, and John bought five tickets and insisted that she hold them.

"Hey, there's a Greek food stand," he said happily. "Want some shashlik?"

"No, I'm not hungry, thanks. I'd like to go look at the animals."

"Okay. If I'm not here in an hour go home and get Frey and come back for me. I'll be at the gate. It's a great day, isn't it! I'll put in an appearance at their booths while I'm at it. Might as well be courteous to our hosts."

"Hosts! We're paying them!"

He threw up his hands, one open and stiff with anger, the other curved in a natural position, painted, and with his class ring on one finger. "Are you starting that again? Go see the animals, for godsake. I'll see you later."

Simultaneously they turned their backs on each other.

As she walked on her attention was caught by a stocky powerful young man whose mop of orange hair clustered in wet curls, ancient Roman fashion, around his freckled face and blazed like a light in the sea of heads. He was talking with intense animation to a familiar figure, and she thought, It's exhausting just to look at him in this heat! But I don't suppose anyone with hair like that could talk any other way about anything. Or is he angry? Yes, it looks like it.

Is that Graham Barstow he's giving it to?

A surge of the crowd obligingly reversed the two and she recognized Barstow's lean face, which was livid with outrage.

To spare him the embarrassment of being seen by her in an ugly argument, she went hastily away, thinking that it was bad taste to shout at someone like Graham. One *conversed* with this patrician, or at worst sent one's second with a formal challenge so that anger could be satisfied in gentlemanly manner in the proper place at the proper time. Not that he was distant and unapproachable. As John had said, he was open and friendly and it was easy to see why he was widely liked. But this young-old man in his middle fifties was complex indeed. A study in opposites.

A closer look at him disclosed that his slenderness was more the stringiness of one who followed a rigorous regimen. His skin, which from a little distance looked tan and smooth, was deeply wrinkled and weathered, dry in this blistering heat with the juicelessness of age, and loose under the eyes and jaw. His dull-gold hair was cut like a medieval page's, fringing the forehead and hanging long and silky to the ear lobes, but it was streaked with gray and sparse at the crown. His deep-set hazel eyes were faded rather than merely light. The kerchief knotted at the hollow of his throat was gay and stylish but did not hide the ropy muscles under his chin—although in point of fact it was not meant to do so. And that bounciness that had irritated John was not the vivid buoyancy of youth but the panic desperation of someone who had lived very well or was going to live very well, and who knew with what cruel speed more than half a century had gone. . . .

Great bursts of laughter drew her to a booth whose signs, in psychedelic color, invited everyone to Bathe The Hippie! Now's Your Chance! Get Him Clean While Water Supply Lasts! Two Buckets Per Customer!

Standing in a ball-and-claw tub was a youth wearing tattered jeans, a leather vest, strings of love beads, a gold hoop in one ear, and on his head what looked at first like a black balloon. From Afro to filthy bare feet he was soaking wet, and he seemed exhausted and sad, as if what he and his companion had conceived as a nose-thumbing money-making joke on the Establishment had boomeranged frighteningly. Nearly all the customers were stodgy, middle-aged, hopeless, and vengeful, and their eyes glittered and narrowed as bucket after bucket of cold water ran down his flinching body and slopped out of the tub into the mud.

Twenty centuries before, Kristin thought, the same guffaws and triumphant obscenities had resounded in the great Circus when blood splashed the sand and heads rolled on it like marbles.

Sickened, she walked quickly past the tawdry booths and hard-eyed barkers, the greedy children and irritable parents, and out beyond the hall onto a spacious sunlit field sweet with hay and clover. At the far side was a long line of stalls and trailers filled with livestock and gear. In the middle was an arena enclosed by a split-rail fence, in which a succession of handsome jumpers was being judged. She joined the spectators, received a lecture on manners and breeding from a knowing type from the Myopia Hunt Club, and applauded generously when an especially magnificent beast collected twenty-three faults on nine hurdles and retired in shame with his tail—in a manner of speaking, she told herself—between his legs.

But it seemed to her that jumping was too mannered and trivial a skill to generate so much blather from the Myopian, and she nodded and strolled away. Her momentary pleasure had fizzled and she knew that there would be none anywhere on the island until the Barstows had departed and left her and John alone. And Frey too, she thought, annoyed that someone as sensitive as Myra to living things should have permitted her coughing runny-eyed Dandie to importune a creature who was plainly ailing.

John grinned at a small boy despairingly pitching baseballs at a clown poster; bought six throws; won a Snoopy dog and an ancient Mickey Mouse watch; awarded them to the child; bought himself and the boy a hot dog and a bag of popcorn; and wandered on happily.

The first animal she saw in the cattle stalls was a gigantic Holstein bull as high as her head that reminded her of Myra. The thought amused her and for a few paces she embroidered it, thinking that she had never stood so close to such a large domestic animal ("That's two tons of very touchy hamburger, lady, so keep your distance," the owner said) or slept in the bed of such a large woman.

Myra was below middle height but her frame was unusually broad and heavy-boned, her muscles strong and well developed from years of gardening and active travel, her hands and feet disproportionately large for the length of her limbs. Nevertheless it would be wrong to describe her build and strength as masculine, because there was nothing masculine about her. She was still very pretty, with large regular features and clear skin. Her eyes were serene, her brow smooth, her soft gray hair massed in a splendid French twist. She dressed with classic simplicity in subtle pastels, and only her slacks were unavoidably mannish. She wore a few fine pieces of antique jewelry, in particular two massive rings that suited her capable hands and called attention to skin and nails that seemed never to have known anything more abrasive than hand lotion and an emory board.

But mere surface details like these were by the way, Kristin mused, as she leaned over the fence and watched a ewe nursing her wobbly-legged offspring. The important thing about Myra Barstow, the essence of this large calm woman, was her resemblance to Ceres, whose strength and genius for life are rooted in and serve her great domain. Myra had stepped right out of Bulfinch. Earth Mother: that was her gestalt.

But she was at least five years older than Graham. After so

many hours together, Kristin was sure of this, just as she was sure that something more than pride had prompted Myra to update the Barstow family tree, and something more than vanity had kept her from inscribing on it her own birth year. Childless for thirty-five years, she slept alone, expending her boundless energy and yearning on a nubile bronchitic dog, a sour-voiced seal point, a canary (in Cambridge with a neighbor), and a houseful of fecund plants.

And kept in her dresser drawer a pile of sexy underwear straight out of a Turkish brothel. . . .

A grubby urchin waved a flag in her face, and she realized that her eyes were full of tears. She walked slowly away, and then her step quickened as resentment shouldered out compassion. This isn't what we came here for, she told herself. John didn't pay all that money to get us tangled into the Barstows' problems. Haven't we got enough of our own?

She ran almost all the way back to the car.

His childish happiness ended abruptly, as if he had heard her justifiable complaint, and as he left the old hall shame stirred in him. He looked at his watch, wondering if she were still at the animal stalls, wondering if he ought to go and look for her. The hot sweet air encouraged him, and as he crossed the field he decided that they ought to pack some lunch, go to a quiet beach for a picnic and a swim, take Frey to a vet—leave him overnight, maybe, to give him a rest from Dandie—and wind up the day with a lobster dinner and a movie. That'll pep her up, he told himself, and tomorrow the Barstows would be gone and they could settle down to enjoy themselves and have some fun. That was all they needed. What was the point in delving into the past? The past was over and done with, there was nothing you could do about it. The important thing was to control your behavior now and in the future. Christ! He at least was trying!

But, because he held a B.A. in history, which encourages the comprehensive view of human behavior, an M.A. in psychology, which encourages an understanding of its dynamics, and an Ed.D. in human relations, which encourages interpersonal communication, it is a moot point whether he was capable of doing even that.

The work horses were being readied for their pulling contest, and he stopped to watch, pleased by the mighty Clydesdales and the rough humor of their owners, the smell of pungent sweat and sweet hay, the masses of heavy accouterments being sorted out and fitted on, the slabs of concrete piled to one side in preparation for loading onto the wooden steel-topped sleds. Caught up in the intense involvement of the spectators, he stayed for one heat, and then, relatively cheerful once more, in a golden honey-scented haze that would have paralyzed the wits of the Delphic Oracle and the conscience of a king, he went through a crowd gathering at the riding arena.

He had to make a detour when a well-spaced file of single-hitch hackney horses, each restrained by a trainer at the bridle, was walked into the ring. Smaller than Morgans, they were finely bred and very nervous, and the posture of the drivers—backs rigid as boards, hands holding the reins in a taut line from chest to bit—magnified their tension. As their trainers released them and they trotted counterclockwise one behind the other with short high-kneed delicate steps, glints of light danced and darted from gleaming hides to oiled leather to polished steel, almost crackling like static electricity, and exaggerating that tension until horses, drivers, trainers, judges, and spectators were united in a charged anxious hush.

"This is not a racing event, ladies and gentlemen," the announcer said through a bullhorn. "Entrants will be judged on performance, quality, manners, soundness, and conformation. First entry—Number Twenty-Four—Barbara Berger!"

A pretty teen-ager, in full fig from cap to boots and scowling in concentration, drove her dainty carriage smartly by him to a round of applause.

"Number Three-Oh-Sev—*Ladies and gentlemen, stand off that fence!*" the announcer shouted angrily as the girl's horse shied away from an idiot who was perched on the top rail swinging his feet over the track. The trainers slipped inside the fence and spread out, alert and strained, ready for anything from their unpredictable charges.

"Number Three-Oh-Seven—Janet Williams!"

"Number Nine—Richard Rose!"

"Number Fifty-Eight—Sam'l Potter!"

John swung around. Sam Potter was a young teacher with whom

he had worked briefly last year when his consulting team had been on the Coast. Well, he thought, I guess he made it to that job back here. Good for him. I wrote him a damn good reference on the strength of that week. A fire-eater, that kid.

"Number Sixty-Six—Douglas Flowers!"
"Number Twelve—Graham Barstow!"
"Number—"
"Number—"

He hesitated, told himself that it would be just a few minutes more, and ran back to watch.

Sam Potter, the angry young man with the bright hair, was grinning broadly now. To him the weighty gravity invested in this gossamer class was a huge joke, and he was good-naturedly aware that he looked ridiculous playing so publicly with his toys. The ripple of amusement that accompanied him suggested that the crowd agreed, since clearly he should have been flying down the Appian Way in an armored chariot at the head of a pack of Vandals and bellowing at a pair of war horses. Nevertheless he had his hands full, his horse being used to audiences but not to such proximity with them, and he had to break out of the line and allow the agitated beast to simmer down in several brisk turns, after which he fell in sedately behind Graham Barstow.

The hackney class was well suited to Barstow's lean classic features and quiet poise. His hair was scarcely ruffled and his casual shirt and gay neckerchief seemed the most formal of hunt club attire. His argument with Sam Potter might never have happened at all.

John was about to turn away, curiosity satisfied and conscience pricking again, when a big balloon drifted out over the arena on a capricious breeze, dropped suddenly in the path of Number Nine, and burst in its face. Terrified, the horse reared and wrenched away so frantically from the exploded thing that the driver nearly lost the reins, and then it collided heavily with Barstow's rig which had been following with proper rapidity.

Taken almost completely unaware, and slammed so hard against the low back of the seat that his spine was badly bruised, Barstow was incapable of reining his horse away in time. Nor could he have done so, because the horses' harnesses had become instantly and hopelessly entangled and there was no place for the wretched beasts to go but up. Lunatic with terror, they reared and screamed, striking at each other with their small sharp hoofs and lunging so wildly and blindly that, had everything but themselves dissolved, they would have been too lost in panic to separate.

And then Barstow's carriage tilted again and flung him off his precarious perch onto the sand, directly in front of Sam Potter.

A meticulous observer with a stop watch would have counted off six seconds by now and no one would have believed him. Violence, fear, instant disaster, compassion, love, seem to last for centuries: Total involvement, if only through the eye, blunts the perception and expands an instant into an aeon. So for six endless seconds, no more, nothing in the world seemed to move except two maddened horses and Graham Barstow writhing in the sand, his arms covering his head.

Suddenly the cosmic gears meshed again, making his urgent struggle plain, and two trainers sprang into the tangle and clutched at the horses' bridles while several others converged on Sam Potter's rig. Sam too had been circling briskly, and his horse, scared not by one charging beast but by a crazy snarl of two horses, two rigs, and a body rolling in his path, had instantly gone mad, rearing and stamping until his hoofs were poised over Graham Barstow's skull.

The sharp hoofs trembled for an instant in a cloud of dust as if held up by all the tiny particles. As they plunged murderously a trainer sailed like a battering ram over Barstow's body and, with a blow of his palms that almost broke his wrists, knocked the animal aside.

You'll have to wait, John thought angrily as if he were talking to Kristin. It's impossible to go picnicking *now!* He shouldered his way to the fence and climbed over it.

He glanced coldly at Sam, who sat shocked and confused in his carriage which a trainer was leading away, and identified himself as Dr. Barstow's friend and tenant.

"This man needs an amb'lance," said one of the judges, a sprightly octogenarian who looked very pleased with the excitement. "If you know where his wife's at, fetch her. We won't wait on her, though, tell her, if the doc comes before she does. We'll send him right along to the hospital. You might better take her straight there. And by the way, Dr. Weiden," he added, "I saw that look you gave young Sam'l. He's a hellraiser, all right, we know him in these parts. But I've seen fracases like this 'un since *I* was a boy. Ben judgin' hoss shows since the Kaiser War. Happens every dern year."

"I'll be back as quick as I can," John said, and ran off, relieved.

He did not have to drive Myra to the hospital. "Thank you, John, but you needn't bother. No need for you to spoil your day. It's happened to him before," she said calmly, putting Dandie into the station wagon. He watched her drive to the exit and stop, and when the ambulance rushed by she turned into the road and followed it away.

He looked at his watch again. Much more than an hour had passed since he and Kristin had arranged to meet at the gate. She was not there now, nor was she likely to be keeping Frey in a hot car while she went looking for him. She had probably stopped and waited a few minutes, and then gone to the vet. But he had better go home, dammit.

He had some difficulty hitching a ride back, and when he reached the top of the hill he found Kristin walking about with her head down, stirring up the dust like a sulky child kicking stones.

Annoyed, he gave her no greeting and no chance to tell him anything. "What's the matter *now?*" he said irritably.

"I wish you'd stop asking me that. Ask yourself for a change. It might help. Myra called a few minutes ago. That Indian flint—the cutting tool on Graham's pegboard—isn't there now, and she knows it didn't come off in Perley's truck because she'd just called him. She asked would I look around here. That's what I was doing, in case you're interested."

"I'm not. I'm hot and tired and I don't give a damn about that flint. It took me a hell of a long time to get back here. I had to ask someone for a ride—and then I had to walk up that hill."

"That's too bad. This whole thing was your idea, remember, not mine. I couldn't come back for you—I never got a chance to leave the house. The phone was ringing when I got here and I've hardly been off it since. Polly called from school. The job finished a week earlier than she expected and she asked if she could come down tomorrow for a few days' rest."

"Sure, why not? The more the merrier! Now what's that look supposed to mean? You didn't tell her no, did you?"

"I said I'd ask you and call her back."

"What's the matter with you, Kris! Don't you want to see your own daughter?"

"Of course I do. But we saw her at Commencement two months ago, and you and I haven't had any time together for—"

"All *right!* But I'd like to see her even if you don't. Let's go in and pack up a lunch."

"What for?" Listlessly she followed him into the kitchen.

"A picnic."

"You make it sound so appealing."

"What would you like, an engraved invitation? Who else called?"

"Josh. He's covered with poison ivy and the camp doctor wants a fancy ointment for him. Something with cortisone, I think. It's expensive and he needs more money."

"I'll wire it to him on the way to the beach. Did you get any ham? Where's the cheese? Hi, Frey, how's the boy?" The big dog had materialized out of nowhere at the familiar kitchen sounds and was ready for a snack. "How about a ham sandwich, fella? You look pretty perky now."

"That makes one of us," Kristin said bleakly. "I don't think we'll have time for the beach. Your chairman called too."

"Who, Nesmith?"

"No, the chairman of your consulting team. He wants to know if you're free to go out to L.A. again." His face lit up. "It's optional, but if you'd care to join them as soon as possible—"

"Like hell it's optional! What did you tell him?"

"What do you think I told him?" she said, despising him. "I said you were on your way."

Chapter IV

The beach under the rocky headland was all but deserted, Kristin saw gratefully as she and Frey descended the long tortuous path late Sunday morning. Thousands of people were being drawn away from all the beaches because of the fair, but few frequented this one at any time because of its singularly unappetizing approach. The road in through dense scrub was hardly more than a faint old wagon track and, at the point where it dwindled to a path bordered by luxuriant poison ivy, most pleasure-seekers gave up in disbelief that anything worth while was at the end of it and backed all the way out.

It could also be reached by way of two fine beaches that strained to meet around the headland, but there were discouraging obstacles to those routes too. East Beach ran into the foot of the cliff whose crumbling base, ceaselessly assaulted by the ocean, was strewn with slippery rocks. West Beach was blocked by a vast fall of granite that was diverting to slither through or climb over but that quickly satisfied most barefooted lovers and explorers. Surprisingly few ventured beyond the sign warning them against being trapped in the cavelike apertures by rising tides.

She knew that someday the island elders in their wisdom would widen and pave the road and probably the path, and put a parking lot like a swollen tumor in between, and issue permits for food stands and souvenir shops, and then trippers would swarm like flies, depositing filth and rubbish everywhere until one more beautiful corner of the world had been corrupted. But now this little crescent-shaped beach, littered only with boulders and deprived of the sun by midafternoon because of the headland's bulk, was nearly empty: only half a dozen cars waited with their noses in the scrub like some weird breed of grazing animal whose strange masters went feeding elsewhere on rare sustenance.

Frey lay down in the shade of a huge boulder, but Kristin spread a blanket on the hot sand, put down her lunch bag, towels, and other odds and ends, and leaned back on her elbows, a limp-brimmed sun hat shading her face. From time to time a couple would wander by, murmuring over little shells and colored pebbles, or seem to float just above the sand, joined only by innocent kisses. A child flying a dragon kite gazed raptly at the gulls wheeling around his alien jewel-colored bird, and so still was he that the sandpipers, though unused to intrusion here, ran back and forth close by him busily pinning wavelets to the sand with their long sharp beaks. Along the shore the water was a pellucid band of emerald, yet precisely where it met another band, of deepest blue, was impossible to determine and unimportant anyway except as one more glorious detail to marvel at. And over all was the unblemished sky, and the sun climbing to its zenith. Slowly Kristin's abraded nerves began to heal and in a little while she rolled over and began to read.

She had driven John to the ferry the afternoon before. "I can't pass this up," he said. "You know how important it is to my career. And anyway, a change from each other wouldn't be the worst thing in the world. And with Polly coming tomorrow . . ." His eyes were fixed on the approaching boat and it was obvious to them both that he could hardly wait to leave. She nodded and he did not bother to give her even a perfunctory kiss as she turned away.

No more amenities, no more gestures. And maybe it's just as well, she thought as she went back to the car. This leave-taking is the first honest thing we've shared in three years—nothing. Nothing to give on either side, and neither of us tried to manufacture anything to give. I wish it had happened two years ago. The doctor was right. How could marriage counseling help when you were forced to go alone?

For a year she had gone alone, trying to restore what she could of the best that they had shared, and steadfastly, maliciously, he had fought her and the doctor, holding his ground as though against a hated enemy, until finally she had stopped going. Well, she would not try anymore. She would not waste time and hope on challenges like the one she had given him in Graham's study. But to continue fighting was unbearable, and to surrender was impossible. Divorce was the sole option now, and she would tell him so when he returned. Life had been precious to her once. It would be again, without him. She took off her wedding ring and put it into her pocket before driving back to the Barstow house.

It was not until dawn, when she and Myra Barstow met in the kitchen, that they had their first friendly chat, occasioned by Frey's passionate acceptance of the collie. She began to like the older woman, but she was glad when they separated, Myra going to the hospital and then to the judging of the exhibits in the old hall, she to the beach for some cosmic therapy.

The intense tranquillity of the place soothed and reassured her, and muted lesser needs like hunger and thirst. It was some time before she closed the book and sat up to consider whether she should eat first or swim first. In the noon hush the shallow water breaking gently on the sand looked like emeralds that had been liquefied and chilled and shot through with golden stripes.

Presently she was floating in it, more contented and at peace than she had been for months, and Frey, who had apparently recovered overnight from the long summer's heat, paddled around her with a serious expression on his face, the graceful plume of his tail moving like a flexible rudder.

"You'll have to wash off before we go," she told him as he dried himself in the sand. His thick coat was salt-sticky and matted with sand, and he looked like a disreputable stray. He gave her what the kids called his "No sweat!" look and sat down on the clean blanket, as careless as royalty, to wait for a snack from the lunch bag.

"Boy, some people!" she said, setting out a paper plate of ham and dog biscuits, and she laughed helplessly when he vacuumed it up in one gulp, got up and shook sand over everything, and went back to his boulder.

More cheerful but unable to eat anything, she put the rest of the food back into the bag, shook out the blanket, lay down again, and opened her book. In a little while she was dozing over it and only the sounds of a quarrel saved her from waking up hours later with a back like a barbecued steak. Blinking groggily, she draped herself in a large damp towel and looked about, resenting the disturbance.

Its source was a new couple some twenty feet away, and most of it issued from the young man with fiercely red hair. Is he always angry? she thought, intrigued. He wore bathing trunks, and now and then he spun a diving mask around his wrist like a hoop. His companion, a shapely girl in jeans and a sleeveless blouse, was leaning back on her elbows and shaking her head vigorously. Occasionally she said something but his passionate eloquence washed over her like surf. He was trying to control himself, that was plain from his anxious glances about them and from his speaking inaudibly much of the time, but Kristin was frankly interested now and wished that, having wakened her with his anger, he would have the goodness to share its cause with her as well. Evidently Frey agreed. He was standing on the blanket, watching and growling deep in his throat.

They were both disappointed when the young man sprang to his feet and strode to the water's edge, his body tense with rage and frustration. As he put on his flippers and mask and dove into the water, the girl clasped her hands around her legs, hid her face in her knees, and began to cry.

Kristin sat in helpless dismay. But a good dog knows when to disregard the niceties of social commerce. Frey trotted over to the weeping girl and gave her a sandy lick. She looked up startled, then threw her arms about his shaggy neck and cried in earnest.

"Oh, you beautiful monster," she snuffled, holding onto him with one arm while searching vainly for a handkerchief.

"Will this do?" Kristin said gently, putting a napkin into her free hand and sitting down beside her.

The girl—she was rather more than that, and very lovely—stared at her with bloodshot eyes. "Oh! Thank you—very much. I'm sorry —we disturbed you—and then I—and then this good Samaritan—" Her eyes overflowed again and she wiped the tears away with a hopeless little gesture.

"Don't apologize. I was in the same condition not too long ago. Frey knows just what to do. He's had lots of practice—lately."

"Then whatever bothered you wasn't as bad as it could've been," the young woman said miserably, putting the napkin away and stroking Frey's great head. "I've been going it alone for a year now and—" She hesitated and Kristin prepared to get up, feeling too burdened by her own distress to want to hear any more, and thinking that whatever assistance she could dredge out of her own pain would be pretty shaky anyway.

"You're all right now?" she said, delicately indicating the wisdom of mutual withdrawal, as Frey returned to his boulder and hid himself away from the sun.

"Yes. You're very kind. Both of you. I'm really very sorry I spoiled your peace—but that cousin of mine spoiled mine! He meant well, he always does. We're great friends although you'd never think so. But he—he has a grievance against someone I'm—someone I love very much. And even if it's a real one—and it is!—it isn't mine. I can't feel the same way he does, can I? *Must* I?"

"No, you can't and you shouldn't. I—I learned that the hard way. People have to deal with their own feelings and their own problems, no matter how closely they're related to people who can't agree with them. I guess the only time it's right to take up the cudgels is in cases of brutality to children or animals or—well, any helpless creature."

"I guess he thinks I'm one of them, then. And maybe he's right. That's just how I feel—helpless."

"Well . . . good-by—and good luck," Kristin said, turning away. As she did, the young woman said "Ah!" and over her upturned face came an expression of such love and joy and yearning that Kristin's breath caught in her throat and she went hastily back to her blanket. Only a voyeur would look again, she thought, keeping her back to the young woman and whoever was coming toward her. Lying down with her eyes scrupulously ahead, she felt for her book and opened it.

A few minutes later, arranging herself more comfortably, she saw the couple walking away, their arms around each other, faces close and touching briefly in a kiss as they neared the end of the beach that ran into the tumbled granite. Something wispy, like butterfly wings, fluttered over the man's shoulder, and she thought, That's funny—I don't think I've ever seen a butterfly on a beach—

And all at once she recognized the tall rangy body and the fair hair, and she knew who was the cause of the argument and the crying. Whatever he had done, however deliberately or unwittingly he had done it, whenever he had done it, Graham Barstow had committed some grave wrong against the angry young man with the orange hair.

She lay back and covered her face with the sun hat, trying to shut out the unwelcome knowledge. But the simple-minded ruse was a failure, and so was the attempt to continue reading words with no meaning. According to its jacket copy the book was irresistibly funny, and she had put it into the lunch bag thinking that she could not afford to pass it up. When you can't laugh, she told herself, you're really beaten. And she had opened it eagerly, hoping to be carried home spent with mirth and henceforth as merry as a grig—whatever a grig was. But she had not cracked one smile in a hundred pages, and as far as she was concerned the Barstows had wasted another of their blue and white bookplates on it. It was a silly piece of work full of harsh sarcasm and pasteboard bores, and after what she had just seen her equilibrium—what there was of it—was more likely to be shattered by going home and having dinner with Graham and Myra.

I'm surprised that Graham's walking around loose in the first place, let alone with that lovely gal, she thought, sitting up and staring at the water. He's got a mild concussion, Myra said this morning, and his back must hurt him terribly too. I'd have thought he'd be resting on the sun deck for a week at least. He's no chicken, after all, though he's certainly trying. That custom-painted Porsche and those clothes . . . And a girl friend young enough to be his daughter. I wonder if Myra knows . . .

What a world we're living in! Age is a dirty word in this culture. Dying's been tacitly abolished. When you say *death,* whisper it behind your hand. It's bad taste, though, to live too long if you can't hide the scars you've gotten from all the slings and arrows.

Myra doesn't seem to be fighting it, though. If you forget about those lace panties in her dresser. I wonder if she's dieting. Some people use the craziest devices for a spur . . . No, they're too sleazy. She'd have Bonwit's best if she were going to have them at all. But they just aren't her style. And she eats very well indeed. She's no glutton, but she hasn't counted calories in years. I think she never did. . . .

What a beautiful woman she is, how patient and forbearing. Graham may be a Boston Brahmin with money and charm coming out of his ears, but he's Peck's bad boy, I bet. She must have had her hands full all these years. The only way she could have kept him in the hospital would be to lock him in there.

She leaned back on her elbows and sighed. Still, she thought, Myra was surprisingly calm about the accident. Graham nearly gets his head kicked in, and she calls from his bed of pain to ask about an old Indian carving knife. And never mentions where she is or why she's there. We may be strangers but control like that is almost frightening. All right, she knew John was on his way home and would tell me all about it, she said, and she knew Graham would feel worse than he already did if she couldn't find that flint and get it back on the board. It's his *pièce des pièces*. But—I don't like that kind of cool.

She did not have to and she knew it, for the simple reason that all of this was none of her business even though it had been thrust in her lap. Well, the three of them would have to endure each other until after dinner because it was the proper thing to do. And then Polly would get off the boat and the Barstows and Dandie and I Chee would board it, and that would be that.

Except that I'll have to spend the next week watering Myra's plants . . . until John gets back . . . Am I still sure of my decision? I won't think about it now. I don't have to think about it now . . . I'm glad I called Polly while he was packing, although I feel a little like a coward for telling her to come . . .

She lay back once more, but purity and peace had gone, and the sun was dropping slowly and would be behind the headland soon. The water was darker now, the air prematurely chill, although on the western side of the island it was as hot as it had been at midday. Hundreds of people were having a gay noisy time there, and the thought made her feel more like an outcast or a prisoner than an independent peace-lover hearing a different drummer.

Sighing, feeling oddly unclean and in need of a hot bath rather than another swim, she called Frey and went down to the water. It was unpleasantly cold now and she shivered as she waded in. Determinedly she swam back and forth as she waited for the dog, but she could not get warm, and Frey, who was going to be a job and a half to brush out if he missed another dunking or "dried" himself in the sand again, was nowhere to be seen.

Irritated and anxious to be gone but dismayed by the social task that faced her, she toweled herself roughly and comforted herself with the knowledge that by bedtime Polly would be here, an ally against the forces that were pressing down on all sides. The world is too much with me, she mused dryly as her eye swept the beach and counted the four people left on it.

From a distance came Frey's bark, sharp and urgent, and she revolved slowly, looking for him. He stood at the bend of the beach around which Graham and the sad young woman had disappeared, and, when she called him, only wagged his tail once and barked again, like a Marine sergeant.

"Now what!" she said as she went toward him, knowing perfectly well that nothing in the world would budge him until he was ready. But when he barked once more she sensed with alarm that his was no frivolous demand, and hurried to his side.

Instantly he went back the way he had come, until the sand was only a slender thread that ended abruptly under the mass of fallen granite. A scattering of stones made the footing difficult, and he waited patiently while his barefooted mistress stumbled and tripped and swore breathlessly behind him. Then he slipped through an opening between two giant rocks into a low, sandy-floored cave formed by the disintegrating escarpment. His short imperative bark resounded terrifyingly in the small enclosure.

"Hold on a sec!" she gasped, hunching her way in and shuddering as she realized the horrible weight of stone tumbled so casually above them. No point trying to catch my breath, she thought. It can't be done. I'm just too scared. What's he up to? "Okay, go!" she said, and her heart seemed to be pounding directly between her ears as she followed him through a narrow and much longer passage into another cave.

This one was paved with large rocks treacherously covered with slimy sea moss and countless barnacles. And it faced the sea, which dashed itself relentlessly and with sinister rhythm against the opening, flinging black drops of spray everywhere, swooshing and sucking and gurgling out again, and rising steadily with each assault to meet the high-water mark four feet up the glistening walls.

Lying prone with his head toward the opening, his fair hair dark with salt water and blood, his face perilously close to the advancing tide, was Graham Barstow. The big dog had tugged him two or three feet up the sloping rocks: his trousers were torn about the ankles and one of his rope-soled shoes was bouncing in and out on the tongues of the waves.

His cheek and the palms of his dragging hands bled as Kristin, grasping his slippery ankles, pulled and heaved him up over the knife-sharp barnacles. Her tender feet also tore and bled, but she felt nothing until she had hauled him through the tight slot onto the sandy floor of the first cave. Sobbing and wheezing and soaking wet, she left Frey to guard him while she made her agonized way back to the beach for help.

Had Frey summoned her as little as half an hour later, they would have been too late.

Chapter V

The admitting nurse, a mass of heartless white starch, took an intricate form out of the drawer, rolled it into the typewriter, and asked it what its name was.

"Kristin Weiden. And my feet are killing—"
"W-y-d-e-n?"
"W-e-i-d-e-n. Look, all I want is—"

"Age?"

"Forty-six. But—"

"Address?"

"Which one? Where I'm staying? Or my home address?"

"Both. Just in case."

"In case of what? Look, all I want—"

"In a minute please, Miss Weiden—"

"Mrs. Mrs. John Weiden."

"Is he your next of kin?"

"My very next. My husband, in fact. We've known each other quite a long time now and—"

"Where does he reside?" the nurse said imperturbably.

Kristin told her. "I live there too, naturally. But look, I've got to get out of here because—"

"Just be patient, Mrs. Weiden. We have to do this first. Children?"

"Two. Daughter twenty-two. Son twenty. And one of them will be here on the—"

"Religion?"

"Relig—! *Look!* My feet are really in bad shape and all I want is to see Dr. Vernon if he's here and—"

"You couldn't have picked a worse time, Mrs. Weiden," the nurse said reproachfully. "It's been a madhouse here since the fair began and everyone's run ragged. And everything seems to get worse at suppertime. You'll just have to be patient."

"I'm really very sorry about that. I would have been delighted to come earlier or later or perhaps on some other day. Which day would be better for you?" Kristin said a little wildly. "If you prefer, I'll go now, and I'll call and make an appointment, how about that?" Tears of pain and shock and anger stung her eyes and she blinked them rapidly away.

"Now now. Please don't make things more difficult. I'm sure it's all very trying but—" said the nurse, and rolled like a tank along her appointed path. "Religion?"

"No preference. And by the way, it's against federal law and the law of this Commonwealth to ask that question."

The tank's headlights went on as if it had suddenly found itself in a strange dark country. "You *must* have a preference," the nurse said severely, her hands still on the keys, her eyes distended with horror. "Everyone must have a preference. Everyone must believe in—in *some*thing!" The transmission appeared to be faltering. "I— my goodness, I've never heard of such a thing! I must put something down. If you died here—!"

"I didn't say I didn't believe in something. I said I didn't have a preference. And I hope you don't think I'd be inconsiderate enough to die here. But if I did," Kristin gritted, standing up and hobbling to the door, "my next of kin would relieve you of all funeral arrangements and responsibilities, what with you people being so busy and all. He's a very thoughtful guy that way—buried several wives, in fact. Volunteered all on his own, just to make things easier, you know. He probably didn't have to, but—" Her face was gray with exhaustion and covered with sweat. "Well, thank you for everything but I think I'll leave now. Some other time, perhaps."

The tank had reached an insurmountable barrier. "Well I never!" the nurse said, her hands falling away from the typewriter as Kristin went out into the hall and limped toward the big glass doors.

She had waited for half an hour and more, biting her lips and clenching her fists against the pain in her bleeding feet, and there was nothing for it but to go home and treat herself. Aspirin and scotch would have to substitute for Dr. Vernon's solicitous hands. And then she would clean and bandage up the pain, which seemed to be a discrete addition to her legs, making her feel taller by an inch. And then, after something to eat—if she could eat!—and a rest, she would drive to the ferry landing and meet Polly. Graham Barstow was being cared for, that was the important thing—unless the hospital staff were holding off until he came to or died, she thought furiously, so that *one* way or another Admitting could type his history first!

The people on the beach had behaved more rationally. "We'd better not risk moving your friend anymore," one man had said. "I'll go sit with him till we get an ambulance." "I'll find a phone," the other man had said, and sped up the path to his car. While they waited, she had washed sand out of the lacerations, wrapped her feet in makeshift bandages, and accepted help in carrying her things back to the car: painful processes anaesthetized by the women's anxious chatter. "I'm all right now," she had told them shakily, when the ambulance came. "Really. I can manage. Thank you for everything. If you'd just see that Mrs. Barstow gets a call at the fair or at home, I'd be very grateful. I'll probably see her at the hospital if you can.get to a phone right away."

But she had seen only a collection of other sufferers in the waiting room, and the nurse with the typewriter and the questionnaire. Whatever medical attention there was was clearly to be found elsewhere.

"Hey! Kris! Where do you think you're going! Here, siddown and take a load off, or you won't be walking for a month." Old Dr. Vernon and a candystriper with a wheel chair caught up with her at the door.

She grinned unsteadily at them. "I could use the rest. What's the prognosis on the admitting nurse?"

The old doctor's eyes sparkled slyly. "God knows. Medical history's in the making, though, judging from the conniption fit she's having. What the hell, Kris! You know the procedure."

"We both know what you think of it, too." She laughed, feeling better already. "I guess I was a little crazy there for a minute. Just tell me what padded cell you put her in and I'll send her a new typewriter."

The candystriper helped her onto the examining table and went out giggling.

"Is Myra Barstow here? Did she get the message all right? I could have called her myself as soon as I got here, considering how long I had to wait," Kristin said. "Although I don't know why I thought I'd get to see you on demand. How did she take it? They were supposed to go home tonight."

"Let's see these feet first. Well well. What've *you* been up to?" His hands, gnarled and brown-spotted with age, were sure and gentle.

"Dancing with my feet beautiful upon the mountains. Ow!"

"Where's that from?"

"The Old Testament, I think. What about Myra?"

40

"She came when he was about to go to x-ray. I sent her home," the doctor said, collecting what he needed and putting everything onto a wheeled tray. "Told her not to come back till seven-thirty. Not that there's anything for her to do or see. He's still out cold. She's very upset, naturally, but she's a strong woman. Co-operative."

"And Graham?"

"Don't know. Not definitively. He got pretty banged up yesterday. Told him to stay put awhile, but he wouldn't, of course. Insisted on leaving this noon. Made her take him back to the fair to get his car. Crazy! What in hell was he doing on that beach? Good thing you were there."

"Ow! Hey! If we hadn't been, Frey and I, it would have been the end for him, I'm sure of that." She avoided the question and shrank from the cold antiseptic. "How do they look? I washed them off before I left the beach."

"Not as bad as they probably feel—*will* feel for a week at least, Twinkletoes. There's worse treatment than salt water and a clean towel. Give you a shot just to make sure, though. And I'd advise you to walk on your hands for a few days, if you must walk. Give yourself a chance to heal. Sun and air will help. Clean 'em with antiseptic, put on fresh ointment and bandages afterward. I'll give you some to take home for morning. Sleeping pills too. And keep dry. At the slightest hint of infection get yourself back in here." He reached for a roll of gauze. "How's the group? This place is like a convention hall. Catch up on all the news. Josh still alive? First time I ever saw that boy, he was ten years old and so banged up falling off a tree I thought somebody'd put 'm through a meat grinder. You, maybe."

She laughed. "Oh, I had more subtle plans than that for his demise! He'd have made a nice specimen for your path' lab. Had any murders lately? Or aren't you the medical examiner anymore?"

"Oh, I'm still the M.E. Haven't had a murder in a long time, though. Other deaths've been pretty straightforward. I'm no medical sleuth, though. Special branch, forensic pathology. Rare birds, those guys. Say, where's everybody. Why're you here by yourself?"

"Josh is in Maine with Outward Bound and poison ivy. He's a giant. Polly just finished at the University of Maine. She's been working all summer in a child psych' clinic. She's coming tonight on the last boat, thank goodness. John had to go to California on a consulting job. The day after we got here. I won't go into the rest. It's been—unbelievable."

"What's with you and him now? Things any better?"

"No. I'm going to divorce him. I'd rather not talk about it right now."

"Hmph! Then tell me what happened at the beach."

"I wish I knew. Frey was wandering around and recognized him, of course. They'd struck up quite a friendship since Friday afternoon. But why ask me?"

"Because you're right in the middle of it. Living in his house. There's been something between him and one of my nurses this past year. One of the finest gals we ever had on this island."

"So?"

"So—I saw that bruise on the back of his head when we cleaned him up for x-ray. It was a very bad one, Kris."

His tired eyes regarded her steadily and she could not evade him this time. "I know. I saw it too. And I saw him—with the girl—before he got it. I tried not to but— And I think," she said slowly, "I think we're both thinking the same thing. Was he alone and did he slip? You said he was still pretty shaky from that horse show. Or was someone with him, and was he struck?"

"And deliberately left there. To drown."

She drew a swift breath and shook her head. "The only thing I'm sure of is that the girl didn't do it. That she wasn't even there when it happened. If you'd seen the look on her face when he came! Hate is the obverse of the coin, that's true, and I believe it. I'm one of the Freudian freaks, as you know. But she couldn't have done such a thing—or been there and watched it done—and then left him there to drown. She didn't have time to work up that much fury. No more than an hour passed between the time they left and Frey found him. No. Even if she did it, she didn't do it. If you know what I mean."

"I do. Brought Kathy Field into the world thirty-four years ago and taken care of her ever since. Trained her, too, after she graduated nursing school! Stake my life on that gal."

"So would I, though I only talked with her a few minutes." She hesitated, then said with a curious reluctance that she could not explain, "She was with someone first, but he left before he saw Graham. At least, he went back into the water—he was skin-diving. Her cousin, she said. They'd been fighting."

"Red-haired chap?" The doctor snorted. "Sam Potter's a hot-tempered one, all right. Never guess he's an artist, would you, and a fine one at that. I delivered him, too, eight years after Kathy—not that he needed any help! Came out like greased lightning and been roaring ever since. No harm in him though. Forthright chap. If he wanted to kill somebody he'd do it openly, the way he does everything else. He's not a sniper or a backstabber. Good lad, basically. Haven't seen much of him, he's been away the past few years."

Unaccountably relieved, she said, "Doctor, if he—if Graham slipped and hit the back of his head, how could he have been on his face when we found him?"

"Don't know. Maybe he didn't pass out immediately. Might've rolled over, tried to crawl or get up, lost consciousness from the effort. Same thing applies if he were struck." He paused to think about it. "Doesn't make sense that way."

"No, it doesn't. Anyone who wanted to kill him—and had the chance to give him such a crack—would have had time to make sure he was out cold and without a chance when the tide came in." She shuddered. "And there was only one blow on his head, wasn't there?"

"Yes, just one. But enough to do the job after his shock and concussion yesterday. He isn't young—although he is to me, I've got twenty years on him—and he doesn't have a heavy skull or frame, either. No, I think he was struck down from behind and looked as if he'd stay put until the water came high enough to drown him."

"Yes, probably. I really don't think he could have slipped. It's hard to slip on that many barnacles! Of course he could have slipped on the seaweed farther up. It never dries out in *there*. But . . . Still, you're the medical champ. Couldn't you tell from the nature of the wound whether he slipped or whether someone struck him?"

"Find me the exact spot he fell on or the blunt instrument that hit him and I'll tell you the answer to that. Don't have time to sleuth, myself. Come on, I'll take you out, see that hero of yours, and then I've got work to do that's more in my line. Here, put this stuff in your bag. And here's a prescription. Sleeping pills and ointment."

"Ow-w-w-w! If I hurt this much after one application, you can keep it!" She flopped into the wheel chair. But she thanked him anyway. It would save Polly a trip to the village first thing in the morning.

"Good thing you've got automatic transmission, Kris. Save one foot some punishment." He opened the car door and tossed her handbag onto the seat. "Hello, big fella," he said to the dog, who scrambled out to greet them.

"This wreck has to have automatic transmission—for John." She grunted as she heaved herself in behind the wheel. "He bought five car raffle tickets at the fair, but the way things are going, the numbers he got will immediately precede or follow the one that wins. There's a weird unity about the events of this vacation, Dr. Vernon. And don't give Frey too much adulation. He's looking awfully smug as it is."

"He can afford to after what he did." The doctor's knees cracked as he bent and shook the offered paw. And then, forgetting Kristin, he put a gentle hand under Frey's graying muzzle and said very softly, so softly that she scarcely caught the words, "You know, Frey, we're getting old, you and I. We're getting old . . ." They gazed at each other, sharing a knowledge she was not yet privy to, and sudden tears spilled down her cheeks as the doctor straightened slowly and opened the back door for the dog.

"Take it easy. Both of you," he said, and left them without another word.

After Myra Barstow fed the dogs and I Chee, she prepared a light supper and served it beautifully, but it did neither of them much good although they ate it all. And then Dandie coughed until she vomited, after which she crouched in a corner looking ashamed of herself.

"Oh dear, that's the third time today," Myra said anxiously as she cleaned up the floor. "She was sick at the Grange. Someone must have given her something behind my back. And she's been coughing all afternoon."

"Myra, I don't know what to say. I've been groaning and complaining while you've done all the work and had all the grief. And now Dandie's sick and Polly's coming. What would you like me to do? If we stay, Polly can help, of course. But if you'd rather be alone, please tell me frankly. All I want is to help any way I can. But I don't know what to do."

Myra's grandmotherly pink-and-white loveliness seemed to have faded. Her round smooth cheeks sagged, her generous mouth was pinched, her eyes lackluster. She smiled slightly and shook her head. "Then I guess I'm just as bad as you are, Kris dear. I just can't grasp this. I can't think ahead or make a plan or tell you what to do. Or even what I'd like you to do. Oh no, I wish you'd stay! You're such a comfort. We're a sad pair, though, aren't we! Things just aren't turning out the way we planned or expected."

"You're so calm, so—"

"I've always been calm so I can't take any credit for that. And anyway, what good would it do to make a fuss? It wouldn't change anything."

"I'm not so sure."

Absently Myra scratched her wrist, then looked at it and sighed. "Poison ivy! I get it every year. The smallest shoot in my garden does it, and they seed no matter what I do." She pushed her chair away from the table and got up heavily. "I haven't cried for years," she said as she began to clear the table. "When I found that—I couldn't have any children, I cried enough to last me all my life. And I never cried again. I just—got busy."

"You didn't want to consider adoption?"

"I did. Graham—didn't. You make a choice—your husband or yourself. And then . . . and then you go on. And now after thirty-five years—"

Kristin sat very still, sensing with dread what was coming yet feeling that she must hear it.

"Now it doesn't seem to matter anymore. I've lost him."

"Oh no, Myra! Surely not! He got a nasty whack but the doctor said—"

"I don't mean losing him that way, Kris. No, not that way . . . No, he's found somebody else, someone—young. That kind of loss hurts more." She was washing dishes in slow motion and her hands almost stopped moving. "Does that sound very awful? Because if you really love someone, you should want their happiness even if you lose your own."

"No, it doesn't sound awful. But the other's a bit too saintly, perhaps. The thing is, a part of us loves and wants to give generously. The other part is angry and doesn't. And neither invalidates the other, you know. Both feelings are real and simultaneous. We're terribly complicated creatures, we humans." It was true for me once, she thought sadly. But I can't give anymore. Only anger. Even if John wanted it, I don't have it to give any longer . . .

"That's what Graham said . . . once. He said people are like night and day. When the sun is shining here, that doesn't mean it isn't nighttime on the other side of the world." She sighed. "But that only makes some decisions harder to come to. Which side do you listen to? Which part of yourself is—stronger?" Defeated, she rinsed a plate and put it into the rack and listlessly picked up another.

"What will you do?" Kristin said after a moment's silence. She looked at her ring finger. The pale circle of skin was darkening now. Soon it would be gone entirely. The love she had had for John could not be so easily eradicated—the memory of it anyway. You could not eradicate the past, nor should you. Much of it had been good. The rest helped you to decide . . .

Myra looked through the window over the sink, then straightened and took a deep breath as if she had just made up her mind about something. "What I've never done before. I shan't back off this time. I won't agree to a divorce or a separation," she said evenly. "Sooner or later he'll forget about—about her." She finished the dishes more briskly now and tidied up the table and the counter tops while Kristin watched, aching for her. "I really don't think you ought to drive, dear," she said when the task was done. "Look,

I'll take Dandie to Dr. Amaral* and then I'll come back and pick you up. We'll both meet Polly and I'll bring you back here before I go to the hospital. I must sit with Graham awhile before I go to bed. Otherwise Polly might be asleep when I get home and I can't wait to meet her."

"Oh, don't worry about that. We'll be up talking for hours."

"You're so lucky. No. Not lucky. Blessed . . . Well, what do you say? I'll drive you tonight and tomorrow we'll decide about the big things."

Kristin stood up and smiled bravely. "See? I'm really better—I could walk all the way to the ferry! No, you go now. And don't worry, we'll be waiting for you. When you get back we'll have a fire and make tea and we'll cheer each other up."

"That sounds lovely. Thank you, dear, you're such a comfort. Come, Dandie. You're going to see your friend, poor baby."

Frey was on the sun deck and Kristin went out to brush him. A few minutes later the new station wagon was off down the hill, I Chee was hunting in the woods, and she and Frey were alone again. His was the only sane companionship on the island, she thought, grooming him lovingly until it grew too dark to see.

She turned off the lights, lingering at the big window to look once more at the vast clear night sky, and out of old habit turned off the lamps in the living room too before limping into the bedroom for her jacket and handbag. But it was too early to leave, and for the first time in three days the bed was inviting. "Not that there's much chance of even closing my eyes, Frey, not with this pain. I'd better set the clock, though, just in case."

She lay in darkness listening to the night sounds. A whippoorwill began to call rapidly, evenly, hypnotically. In two minutes she was fast asleep.

When the alarm clock rang she awoke feeling astonishingly refreshed, even cheerful, but she dreaded having to stand up. That first moment—! As she urged herself to grin and bear it Frey began a staccato codelike growl.

The whippoorwill's persistent wail broke off in the middle of a phrase. Annoyed, she thought, I've still got a few minutes. I'll wait

---

* Americanized pronunciation: *Am*-er-al

for that damn bird to drop the other shoe and then I'll positively turn on the light and get going. Maybe I should have let Myra drive me . . . Maybe I Chee got him, poor thing.

Frey got up and growled again, tilting his head from side to side, intent on something beyond her power to hear. Hackles raised, he tiptoed to the door and stopped, a quivering line from his nose to the white spot on the tip of his tail, his lips drawn back in an ugly snarl. Plainly he meant business. He had always been alert but discriminating and, after what had happened at the beach, Kristin was frightened. And doubly frightened because of her relative helplessness. She swung her legs over the side of the bed, put on her sneakers, and tried to stand while avoiding all contact with the floor. To reach him seemed utterly impossible, but adrenaline dulled the outraged tissues of her feet and before she could decide how in the world she was going to manage, she was at his side.

Her hand trembled as she leaned on his bull-like neck and strained to hear what he was hearing, but the pounding of her heart roared in her ears, her mouth dried up, and all she could be certain of was that she was terrified.

A small metallic scratching sound came from the front of the house. It must be I Chee, she thought, back from hunting, ready for warmth and company, balancing on the sun deck railing and reaching for the doorknob. She smiled, listening for the ugly cry he always gave when he tried to get in, as if he were obliged to admit that his excellence would be enhanced by the acquisition of a thumb.

This time there was no such complaint—yet all at once her fear vanished.

Say an intruder was on the sun deck trying to force the lock or find the keyhole. When she told Frey to go, he would erupt like a one-hundred-fifty-pound volcano fanged and clawed. And if the intruder were armed, he would discover that he might as well be carrying a water pistol as a machine gun for all the good it would do him.

That this expectation was based on truth was less true than that it was a defiant answer to Dr. Vernon, but she did not think of that until much later. Almost relaxed now, even prepared to enjoy the rout, she tugged at Frey's collar and they padded out silently to the wall between the living-room picture window and the steps to the kitchen.

There was no question now that someone was seeking entry from the sun deck. The knob was being manipulated in a way that I Chee could never manage, and there were small brittle sounds as though a piece of plastic were being forced against the latch. Between the intruder and his ambushers was a distance of less than three feet, and Kristin was sure that she could hear him breathing.

She was about to object that he was taking much too long when Frey decided that he had, and bounded down the steps. Barking furiously, he leaped at the dark figure bent behind the barrier of small panes, but his claws only hit the moldings and clattered against the glass. Kristin caught a glimpse through the big window of a shapeless form vaulting the railing. It crashed into the brush and disappeared.

"We'd have nailed him if you'd kept your big mouth shut," she told the dog a few minutes later as they drove away. "The only satisfaction I've got is knowing he knows you're here, so it isn't likely he'll try again. He must have thought you were the Creature rising out of the Lagoon!"

She wondered, belatedly, who the intruder was. Probably that fireball with the orange hair, Kathy Field's cousin Sam. Sam the artist. No, not so probably, she thought, remembering what Dr. Vernon had said. Hot-tempered, yes. She had seen that herself. But forthright, too, and with no harm in him. The doctor knew what he was talking about, so it was improbable that the young man would force a lock and sneak around in darkness to get whatever he wanted here. No. *He* would ring the bell—kick the door down, more likely!—and walk right in and demand what he so urgently required.

Not a contemporary sort of character, she thought. People rarely dealt with each other honestly, without guile, unconscious or otherwise. They hid in darkness, behind masks, and went through grotesque motions called communication. Not that deviousness was new, of course. Nothing was new, and it was pointless to mourn nostalgically for purity of converse. Had it ever, in fact, existed anywhere since humans had begun to congregate? All the same, the

49

young man she had seen twice and would probably never see again was not a contemporary character. She realized suddenly that she liked him and wished him well.

Her thoughts drifted to other matters. For instance, John would say he's having a much worse time of it than I am, she told herself, and knew that she no longer cared. She had made an observation as unimportant, as casual, as that today was Sunday.

They were halfway to the ferry now, and the pain in her feet was throbbing again like an orchestra of berserk drums. "If you could only talk, Frey," she gasped, "you'd have told me what you had in mind and I could have put my shoes on first!"

But by the time they reached the clustering village lights, parked, and made their way through the crowd on the wharf, the throbbing had relocated in her chest. With one hand on the dog's powerful neck she was able to walk without unbearable discomfort to the barrier behind which people were watching the approaching boat.

It was depressing to look at the cars lined up along the side of the wharf. The Barstows should have been in that line, Myra in the big wagon with Dandie and I Chee, Graham in his bright yellow bug, waiting to board the boat and go home to Cambridge. Unhappy, perhaps, and divided—from his wife and his mistress— but at least physically intact. She shuddered, seeing again the bleeding cheek and battered head, the soaked unconscious body left close to death by—and she was sure of this now—by a murderer as cruel and monstrously deliberate as any she had ever heard of.

Absently, her gaze turned inward, she was stroking Frey's head when the touch of a strange hand startled her. The two youths she had seen at the fair were admiring the huge beautiful animal, and the one with the Afro and love beads was pinching up the layer of loose skin on the back of Frey's neck. His index finger, Kristin noticed, was missing.

"Gee, sorry!" he said, letting go as the dog's upper lip quivered. "Man, he's big. Big enough to ride. He could carry quite a load."

"Yes," Kristin said. "Including another one of your fingers. Every now and then he takes issue with certain kinds of liberties."

"Huh?"

"He doesn't like to be touched that way."

"Say, he's the hero dog, ain't he. Man, yuh could make plenny bread with a dog like that, hey, Jack?"

"Man, you know it! But I ain't that crazy!" his companion said nervously. "Christ! I wish they'd hurry up!" He was sweating freely in the cool air.

Frey was used to homage and usually lapped it up, but for once he was preoccupied. He acknowledged the two youths with a wag of his tail and ignored them, pressing forward with the rest as passengers began waving and shouting from the sun deck.

The broad flat-bottomed boat, as stolid and ungainly a vessel as had ever come down the ways, nosed slowly past the two bundles of pilings as if it had changed its mind and decided not to stop. But then it sounded a cheerful blast and, amid a churning that turned the green-black water a sickly yellow under the powerful lights, backed between the pilings into its slip. As the counterweights were lowered and the steel ramp creaked up to meet the bow, a crewman skipped nimbly across the gap and ran down to move aside one of the two stanchions that held a heavy chain across the foot of the ramp.

Scores of foot passengers came clattering off first, and Kristin scanned their faces eagerly. The two youths next to her called out to a man who held a white German shepherd on a tight lead, and he ran toward them. The dog followed with difficulty because of a large bandage on the side of its chest and it pulled against the lead, trying to sit down. Kristin cried out in protest as the man yanked it along, but Frey, with a strange singleness of purpose, was indifferent to the handsome miserable beast. And then she forgot about them as a familiar figure, groggy and tousle-haired from sleeping, emerged and stopped uncertainly on the ramp, blinking under the lights.

"There she is! There's Polly!" Kristin said, and pushed ahead impatiently. But with that "Why wait?" look on his face Frey nosed through the crowd, ducked under the barrier, and bounded away.

Between him and the uptilted ramp was the chain between the stanchions which served as a guide to offloading traffic. The huge dog cleared it easily and soared like a hairy butterfly toward the tall slender girl who came slowly down, laden with baggage. She smiled and her step quickened as she saw him and called his name.

He strained to meet her, his front paws outstretched, his thick plume of a tail streaming behind him, as he rose in a slow parabola like a canine Pegasus. For an instant he seemed to float effortlessly, weightlessly, on the stiff breeze coming off the water.

And then a wrenching spasm shook his body, and at the peak of his flight his tired heart burst with joy.

Chapter VI

There was no moon, no gleaming track across the water, no glow on the horizon, no running lights of sea- or aircraft blinking by, no friendly beam poking through the trees from any dwelling tucked into the surrounding hills and meadows. And the night-blue sky stretched and stretched to uncharted distances, pulling the stars with it until they were too far away to glitter. On this unusually dark night the Barstow house appeared to float in a little wash of pale gold: Polly had run shuddering from room to room turning on the lamps to keep the darkness out and dissipate the peculiar gloom within.

Then, having gone out again for firewood, she had built a small fire, tuned the radio console to a late concert station, and prepared a tea tray which stood well laden and tempting on the slab of driftwood in front of the couch.

But her protest had made no essential difference in or to this contrary house, and only I Chee dozing in his basket by the hearth was entirely and predictably comfortable. For the darkness pressed down so relentlessly that the lamplight shining out through the windows seemed blocked by an invisible wall. The wind moved through the trees in restless gusts and backed down the chimney, puffing smoke into the room and intensifying rather than masking the odor of damp potting soil. And the whippoorwill, once again engrossed in self-pity, complained tiresomely above the music in off-key counterpoint.

There seems to be no way to please this house or cheer it up, she thought, puzzled. All she knew about its owners was that Graham Barstow was in the hospital with his wife by his side, and that her mother and her dog had rescued him from drowning in a cave. But this alone could not account for an atmosphere she sensed but could not yet identify as tainted.

What's happened here? What are these people like? She looked at Kristin, who was sitting with her bandaged feet propped on a hassock, gazing at the fire.

Kristin had not moved or spoken since accepting a cup of tea sometime before with the irrelevant remark that the day had passed very quickly. The tea was cold and untouched in her hands. Her short curly hair was wildly ruffled, her thin cheeks hollow from fatigue and strain, her gray eyes blank as she looked into the past and the future and grieved silently.

The girl, so very like the mother, swallowed her questions with her sandwich and took the teacup out of the limp hands. Having had little to eat during a complicated day-long journey, she ate another sandwich, but at length she pushed the plates away and stared at the fire that sizzled and crackled on the grate, its cheerfulness confined behind the screen.

She's finally taken her ring off, Polly thought sadly, resignedly. I wondered when she would. She hasn't said a word about Dad, not one. Not that she has to. It's all been said. I've watched it coming . . . He's an inadequate man—she's not perfect either—my god, who is?—but I love him, I love them both . . . He gave me a lot in his own way . . . But you can't make a person change or learn or grow. You can only change yourself . . . I wonder if he'll call . . .

When the telephone in the kitchen shattered the silence she jumped up and ran to answer it. The caller was Dr. Vernon, still hard at work at ten-thirty in a hospital totally unequipped to serve the island population at the height of the season. His was the last voice she expected to hear, but she had been his summer patient for ten years and loved him for his staunchness and generosity. She greeted him with affection.

"Glad you're here, young lady," he said grimly. "How's your mother taking it? The dog, I mean."

"Oh. You heard."

"Hear everything sooner or later. Not surprised, though. I could tell. He looked a lot different last year. These big dogs—ten, twelve years is about it. I'm sorry. He was a good fella."

"But how—"

"Police were here. Seems they took over at the ferry."

Fresh tears rolled down the girl's face. "Yes, they were wonderful. They took him to a vet—he'll be—he'll be cremated there. What with Mom's feet and—and all, we were pretty helpless. He's—he was pretty heavy. It all happened—it was all over so *fast!* We just—we weren't ready. He hadn't been sick. Just—tired. Mom's been sitting like a statue since we got home."

"Nobody's ever ready, even when they are. You were lucky and he was lucky. He didn't suffer. It was a merciful death. A clean death. Not like—" He stopped abruptly.

"Dr. Vernon, what's wrong? Why were the police there? What is it? What happened?"

"It's Barstow. Your mother told you about him, of course."

"Yes, but—but that was an accident. Wasn't it? Surely they don't suspect that Mother had anything to do with it!"

Roused at last, Kristin put her feet on the floor as a cold hand closed around her heart.

"No no, certainly not," the doctor said testily, as though she should have known better than to say such a thing. "Polly, Barstow's dead."

"Oh *no!* Oh my god! What—? Mom!" By now Kristin was halfway across the room. "Just a minute, Doctor! She's coming."

Kristin took the receiver with a cold stiff hand and shook her head impatiently when the girl motioned her to a chair. "Hello, Doctor. Don't any other doctors work there anymore? Graham's dead, isn't he. What can I do?" Her voice was steady, almost detached. She might have been inquiring about what to bring to the hospital benefit.

"Wish you didn't have to do anything, Kris, but I need your help. Polly's, rather. With his wife. Best I could do was give her a sedative. But she'll have to go home. We're full up here and that's that. Not a bed to be had." Not even her husband's, he thought swiftly. "She's in no condition to drive, of course. I've released his things. Polly can take them too."

"I'll come for her . . . No, it's all right. I might as well keep busy. I'm just one of the walking wounded anyway. And Polly doesn't know the way as well as I do . . . Well, all right, she can do the driving. We'll be right over. But I don't get it. I thought—well, I don't know what I thought. I thought he just had a bad concussion. Maybe a bad fracture. You weren't too sure about his condition but did you think it was that bad?"

"No."

Even in such circumstances and even for him, such brusqueness was unusual. She said directly, "Something's up. You'd better tell me. I'd better be prepared."

"I agree. Kris, Barstow didn't die of a skull fracture—and he had a serious one this time—either by accident or any other way, *cave*-wise. He was murdered tonight. Stabbed through the heart while he was still unconscious."

The doctor had left Myra Barstow in a squashy old armchair in his office, sedated, spent from shock and an interview with a state police detective, the village police chief, and himself in his official capacity as a state medical examiner.

Her husband, Myra had told them, was still unconscious but breathing normally as far as she could tell when she got to his room. At least, he looked quite peacefully asleep.

Yes, the intravenous equipment was working properly. At about ten past eight Miss Field—

"Katherine Field? She was on duty there?" Kristin said. "My god!"

"We were so shorthanded that even if I'd known, I couldn't've done a thing about it," Dr. Vernon said. "Head nurse didn't know anything or she wouldn't've allowed it. Sensible old gal."

"Have the police—do they—?"

"I don't know, Kris, I just don't know. She did a damfool thing—she left! But she didn't do it. Couldn't've! Nonsense!"

"Well anyway, go on. What else did Myra say?"

Miss Field came in to check the I.V. and connected a new bottle. She left at eight-fifteen, saying she would be back shortly to check it again.

No, no one else came in. Someone did knock on the door just as Miss Field was leaving, and she heard her say something like, "No, not now," and go out and close the door. She didn't know who it was. Another nurse, probably.

Anyway, she sat watching Graham for perhaps fifteen minutes, holding his hand, talking to him, trying to bring him around, but after sitting for almost an hour she was stiff and uncomfortable and at eight-thirty she went out, first to the rest room and then to the cafeteria to get a cup of coffee.

She was gone for about fifteen minutes, maybe less. She bought another cup of coffee to take back, and when she returned Miss Field was at Graham's door. Well, it was open a foot or two and Miss Field had her hand on the knob. She might have been going in or just coming out, but when she saw Myra she turned and ran down the hall.

And then she, Myra, went in and the first thing she saw was the expression on Graham's face. He had looked so peaceful and handsome, and now his face was contorted. And there was something dark sticking up out of his white hospital gown. You could see it very clearly because his bed faced the door, and it certainly had not been there when she left! And when she went nearer she could see what it was—the old Indian flint cutting tool that Graham had found on the hill and that was missing from his pegboard exhibit at the fair.

Then she dropped the coffee and ran out crying for help.

Yes, there were people in the hall—a few patients, some visitors—but no one she recognized. Miss Field was not on the floor.

When she'd first arrived she had seen Sam Potter, a former student of her husband's, downstairs in the lobby talking with Miss Field.

No, she had not spoken with them. She was anxious about her

56

husband, and in any case she had nothing to say to Sam Potter, whose hard feeling about her husband was no secret. He had quarreled publicly with Graham at the fair the day before, and almost killed him later during the horse show.

Well, it could have been an accident, of course. That sort of thing happened all the time with hackneys, and she had always hoped that Graham would give the hobby up. He wasn't *young* anymore.

Oh no, it was not the first accident he'd had with hackneys. He'd had one at the fair a year ago and had spent a day or two right here in the hospital.

No, the Potter boy had not been involved. In fact he and Graham had never been together in previous shows.

Well, actually, she really could not describe their quarrel *as* a quarrel. It took two to quarrel, after all. More of a misunderstanding on the young man's part, regarding his doctoral dissertation. Graham had been his adviser and had not approved it, and had simply given up trying to explain why. He'd been so patient, he always was, and his students at the university loved him. But Sam Potter was like a dog worrying a bone. He just wouldn't give up, wouldn't accept reality. These young people! Always in such a hurry! Always wanting something for nothing—or too soon. Of course it had been a bad blow, an awful disappointment, working so hard and so long on his paper only to find that it was unacceptable. But Sam Potter wasn't the first doctoral candidate to have to start over. Graham himself had had to rework a large part of his own dissertation. But young people seemed to have no sticking power anymore.

No, of course she didn't know Graham was going to the beach— or why—after leaving the hospital at noon. At his insistence she drove him back to the fair grounds to get his car. He had said he was going home to rest, and in a way she was almost glad he'd left before the judging—he didn't even go into the Grange Hall—because this gave her time to go on looking for the missing flint. He was always extremely possessive about his things. But she couldn't find it, so she went home to see how he was feeling. But he wasn't there. Restless and worried, she took her sick dog for a little walk, which was why she'd missed the calls from the fair and the people at the beach. But they'd been so kind—they'd kept trying until they got her. Everyone was so kind . . .

She had been allowed to see Graham just for a moment before they took him for x-rays. Then Dr. Vernon had sent her home, so her first really good look at him was after supper and a trip to the vet, Dr. Amaral, when she came back at seven forty-five.

No, she couldn't think of anything else. The Indian flint? Well, the Potter boy had been angry about that too. Something about its proper ownership—exactly where Graham had discovered it or where it should be housed. The hill had been an Indian burying ground and the Island Historical Society naturally wanted all finds in their museum. Well, but Graham had given them everything he'd ever found except this one thing. And she never thought it mattered. Until now . . .

"And then she broke down," Vernon said. "I gave her a shot and let her rest while I examined the body and so on. Then I called you." He looked at her critically. "You're all in. Get Mrs. Barstow to bed, and then you take a sleeping pill and pack it in," he said severely.

She smiled wanly. "Pack it in yourself. You look exhausted."

"I am. Been quite a day. Here, take my arm. Come along, Polly, we'll go get her. His things are in my office too. You can take them. Quiet here now, thank god. In forty years of practice I've never had a *patient* die of murder! And there's something else about it that bugs me."

"Like who killed him, to begin with," Kristin said somberly, and winced as they walked to the elevator. "Because it wasn't Kathy Field or Sam. It couldn't be!"

"Wasn't what I meant—not that I wouldn't like to know." He pushed the button with an arthritic finger and the door closed soundlessly on the empty peaceful lobby.

"She really nailed him, didn't she," Kristin said in dismay.

"Sam? Looks like it. What's more, he was the one who tried getting into Barstow's room! But dammit, Kris, I know that boy! If he were planning to commit a murder he'd hire a hall and sell tickets!" He shook his head angrily and the light danced off his bald crown. "I guess they're looking for him. Guess!" He snorted.

"I know they're looking for him! And Kathy! An aide saw him on the floor and thought he was *cute!* She didn't know who he was, but one word about that hair and *I* did! God, what a day!" His shoulders had been bent long ago by thousands like it.

It was not until they reached his office door, behind which Myra sat in flaccid misery, that Kristin said hesitantly, "I was thinking of going home tomorrow or Tuesday if I can get car space on the boat, Doctor. After I take care of—of Frey, I mean. I had planned to stay if they'd left tonight but—but now—well, what do you think? Can I leave her alone? I don't want to walk out on her but—I've had it."

He took his hand off the knob and rubbed his eyes wearily. "Police asked her about relatives, anyone who could come and help till this is over. But the only one she wants is in France. It'd take several days for him to make arrangements to get here, she said. I don't know, Kris. She'd be alone. But I can't tell you what to do. God knows you're not obligated to stay but—"

"But I guess we'll have to, won't we." Her eyes filled with tears.

"It's all right, Mom," Polly whispered, giving her a hug. "It's all right. I'm here. I'll help."

She opened the door with a firm young hand.

The station wagon all but drove itself, but every inch of the ride home was horrible. Myra lolled on the front seat, stupid from shock and sedation, and Dandie whimpered in the back.

What am I going to *do* with them? Kristin asked herself, and glanced in the rear-view mirror for the hundredth time at Polly following in the old Chevrolet. Poor darling, what a vacation for her after the work she's been putting in. Well, it can't be helped. I hope she can drive Graham's bug, unless the police are nice enough to drive it back for Myra . . . It must be on the highway near the end of West Beach . . . He saw Katherine Field in the hospital last night or early this morning. He planned to leave the hospital at noon and meet her on the little beach when she was off duty. And he came through the caves to where she was waiting . . . How come Sam Potter was with her? Did he want to see Graham too? Did he swim away and then swim into the cave and lie in

59

wait for him . . . ? They all seem to know those little caves. Graham was used to them by now, he'd never have slipped. Not in rope-soled shoes . . .

That's a very hot little car, that Porsche. There can't be many like it on the island, and the beaches weren't too crowded today, so either someone with a beef against him knew he'd be there and followed him, or happened to be cruising down the road and saw that yellow bug and went looking for him. He was fully dressed, he'd have stood out like a sore thumb on the beach . . .

And the murderer saw him . . . saw him going into the caves . . . and followed slowly, sort of meandering casually . . . and then snuck inside too, and waited . . .

But Kathy Field was with Graham—

Oh nonsense! She couldn't have killed him! *No.* But they talked awhile, probably about his divorcing Myra, and she left him there thinking things over, and then—

Oh god! I'm no good at this!

Myra's safety belts had not been fastened on and she was sliding on the seat. Kristin turned into the old road as if she were taking a hairpin curve in a vehicle loaded with fine crystal—and smiled involuntarily at the Chevrolet, which hissed and steamed along behind like a faithful dragon.

The next twenty minutes were much worse. Myra's heavy body hung like dead weight between them as they helped her into the house, and Kristin's feet, crushed with every step, felt like blobs of fire.

And then Myra had to be undressed and toileted and washed, a peculiarly distasteful task since she was neither an utter stranger nor someone close and loved in whose terrible bereavement they had a genuine share. Intimacy had been thrust on them and their very natural instinct was to recoil from it. But calamity had engulfed them and their schooled response was to unite against it. So they did what had to be done, quietly and gently, their voices soft and reassuring, and left her in her own bed with Dandie trembling beside her, rather than in the back bedroom where the murdered man had slept alone for so long.

"Sleep now," Kristin whispered, stroking Myra's forehead. "Sleep now."

She noticed, as she gathered her small belongings, that her wedding ring was not on the dresser. Its absence puzzled her because she had put it there and left it there on Saturday evening, but she felt no twinge of loss or regret. Polly closed her suitcase and picked it up, and they tiptoed out and closed the door.

"That goes for you too, Mom," Polly said, putting the suitcase down in the back room. "It's been a heavy day. Come on." She pulled out the trundle bed. "Where are the sheets and blankets?"

"In the hall linen closet next to the bathroom. Pillows are here on the closet shelf." She opened the door and squinted. "That's funny . . ."

"What's funny? Is someone sleeping in there?"

"Where?"

"On the shelf."

"Very funny."

"Well, what *is* so funny?"

"About what?"

"*I* don't know. You opened the closet and said something was funny."

"Oh. Sorry. I'm not sure. It looks different, is all. We looked into this one and Myra's and decided we couldn't unpack—there just wasn't any room."

"How does it look different?" the girl said, coming over to look. "It seems pretty full to me."

"Well, it was really full before. You'd almost think Graham was planning to live here, though I don't see how—he was going to start working in Hollybrook next month. But it looks as if he moved everything he owned to this house. Anyway, I'm sure something's missing, though I'm not sure what."

"The stuff we brought from the hospital?"

"No, much more than two pairs of slacks. It's a now-you-see-it-now-you-don't thing. I know that I know what it is—what*ever* it is—but I don't know what it is that I know."

Polly sighed and returned to the bedmaking as Kristin opened the dresser drawers, looked into each without touching anything, and then bent over her suitcase and made a hasty inventory. "God!" She straightened with an effort and limped out of the room.

Polly found her staring at the wall of books and then at everything else in the room as though she were not merely from another culture but from another planet. "Polly," she said, her eyes closed in concentration, "was there a covered cloisonné dish on Myra's dresser? A lovely thing. For her jewelry. And an antique silver-backed hairbrush with a fancy letter B on it?"

"No, nothing like that. Or in the bathroom either. Why?"

"Something's missing from Graham's closet. And my new bathing suit—with the tags still on it—isn't in my suitcase." She lowered her voice as they went back to the bedroom. "And my new mini-hair dryer and the little radio are gone too. Even my ring is gone. And some books aren't on the shelves either. I know, because I practically memorized them before I picked one to take to the beach this morning. It was awful, too," she added, flopping onto the bed. "And I bet there's a bunch of other small items gone. Polly, whoever tried breaking in just before we—before I went to get you, came back just after I left."

"Are you sure?"

"Absolutely certain."

"But why? How? He heard you and ran. And Frey—Frey was big and loud and must've scared him to death."

"Because I'm an idiot, that's why. First I turned out every light in the house, the way I've done ever since the War, and I fell asleep, so the house seemed empty. Even with the car out back, assuming he saw it. Then we scared him off, but I never opened the door so Frey didn't get a chance to chase him. I had to go for you, and god knows when he would have come back if I let him go. I couldn't wait for him and I couldn't go with him, not with these feet. Anyway, then I turned a few lights on the way people do when they want to make a house look occupied, and then we left. And that car makes as much noise as a truck now, so he must have known, once he was a hundred feet down the hill and knew he wasn't being chased, that it was safe to try again. Because those things are gone, Polly. Small things of some value that could be carried easily and disposed of easily. By somebody who looks like having had lots of practice."

"Do you want to call the police? Maybe you should, Mom. Maybe they can find fingerprints before we smear everything up."

"No. Anybody that quick and clever would wear gloves. And anyway I don't care. I don't want them clumping through the house. Myra's had enough. And so have I. And you too. Thank you, Polly, you've been a darling. I couldn't have managed without you."

"Well then, how about copping some z's? It's about time."

"I will. Soon. No, don't fuss—I think I'll have that tea now. With some scotch—if our thief wasn't above stealing an open bottle. You pop off. I'll be in, in a bit."

She could not remember a time when she had been more exhausted, yet she was wide awake after a cup of hot tea heavily laced with whiskey. And after undressing and washing and taking one of the sleeping pills Dr. Vernon had given her, she lay in the narrow bed staring for half an hour at a ceiling she could not see.

Presently her ankle began to itch and she scratched it, making it worse. The itch spread, creeping from ankle to knee with an awful, sure slowness, and she closed her eyes determinedly, trying to escape from it into sleep. But every nerve in her body was screaming from this new and exquisite agony and she could not ignore it. Oh *no!* she thought, suspicious, and got out of bed and turned on the light to look.

Poison ivy.

This *too!*

I must have gotten it when I stumbled up the beach path with Frey and went to the hospital, she told herself, applying hot packs in the bathroom. If she had not been so furious she would have burst out laughing. Of all the anticlimaxes to murder that the Backroom Boys up there somewhere in the Ironical Department could devise, poison ivy was the meanest!

She chided herself for being so self-centered. Josh had said that he'd been out of action for three days with a rash all over his body almost bad enough to hospitalize him. Myra had it too. And if John were here, *he* would have had it by now. He'd gotten it every summer since she'd known him.

This thought, and fifteen more minutes of wet towels wrung out but hot enough to burn, quieted the hysteria and the itching. But still she could not sleep. Her mind was a jumble of all that had happened since Friday afternoon; she could not fix on anything. And always behind her closed eyelids was a picture of Frey leaping over the chain, and in her ears the dreadful sound of his great body hitting the iron ramp, and then her tears and Polly's shining diamondlike on his coat, smooth and silky from his last brushing, and the onlookers whispering about the hero dog who had saved a man from drowning, and, finally, the police carrying him away. By tomorrow all that would be left of him would be a collar, a name tag, a little pile of gray dust and bits of bone, and memories of a love and loyalty no less valuable and necessary in this insane world for having stood on four feet instead of two. Stinging tears hurt her eyes and ran down her cheeks.

Once again she flung off the covers, but this time she put on a robe, took a blanket from the bed, and went into the living room. I'll read for a while, she thought. Maybe I'll be able to fall asleep on the couch. But the hothouse atmosphere of the room choked her, and in a new burst of temper she went out to the sun deck without even bothering to turn on a light. Wrapped in the blanket, she sat on the weathered deacon's bench, put her feet up, and began to review her situation.

It appeared to consist principally of anger, which she could not sleep off or walk off or work off, and within moments it became so diffuse yet so intense that to sit quietly and contain it was equally impossible.

And then an iron vise fastened on her arm and a low voice said in her ear, "Be quiet. Sit still. Or you'll be sorry."

"I actually didn't stop to think what I was saying," she told the detective much later. "I didn't even think about my feet. I wasn't even scared, I was so furious! That wild-haired lunatic was so taken aback that if he'd had a loaded gun in his hand he wouldn't have known what to do with it!"

"What *did* you say?"

"I said—uh—'That's what you think, you son of a bitch! Who do you think you're talking to!' And then I jumped up and punched him—in the chest! Just about a foot higher and I think I'd have knocked him flat!"

Sam Potter thought so too.

Chapter VII

Sam Potter's life thus far was punctuated by three major experiences in stress. He had once spent several seconds eyeballing it with a shark at five fathoms. His parachute had opened tardily in a sky dive. His brakes had failed one day at a busy grade crossing. And now, attacked on the Barstows' sun deck by an insomniac with a splendid right that flashed out of a blanket like a bolt of lightning, he experienced once again that ineffable sense of strain.

Breathless and utterly astounded, he fell back a step or two and squinted, trying to see Kristin's face, and she instantly recognized his stocky body and the vigorous round of his skull.

I've nothing to fear from this crazy guy, she told herself, picking up the blanket and wrapping herself in it. She stood waiting, regal as an Indian, wondering what he was going to say and thinking that nothing he could say would surprise her.

"Well, who *am* I talking to?" he demanded. "And what in hell're you sitting out here for at this time of night? You scared the bejesus out of me!"

"*I*—! Boy, you've got gall. Don't push me, Sam Potter. I'm not in the mood to be pushed. Just watch out what you say next or I'll punch you in the mouth. Now sit down. I can't ask you in, one way and another, but you've got some explaining to do. And some decisions to make. The police must be combing the whole island looking for you. You probably know why."

"Jesus Christ, you're something else! Hold it, hold it! That's a compliment! Okay, for what it's worth, I'm sorry. Not to put too fine a point on it, I was trespassing."

"According to Dr. Vernon, who's a great fan of yours, it would have been more in character to barge right in. I was told skulking wasn't your style, Sam." Her voice, though still a little tart, was low and she was quite composed. This too surprised her since she had never expected to see him here or anywhere else. But, as she had told the doctor, there was in the events of the past two and a half days a lunatic unity into which this strange interview fitted very nicely.

"It isn't," he said ruefully. "But then, I didn't expect anybody to be here." She made an impatient little gesture and he added hurriedly, "Not that that changes anything, of course. I don't mean that. I mean—" He sighed and leaned back, exhausted and defeated for the second time in his twenty-six years. "I don't know what I mean. It's all—a mess. A total lousy mess."

True, she thought. Graham Barstow's dead, murdered, and Myra has served you to the police on a silver platter. And then there's your doctorate. Your professional goals. Your future.

"It seems to be coming at you from all sides," she said softly, as though she were talking to herself about her own predicament.

"Yeah . . . that's it. Like a bombardment . . . And you get numb . . ."

"Yes. But it really keeps on hurting. You can still feel it." Her eyes sparkled with tears and she blinked them away.

He did not see the tears. He only heard her recognize and echo his own pain, and he sat up. "Say, are you a shrink? You sound like one."

She smiled wryly. "Now that *is* a compliment. No, I'm not a shrink, I'm a textile designer. But I've learned quite a bit about human relations over the years. A professor's wife has to be up on things like that. I'm Kristin Weiden."

He stared at her in consternation. "Oh my god! Oh my aching—! It figures—it's all I need! Do you know who you are? You're John Weiden's wife, that's who you are! He wrote me a swell recommendation—I just came east and got a job in Hollybrook. System-wide director of the art program. God knows how long I'll keep it!"

Another surprise. "You know John? Were you his student as well as Graham's?"

"No. John's consulting team was helping me turn my school upside down out on the Coast last year. He didn't mention me? When he comes out and finds me here—!"

"He had to go back to California the day after we got here," she said, and marveled at how little it mattered now.

"That's rough. No, I was Barstow's student—doctoral advisee. And after what happened between us, it was a shocker finding out *he's* —he *was*—going to be the new curriculum superintendent in Hollybrook. I knew he was leaving the university but I didn't know where he was going till I got back here. Didn't he mention me either?"

"No. And from what Myra told the police tonight, I'd guess he didn't even want to think about you."

"That's understandable, Mrs. Weiden. Every time he did think about me his conscience hurt like hell. Only, it didn't hurt him enough, the bastard. God, what a world! Talk about small! Between the two of us, we've brought a lot of people together. And what a parlay—all the way to murder!"

"With you the front runner," she said bluntly. "Well, now that we've been introduced, let's talk. It'll be dawn soon, for one thing."

"How'd you know my name?"

"I saw you at the fair arguing with Graham on Saturday. And then I saw you on the beach yesterday arguing with your cousin Kathy. I talked to her after you roared off—"

"So you were the gal with the dog and the handkerchief! She told me about you but she didn't know who you were."

"I didn't know who you both were until Dr. Vernon told me. He said you were a painter—a fine one."

He laughed at the dubious note in her voice. "I'm hanging at the fair—too bad you didn't see my stuff. I'd brought a few things to school to liven up the place but I need the money, what with all this cross-country moving, and I thought they'd sell so I carted them down here Friday night. I can always do some more."

Like turning on a tap, she thought, smiling, and speculated that the "stuff" was probably crude, phony, and far-out, featuring black whorls on puce backgrounds titled *Conflict*. More than likely Sam merited hanging. Her smile faded at the word. "I also saw Graham on the beach with Kathy—and—and afterward."

"Yes, I know. And I heard about Frey too—the news is all over the island. I'm very sorry about that. But someday—"

"No. No, I'll never have another dog."

"Well, maybe. It was a great thing he did. God, those caves are tricky places."

"Sam, did you—?"

"No, I didn't. I was snorkeling off West Beach and I plowed around the corner because Kathy had told me she was going to meet Barstow there. It's a good swim anyway, I've done it lots of times. I had the idea that she'd help get him to change his mind and give me a break. I'll go into about what in a minute. Anyway, I told her what I wanted and she objected, which was understandable. But that's why we had a fight. I gave up and took off."

"Where did you go after you left her?"

"No place. I swam back and got my things and drove around looking for something to sketch or paint that appealed to me. But I didn't see anything interesting and the light wasn't what I wanted anyway. Well, I did see the most perfect cedar I've *ever* seen. Very satisfying tree, the cedar . . . boy, that was some tree . . . Then I went home to wash and change and go have supper with Kathy. She's been on night duty all week but she was going back on the floor early because they're so shorthanded. We had a lot to talk about, and I was going to drive her over."

"So you have no alibi, then, for the time he was in the cave. Neither does she, for that matter."

"No. She said she left him there. To think, she said. He liked sitting on those crazy barnacles, looking out at the water. Say, you're assuming he was deliberately attacked."

"After what's just happened to him, Sam, it's very hard not to."

"Yeah. Very. How'd you know I knew about it—the murder? Did you speak to Kathy?"

"No. I had to bring Myra home and Dr. Vernon told me you were missing and she was too. He said you didn't do it."

"But I could have. Yes, well, there again, so could Kathy. And she didn't do it either. And anyway, neither of us knew what

68

had happened to him in the cave, so when we got to the hospital and saw Myra coming in again, we wondered what in hell was going on and Kathy went up after her. She said later that she had a feeling something was wrong, and when she saw his chart at the desk again she almost collapsed. She's out of her skull now. She really loved that guy. I'm still too bitter against him to have any grief but I'm not about to say I'm glad he's dead. Apart from its making my claim harder to establish, what happened to him was bad news. Not that it's easier to die wide awake watching someone coming at you with a deadly weapon! But this! It's on a level with putting needles and razor blades in kids' trick-or-treat candy!"

"Sam, Kathy only said she couldn't side with you although you had a justifiable grievance against Graham. Myra said it was about your doctoral fiasco," and she told him what Myra had said.

"Well, that's partly true, but if it's all the information the police ever got, they'd think I was a paranoid punk who brooded until I was thirsting for Barstow's blood. I *had* done a lot of work and he *was* my adviser and he *didn't* approve it and I *did* quit. What Myra didn't say—and she's a great gal, everyone liked her—liked them both—they used to give great parties for his gang—but her sun rose and set on the good doctor so naturally she'd see it his way. Especially if it was all he ever told her. But what she didn't say or didn't know is this—he *stole* my work! Every idea I had, every plan I discussed with him before I went to Cal, and after I came back two years ago for my year of residency—everything went into his new book! He said that, as his research assistant, my work was ancillary to his. That it was understood that my topic was part of his whole project. He was a great guy so I can't account for what he did. There was no bad feeling between us so it couldn't have been malice. And he was damn smart, very very sharp, so it's even harder to put it down to a simple misunderstanding of what I was doing, and who and what I was doing it for. To say nothing of the fact that my notes predate becoming his assistant. John could testify to that because my work was part of what his team was concerned with. Barstow said it would be impossible for me to prove it since he'd discussed the same stuff the year before. Well, he did—but that's because *I* was the one who began it! And I'd worked a good part of it out before I went out west. But like a fool I believed him. He was so *sure*. I never even bothered to check it out with a lawyer. No money anyway. So I did quit—because I needed to make a few bucks before going someplace else and starting all over again. And there was also the mere matter of my state of mind. I was mad enough to kill him with my bare hands and I thought I better take off before I did! God! I had to go back to Cal and teach this past year just to get my sanity back!"

"Some people would say that proved you were crazy. But is it possible that you misunderstood him?"

"Sure. Anything's possible. Tomorrow our glorious leader will disband the army and throw away the bombs because he got a postcard from me. Look. Four years ago I started developing that dissertation. Then I got a job in Cal and developed it further. Then I came back two years ago to finish my course work *and* everything else. And I was almost done last year when he gave me the shaft. I'd taken a leave of absence so I went back out west again. And when one of my buddies at the university wrote and told me Barstow's new book was going to the galleys and would be ready for final corrections this summer, I started to boil again. I'd heard about the job in Hollybrook and I wrote to John for a reference because he knew something about my administrative style and ideas when he was out there, and it worked out beautifully, and I came back. I thought that if I were on the scene, I could get my hands on those galleys—maybe even snag his working copy somehow—and get a lawyer *this* trip and go back to the university with the proof and be reinstated. *My* stuff, all my papers, everything's down the hill in my old room. You could see for yourself if you compared the two. *If!*"

"I don't get it, Sam. He couldn't have been your only adviser. Wasn't there someone else to turn to?"

"No. Oh, I had three other readers on my advisory committee but he was the senior member and no one would even listen to me. Christ, what a scandal it would've made! It wasn't that they didn't believe me. They didn't want to! I could go into the politics of the thing but it would take too long, and as you said, it's beginning to get light now and I wouldn't want Myra to see me here. That'd be too much, poor gal."

A gleaming band of delicate golden pink was pulsating on the horizon, and, even as they looked, the black ocean began to lighten and one by one the stars winked out.

"All I'll say at this point," he went on, "and you can take my word or not as you choose, is that Barstow had the leverage and he used it. He sort of bad-mouthed me in a very charming way —his way. But you know him, so you know what I mean. I hate to disillusion you, but the Groves of Academe are full of sharpshooters and cutthroats and opportunists just like in the world of business. I'm one of many this has happened to. John must've told you about things like this—he's been around."

"I've heard of it but I guess I never really believed it. Did any of this have anything to do with Graham's resignation?"

"This? God, no. *He* didn't have to leave. He was up for provost—and he'd've been president sooner or later. No, the reason why he left was all tied up with Kathy. The university and advancement—that was age, that was his wife who's older than he is—was. Hollybrook was the beginning of a whole new life, a new wife, youth, the works. Do you know what he was planning to do? Kathy told me yesterday at the beach. Live here, with her, and fly a chopper back and forth to Hollybrook! He had plenty of bread. Yeah, he really had it made. For the first time in his life, he told Kathy, he was happy. For that I'm sorry. He had a plan. It was all mapped out—and now it's all wiped out. I'd be sorry on principle."

"When did he meet her, before or after you returned to California?"

"Just after I went back. She was his nurse—he'd gotten banged up in the horse show. I guess you know about that."

"Yes, I heard. Did he know you and she were cousins when he stole your work?"

"Not from me. I had no reason to tell him that. We weren't on close personal terms although he knew I was an islander. Until Friday night I didn't even know *they* knew each other! She must have told him about the family—my parents were born here, died here too when I was a kid—I grew up with my grandmother and her sister—and she probably told him I'd be in Hollybrook, because I called home when I got back last week. But he went ahead anyway and of course he never told her. It isn't the sort of thing he'd tell anyone!"

"When did she tell him she knew? I assume she knew last year."

"She knew before she met him who he was and what he'd done to me, but she fell for him anyway. That's the way life is. But she never told me about him because she didn't want a hassle. When I got the whole story Friday night I was furious and insisted she speak to him. So she finally told him she'd known for a year and more what he'd done. That was one of the things *they* argued about! But while I was away this past year, all I knew was that my grandmother and my aunt were very upset about something—which is one more reason I wanted to come home. They wouldn't tell me either, because they're closemouthed Yankees to begin with, and because I was so far away and Kathy was here and having plenty of her own troubles. All I was told was that she was in love with a married man who couldn't get a divorce—or maybe didn't want one. So all things considered, I thought that if I could get hold of those galleys I'd be sitting pretty. I assumed they'd be here because he was planning to move down here, as I told you, and Kathy said he'd moved practically all his stuff down here by now. He scooped me! To go out of the university in a blaze of academic glory, I suppose. Who knows? I asked him if he'd at least give me credit as co-author—I stooped that low!—and he said no. That was yesterday not long before the horse show. Another nice bit for the police! *I* didn't know he was going to be at the fair or in the show. I just bumped into him there."

"Well now, contrary to Myra, you don't give up all that easily, Sam. You're into housebreaking, too. For the third time. Or didn't you have anything to do with the first two tries? You could have made it over here by eight-thirty when you left the hospital."

"*Three?*"

"Last night at eight-thirty—but that was only an attempt which we scotched, Frey and I. And then right after that when we went out. And now. Two and one is three."

"*Uh*-uh! Whoever it was, it wasn't me. What with thrashing things out with Kathy and my grandmother and aunt, and wanting to see a few old friends, have some fun at the fair—see if I could still drive—and all that swimming—I was pretty busy, and at eight-thirty last night I was still at the hospital—oh god!"

"Oh Sam, *no!* Are you—are you sure?"

He looked at her bleakly. "Sure I'm sure. Funny, isn't it. I'm trying so hard to square myself with you that I save the police the trouble of putting the rope around my neck!"

"But—but maybe you were with someone when Graham was murdered. Think, Sam! Myra got there at a quarter to eight. At eight-thirty she went out of his room for coffee and was back in fifteen minutes. And found him dead."

"Okay . . . We saw her arrive. I told Kathy I'd be around awhile—check in with some old buddies I went to school with. Steve Black's the hospital pathologist and his wife Charlotte's a lab tech. So Kathy went upstairs and I went downstairs. But Steve and Charlotte were busy as hell, mainly on account of the fair. There's an epidemic of salmonella going around now and Steve was helping her do tests on fecal specimens. They could hardly keep up with all the work and they'd gone right through suppertime. That place is so understaffed, it'd make you sick! Anyway, they were ragged and they said they'd quit at eight-thirty ready or not, and meet me in the cafeteria and have a bite before they went home and dropped. So then I went upstairs to Barstow's room. That was at about eight-fifteen."

"It's pure hindsight, of course, but why didn't you go up with a loaded shotgun? You're crazy, Sam."

"Yeah. But I felt lousy about Barstow and Myra and the way she looked at me, and I had a stupid idea of apologizing to her— though I'm not sure about what. *I* didn't do anything to him! Maybe I was thinking about Kathy. Maybe I wanted to make a gesture. *I* don't know! Anyway, I knocked on his door just as Kathy was coming out, and I asked to see them—Myra, anyway, and she said no. She looked like hell and she answered me like a stranger. So I went out to my car to relax and wait for Steve and Charl, and I started thinking, and that's when I decided to break in here. I figured, knowing Myra, that she'd stay with him all night, and I didn't know they had company. I thought I'd have a good chance. But I was pretty bushed what with everything that had happened, and I dozed off. When I woke up and looked at my watch it was past eight forty-five and I ran back to the caf. Steve and Charl weren't there so I waited ten minutes and had some coffee, but they didn't show up so I went to their labs and they weren't there either. By then it was five after nine and I decided to take off and come up here, and I was just leaving when I heard someone crying. It was Kathy, in a back corner of the path lab. Well, I took her out of there and we drove around talking half the night and I got the whole story. Then I took her back to her apartment and came home and left the car there and came up here. I figured that if Myra *were* here, she'd be too sedated to notice anything. And as I said, I didn't know they had company. Barstow hadn't told Kathy so naturally she didn't tell me. Lousy communication. Too many people didn't tell each other too many things for too damned long!"

"I agree. And that's some story," Kristin said soberly. "Unless someone just happened to see you sleeping in your car, it doesn't matter whom you were with or what you were doing from eight-thirty to eight forty-five. It wouldn't make any difference."

"No. I guess it wouldn't . . ."

As they sat in silence, thinking, a chewink chirped softly and the great bowl of the sky shrank and lightened to a pearl gray and came closer to meet the rising sun. Out of the trees below floated bands of silvery mist that caught a tinge of pink—and shredded away. And then the brilliant red limb of the sun appeared on the edge of the water.

"Ah . . . look!" He turned to her, smiling, and her heart lifted at the sight of his face. It was as smooth and pure as a child's with wonder and joy. "I live just down the road," he said confidingly. "You've seen the old sign—Potter and Todd? That's my grandmother and her sister. When I was a kid I used to come up here to watch this. I learned to paint up here. What a place! I had the wildest fantasies about the Indians that were buried right under my feet, and I tried to paint them the way *I* thought they ought to look! I used to dig around a little too, and when I found something—oh wow!"

She smiled back at him, sharing his pleasure, liking him. But what he had just said reminded her of something else and she said seriously, "I hate to spoil this—but did you ever see the Indian cutting tool Graham had? It was part of his collection of island things."

"A cutting tool? Oh, the flint knife. Sure. In his office at the university. He brought it in one day just before I went back to the Coast and put it on his pegboard. Why?"

"Myra said you argued with him about that, too."

"I told him what I thought, if that's an argument. He told me where he found it and I knew the exact spot. On my grandmother's property where it abuts his. He owns the top of the hill but she owns all the rest. And anyway, it was a good one, it should've been in the museum here. He got miffed when I said so. I never saw it anyplace else. It was still sharp enough to do plenty of damage with, too. Why do you ask?"

"Because that's what he was killed with, Sam."

He stared at her. "That's what—? The murder weapon? All Kathy saw was that he'd been stabbed, she didn't know with what. Christ! What next!"

"Good question. Sam, what are we going to do?" Neither noticed her use of the plural.

"What *can* I do? I didn't kill him, but I guess I'm licked. I'm just sorry you're involved. Are you close to them?"

"I never met them until Friday afternoon. And now I'm stuck. I can't leave her alone and I don't want to stay. At least, I didn't till now."

He inferred that her loyalty was to Myra, and nodded. "Well, thanks for listening." He got up and gave her a suddenly shy smile. "I better take off. And you go get some sleep. You must be bushed." But he stood there as if waiting to be dismissed.

"Sam, what *was* the subject of your dissertation?"

"Huh? Oh." He grinned. "It's a beaut. You ready for this?"

She laughed. "As ready as I'll ever be. I've seen a lot of thesis titles."

He took a deep breath. "'A Rationale and Model for the Supervision of Teachers in a Comprehensive Approach to Multimedia Experiences in the Art Curriculum K Through Twelve. Including a Plan for an In-Service Training Program for, and Evaluation of, Teachers Carrying It Out.'"

"Is that *all?*" I bet the temperature rises when this fireball's around, she thought. Ideas burst out of him like the Fourth of July.

"Everything but the kitchen sink. I think big. At least," he said slowly, "I did. Ah well." He looked up at the sky. "Anyway, it's going to be a fine day. Thanks, Mrs. Weiden—"

"Please call me Kristin."

His deep blue eyes, candid and curious, appraised her thoughtfully. "Kristin. A good name for you. Crisp but sweet. Like an apple. Thank you, Kristin, I appreciate—well, thanks."

"Sam, please try not to worry. I'll help if I can. I'll do some scouting around—"

"For the galleys?"

"Don't get your hopes up, but I'll try."

"If I'm—not around, you can get my papers from my grandmother. Those ladies are both nuts. You'll like them."

"The way things have been going, I'm not sure I want to meet any more lunatics than I already know, Samuel."

"Good morning," Polly said from the doorway, and came out onto the sun deck looking puzzled, her lips tremulous with a dozen questions. Her short curls shone in the young light, and her clear gray eyes were moist from sleep.

Sam swung around and stared.

And again Kristin saw that look of extraordinary happiness spread over his round freckled face.

She smiled.

Chapter VIII

"I don't think I can sleep," Kristin said, crawling under the covers, "but if I do and Myra gets up—well, you know what to do. Or are you going back to bed too?"

The girl bent and kissed her. "No. I'm fine. I'll get dressed and have breakfast. If she needs anything I'll be ready. And—uh—Sam

—I mean, if Mr. Potter should call—I mean if the police—" She colored under Kristin's wry glance. "You just get some rest."

"That'll be the day." She wriggled and turned irritably on the narrow bed, then with a great sigh gave up the struggle for comfort. There were too many things to think about—in the bed that Graham Barstow had slept in.

Nevertheless she fell asleep instantly and when Polly came in two hours later with the news that it was eight-fifteen and the police were coming at nine, she got up feeling much better. "I actually feel I've been asleep for a week. I must have slept fast, but I can't walk fast!" She hobbled about, washing and dressing, and then they went into the kitchen.

"Hungry, Mom? What would you like to eat? Here's some coffee to start with. How about an omelet? Scrambled eggs? I could make a big batch for all of us. I ate a while ago but I'm still starved." She cracked an egg into a bowl but regarded it with sudden loathing. "Mom, what are we going to do?"

Kristin moved painfully to the other side of the table, reached for her cup, and stared out at the glittering ocean. Her rash had begun to itch again and the effort to keep from tearing the skin off her leg was making her stomach flip with nausea. "I don't know. Take one thing at a time, I guess. I'm not hungry. And I've got to fix my feet before the police come."

The door of the master bedroom opened, and she lowered her voice. "And I hope she goes out or does some gardening or something. I want to call Dr. Vernon and I've *got* to get into Graham's desk!"

But when Myra Barstow came down the steps into the kitchen, the only thing that seemed to matter now was how to help this woman who looked, despite her long drugged sleep, as if she had spent the night in a private and terrible agony.

Washing, anointing, and bandaging her feet had been a painful task, and putting hot packs on her leg was a tedious one. The toilet tank was leaking all over the floor and the sink was stopped up and drained slowly, which meant that she would have to do something else she didn't want to do—ask Perley Stokes to send his son

Toby to fix the plumbing again. And you're making everything worse, she told herself sternly, by thinking what you're thinking.

Which was that Myra was not behaving in the manner for which she had primed herself, so that she was also smarting with irrational resentment.

For Myra, perfectly groomed as usual and dressed in cotton slacks and a long-sleeved shirt for outdoor work, had taken over the kitchen and made a hearty breakfast for all of them (and she had obediently eaten it). Except that Myra regretted Kristin's loss while under her roof, the news of the burglary did not concern her: This sort of thing was now very common on the island and she and Graham had often wondered when their turn would come. She was more concerned with Dandie, whose bronchitis and fever were responding to cough medicine, a walloping twelve cc. of sulfa-dimethoxine, and streptomycin. She was clearly impressed by Polly and questioned her with quiet affectionate interest about her college work and career plans, and her sole and oblique reference to Graham's murder was the comment that she had been neglecting her garden. "If you'll do the dishes, dear," she said to the girl, "I'd better get busy. I haven't touched it for two weeks. It's still too early to do—anything else." And she was now outside weeding, snipping, watering, alone with her misery and looking as normal as bread and butter.

And Kristin, waiting irritably for the basin to drain, thought, What are we bothering to stay for! She continued with the hot packs, which soothed her rash and resentment but fired up her self-reproach —which increased her bad temper.

Rarely is the human genius for suffering this kind of self-inflicted pain frustrated by the arrival of the police.

State Police Detective Lieutenant Matthew Amaral and village Police Chief Philip Trueblood were not on the best of terms. Amaral, a handsome swarthy large man in his middle forties, wore a conservative suit with enviable flair, whereas Trueblood, dumpy and blurry-featured except for his protruding pale eyes, was all too conscious that he looked as distinguished in his blue tunic and trousers as he had in his diapers. But what really gave Trueblood a pain was that Amaral, once a lowly member of his force, had defected some years ago to the wider world of Greater Boston and the State Police and now, having recently returned to the island, ranked him in felony investigations requiring the knowledge and technical equipment he was forced to ask for. The disgruntled police chief could almost be heard protesting that it wasn't fair.

The younger man *had* heard him many times and at length, and with a weary shrug of his well-tailored shoulders had finally told Trueblood to go to hell. But now he faded into the background, and Trueblood whipped out his notebook, seizing the initiative with a truculent officiousness that amused Polly, frightened Myra, and exasperated Kristin.

He went for Polly first. "You're not a witness, young lady. Never met deceased. So I won't be needin' you. You can go if you want to."

"I don't want to."

"Then don't interrupt. Now. Mrs. Barstow. Glad to see you lookin' better. Few things I want to clear up with you 'n' then I'd be obliged if you'd come down to the station 'n' sign a statement."

"Why?" Kristin said.

"Material witness, that's why! Same goes for you too. And you'll both be appearin' at the inquest."

Lieutenant Amaral shook his head.

Myra turned very white. "But I told you all I knew last night. At the hospital."

"May *be*. May *be*. But you were pretty upset last night. Anybody'd be. Never know what you might overlook when you're in a state. So we'll go over it again. Till I'm sure I've got it *all*." He gave her a searching look and she winced as if he had thrown something at her. " 'N' by the way," he said, taking a small envelope from his notebook, "this is for you. Wife's first cousin judged your exhibits while you were out 'n' thought you'd like to have your ribbons as a souvenir. First prize for *you* and special mention for the doctor. But I guess it don't matter much now."

"No," Myra whispered. Two tears rolled down her cheeks which looked as lifeless as dead flowers in her garden. "No, it doesn't matter anymore."

"The Lord giveth, ma'am. The Lord giveth 'n' taketh away.

Nothin' we can do about that. Now, where were you 'n' what were you doin' last night from seven forty-five on?"

Myra repeated in a low faltering voice what she had said the night before, adding and omitting nothing to change the account the doctor had given Kristin.

"You say your husband was calm 'n' peaceful when you went out for coffee but looked contorted in the face when you got back," Trueblood said, and pounced like a cat. "How do you account for that?"

She stared at him.

"Well? How do you account for it?"

"How should I account for it? How can I account for it? I'm not a doctor. He was in pain. He was stabbed. He—it hurt. It must have hurt. It must have hurt him terribly!" She began rubbing at the rash under her long sleeves. "How do *you* account for it?"

Trueblood's face went blank and stupid, but evidently his power of concentration was inhibited by the gaze of four pairs of eyes. He flushed deeply. "*I'm* supposed to be askin' the questions. Now, he'd been unconscious for four, five hours. Was he movin'? Mumblin'?"

"No. No. He was quiet. I talked to him. I kept talking to him. I thought the sound of my voice—they say it helps bring them around—I talked to him. I held his hand. He didn't move."

"Hmmmm." Plainly at a loss, Trueblood made a great show of consulting his notebook. "Any enemies besides Sam'l Potter?"

"My husband had no enemies. He wasn't that sort of person. He didn't live that sort of life. He was a teacher and scholar. His is one of the Commonwealth's first families and it was an honor and a privilege to be associated with him."

"From what you said before, Sam'l Potter wouldn't think so."

"The Potter boy is a misguided young man. But certainly my husband did not consider him an enemy, no matter what he has done. He has a very quick temper, certainly."

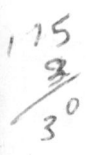

"And he was plenty visible past couple of days, too. Violent argument with the doctor before the hoss show. Come within an ace o' killin' him *at* the hoss show. Was on the beach near that cave yesterday afternoon. And tried to get in to see the doctor last night, accordin' to the nurse's description of him. Oh yes, he was there. And the murder weapon, which was missin' off the doctor's pegboard—Sam'l disputed ownership of that with him, didn't you say?"

Polly gasped.

Myra's broad shoulders rose and fell helplessly.

"You're not co-operatin'," Trueblood said resentfully.

"What do you want her to *do?*" Kristin said. "Be judge and jury and condemn Sam to death?"

The police chief ignored this and directed his boiled gaze at Polly. "What do you know about Potter, young lady? Noticed you jumped just then. What's Sam Potter to you?"

"The first I knew about any of this was last night when my mother picked me up at the ferry," the girl said, calmly equivocal. Kristin smiled behind her hand.

"Hmmmmm. One more question, Mrs. Barstow. Sometimes a wife don't know or don't like to say everything a man's been up to. Speak well o' the dead, y'know. Keep things under the rug. All very well, very understandable too. But *not* in a murder case, y'know. Now, was the doctor playin' around? Any gals on his string? Plenty opportunity in a big school—young women, pretty women, jealous women, under his nose all day—" The tip of his tongue flicked the corners of his lips and his eyes narrowed in a kind of silent snigger. All four of them looked at him contemptuously but he was too absorbed in his Arabian Nights fantasy to notice.

Myra stood up. "My husband and I were happily married for thirty-five years," she said with dignity, "and *no one* was going to come between *us*. I've answered your questions. I have nothing else to say. There's nothing else I can say. When you're ready I'll go to your office and sign a statement. I have to take my dog for another shot, and then I'm going to arrange for my husband's burial. You'll find me in my garden."

Afraid that he might not, he jumped up and followed her and Dandie out of the house. Presently two cars were heard going down the hill. Then all was silent again.

Now what am I supposed to say? Kristin thought during the silence. Myra had said nothing about Graham's plan to divorce her and marry Kathy Field. And nothing about the real reason for

Sam's murderous anger toward his former adviser: the imminent publication of Barstow's book plagiarizing his dissertation.

But at least six people on this island know about the one, she told herself, and at least five know about the other. And some of them know, I'm sure, that I know. And they know who I saw on the beach yesterday. Suppose one of them says something? What am I supposed to do, back Myra up—which amounts to protecting Kathy and Sam? Which also amounts to lying and suppressing evidence? Or tell what I know and let the chips fall where they may? After all, I'm not the judge and the jury either. And I'm not really involved in the nitty-gritty of all this. Naturally Myra wants to protect Graham's name. In her place I would do the same. But I'm not, and this isn't any of my business.

And I don't like the look in that detective's eye. He's sitting there huge and handsome, waiting to pounce the way Trueblood did. How do I know what he's thinking about? How do I know *he* didn't see me on the beach yesterday? He looks familiar . . . I wonder if he's related to the vet . . . No, I don't think so—he's twice as big as Dr. Amaral, if I remember correctly after two years . . .

Oh god, I wish I knew what to do . . .

Well, what *are* you going to do?

I guess I'll just have to lie . . .

Of course.

She smiled sunnily. Sometimes there was nothing else to do but lie. In the interests of Truth and Justice, naturally. The irony appealed to her perverse humor, a development of the past three years. She looked at Lieutenant Amaral, took his measure, dismissed him, and waited serenely to be questioned.

Matt Amaral was anything but vain, complacent, or a fool. He disliked seeing Phil Trueblood upset people and make an ass of himself besides. But in doing so, Phil left him as free as a fly on a wall to observe witnesses, and he was aware that this angular attractive cranky woman had written him off along with the chief. Well, she'd find out soon that she'd made a mistake, the same one that many others had made. Disarmingly, with the perception of a mind reader, he approached from another direction.

"You're quite right, Mrs. Weiden, you did see me." And you

weren't wearing a wedding ring last night either. Now why? he thought, moving to the chair Trueblood had vacated. "Last night at the ferry," he said kindly. "I was talking with two troopers on duty. They carried Frey to my car and I took him to the hospital. I'm very sorry. He was a fine animal. A brave one."

His sincerity was patent, and grief spilled out of her eyes once more. Presently she said, "I'm sorry. Polly, would you make some coffee? You'll have some, Lieutenant? You know, apart from everything else, it was the first time I'd seen death, witnessed it, so it hit me harder even than Graham's—Dr. Barstow's—ever could. And I feel bad enough about him. It haunts me—he was a fine-looking man and I can't picture him looking any way except the way I saw him. Even in the cave he looked good. Why was Trueblood upsetting Myra with all that fuss about the expression on his face? The only thing I can think of is that he wasn't as unconscious as she thought he was."

"You knew him well?"

"I didn't know either of them at all." Quickly she explained the reason for their connection. "But from what I did see of him, I liked him very much. And Myra's been wonderful, as you saw for yourself."

"And very generous."

"Generous? About what? To whom?"

"To Sam Potter."

"Well, I agree with her," Kristin said impetuously, and could have bitten her tongue off. "I mean, I guess she ought to know. And I don't think much of your allowing Trueblood to try coercing her into making damaging statements about him."

"I didn't. Chief Trueblood is free to ask any questions he thinks fit. He doesn't need my approval or permission. But the fact is that, whether she liked Sam Potter once, she doesn't now. And what Trueblood said is more than enough to arrest him on probable cause."

She scowled at him. "I don't know what you're getting at. Unless —if Myra's right, if Graham led such a blameless life, then the only known person with a beef against him *is* Sam Potter. You might say she's grinding an ax by damning him with faint praise, so to speak. But I don't think Myra's that subtle and I haven't seen any reason why she'd want to be. For total strangers we've covered a lot of ground since Friday afternoon. Have you seen Sam yet, by any chance?"

"Have you?"

She began to suspect that she had been wrong about him. "I haven't had the pleasure of a formal introduction," she said caustically and with perfect truth. "But," hastily steering him away from her transparent ambiguity, "there *is* someone I'd like to meet and that's whoever broke in here last night."

"When? What happened?"

She kept him waiting while she served with studied elegance the instant coffee Polly brought in.

"I'm going for a walk. Down the hill," the girl said pointedly, at which the lieutenant's lips twitched. "Is there anything else I can get you, Mom?" But she was already in the hall and a moment later she was gone.

Seeing the lieutenant's lips twitch again, Kristin hastily told him what had happened and what she knew to be missing. His next comment gave her a sharp twinge of guilt, as well as pain.

"Between all the excitement of the rescue and then that attempt to break in the first time, I guess it was too much for Frey, poor fella . . . I saw him flying through the air last night, you know . . . Well. Did the Barstows ever say anything about previous incidents like this?"

"No. But I gather it was only a question of time until it happened here too."

"When did you tell her about it? She didn't mention it."

"At breakfast. She wasn't concerned. In the circumstances I wouldn't expect her to be."

"Who looks after this property? Who else has a key besides the Barstows?"

"Perley Stokes does. He's a—"

"I know who he is. His farm's at the bottom of this hill, by the way. You saw him?"

"He dropped in shortly after we got here to see if everything was all right. I didn't like him."

"Why?"

84

"He—slithered. Like a snake. All of a sudden he was here, and all of a sudden he was gone. And he said something . . ." She frowned in thought. "I can't remember. But he seemed a very snoopy type. I had the feeling that he knew everything that was in this house. Something about him jarred me. I hope his son isn't a chip off the old block—I have to call him about the plumbing. Are you thinking Perley was here last night? Or his son? Because that wouldn't make sense."

"No. It wouldn't. Perley has a key, as you say, and he knew who'd be here, and when. Presumably Toby would too. He's never been a favorite of mine but I don't know of anything against him. I know Perley from way back. He's honest. But even if he weren't, he could always move around in the woods like an Indian. He still can—I go hunting with him sometimes. Nope, it had to be someone else went crashing down the hill."

"Who, for instance?"

"A local, probably. Someone who knew Barstow was in the hospital, with his wife at his side. Someone who didn't know you were here or who thought you'd be out with her. You couldn't recognize him? Describe him?"

"I can't even be sure it was a man. It could have been a woman."

"It's very possible. The way things have been going," he said cryptically.

"Lieutenant, would you please tell me what's on your mind? I can't stand not knowing."

"Now you know how you make me feel!" He laughed, all at once becoming human, accessible. And the complicated expression on his face was particularly welcome to her in her unhappiness, for he was looking at her fully, frankly, approvingly, as a man looks at a woman. And as one looks at an adversary worthy of respect.

"Well?" she said, coloring.

"Well. Drugs. Or rather money for drugs. Breaking and entering's on the increase, especially in the summer homes. TV sets, radios, personal belongings—everything's converted into money for drugs. Off season it's the locals, mainly kids. During the season any resort's a sitting duck and plenty of off-islanders come over on the boat—lots of them as foot passengers carrying a lot of junk that'll hold more small stuff—or they cruise over from the mainland in small craft, pick up what they can as fast as they can, and take off. They may or may not have the help of the islanders. And we've had no luck tracing stolen cars, either."

"It doesn't sound as though you can do very much about it."

"No, we can't. Not yet anyway. And in this case we don't know if it was just another burglary or if it's related to Barstow's murder."

"Stymied."

"Don't look so pleased."

"You think I do? Well, I'm not. I was here. And what with one thing and another, I wouldn't be happy no matter how it could be explained. Any of it," she added forlornly.

"No," he said, considering her. "No, I don't think you would be. I'm sorry. I shouldn't have said that."

She discovered that she was oddly disappointed when he got up to leave.

"I'll send someone up here to take your statement, for the record, so you can stay off your feet. We got the information elsewhere but I'd like it in your own words. And make another one about the robbery, itemized. Mrs. Barstow will have to help when she feels up to it."

"Do I really have to appear at an inquest?"

"Grand jury hearing, not an inquest. I'll let you know."

"And what about funeral arrangements for Graham?"

"That's up to the medical examiner. Dr. Vernon will decide when he's ready to release the body. He isn't yet."

"It's a terrible mess, isn't it, Lieutenant."

"Yes. But all the same," he said over his shoulder as he went out into the hall, "all the same you're pleased about something."

"Oh? What?"

He turned suddenly, catching her off guard by his disturbing nearness and the mischievous gleam in his large dark eyes. "Yes. That you've successfully kept from me two facts. You and your daughter met Sam Potter—informally—and think he's innocent even though he's in a damned compromising spot. And also, you know Mrs. Barstow was lying. She and her husband weren't all that happy together. Probably because of Kathy Field. You and Frey met her on the beach yesterday, remember? After Sam took off. Well, I saw Kathy very early this morning." He grinned down at her. "Nice try," he said, opening the screen door.

Chagrined but game, she said, "I thought so. What are you going to do now?"

"Arrest Sam for murder," he said cheerfully, and closed the door behind him.

Chapter IX

She stopped short on the threshold of the dead man's study as if someone had collared her.

First things first, said intuition, and flitted away.

But what's more important than going through Graham's desk? she argued. Here's the time and opportunity I've been waiting for. I'd be crazy to pass it up.

No.

What are you talking about! The lieutenant is about to throw Sam in jail and you're wasting time talking to yourself.

All right, look. Suppose the galleys and maybe the working copy *are* in Graham's desk, or in that file cabinet in his closet, and you find incontrovertible evidence of plagiarism, just as Sam claims. All you'd accomplish would be to confirm his motive for murder. Obviously that detective got the story from Katherine Field.

Oh. Yes. I should have realized . . .

I wonder what I ought to do . . .

She sat on the floor and gazed hungrily, like a pauper at a Christmas display, at Graham Barstow's desk.

"I'd probably do better to find out if someone saw Sam sleeping in his car," she said aloud. "And I'd better go shopping for a few things, too, *and* take the trash to the dump *and* see Toby Stokes about the bathroom."

She hobbled into the kitchen and took the telephone directory off the top of the refrigerator.

Katherine Field was not at her apartment. Or on duty.

"How the hell do I know where she is! This is supposed to be my day off!" Dr. Vernon snapped over the sounds of an angry argument. "This goddam murder! If you knew what we were into, Kris! Me, my pathologist, the police, even the funeral director—! Try her grandmother's—" and hung up even as he plunged back into the debate.

"Now that you mention it," she snapped back, "I would like to know!" and slammed the phone down so hard that it fell off the wall cradle and swung like a pendulum. She looked at it thoughtfully.

Not more than ten minutes ago Lieutenant Amaral had gone down the hill to arrest Sam. Very likely he was still there. You didn't whisk a person away to jail in the time it took to say, "I arrest you for the crime of murder." If she called now, asking for Katherine Field, he would know it and he would want to know what she had in mind. And if she stopped by on her round of chores, he would certainly find out.

The thought of seeing him again did not displease her. But as she replaced the phone she thought, No. I didn't do very well in the first round. I'll be much more careful from now on.

Let's see. The Stokes farm first. Better to stop there rather than call, because Toby was probably out plumbing and Perley would be working outside. If she couldn't find him she could leave a note. Then shopping for a few items in the village supermarket. Then—to the vet for Frey's ashes . . . It would be a good time to get them. Myra had said the doctor had no office hours in the morning. There would be no one there to see her cry . . .

And then to the dump with three days' accumulation of trash and garbage. I should be back in a hour and a half and then I'll call down the hill and see if Kathy Field is there. The lieutenant should be busy someplace else by then. And if he wants to send someone to take down my statement he'll have to make an appointment. I can't sit around here waiting. And there's another thing. I've got to see Dr. Vernon today if it's the last thing I do. I'm going to make that old curmudgeon sit still long enough to tell me what's so mysterious about Graham Barstow's death by stabbing.

She had just loaded the trash into the back of the car when Katherine Field and Polly came puffing up the hill.

"I wanted to see you again," Katherine said, winking back tears, "to thank you for being so good to Sam. Matt—Lieutenant Amaral —just took him away. I wouldn't have come up here—I never have yet, I wouldn't—but Polly told me where Mrs. Barstow's gone, and I knew it would be—all right. Besides, I expected you to be lying down, so I didn't want to call. You shouldn't be walking on those feet, Mrs. Weiden."

"Believe me, if I had any others, I wouldn't. And please call me Kristin. And don't fuss—either of you," she added swiftly as Polly saw the trash and opened her mouth to protest. "I have a few things to do," she said flatly, limping around the car, "and I'm going to do them, and that's that," and plunked herself behind the wheel. "I was trying to call you, Kathy, to tell you how sorry I am—about everything. Although there's nothing much to say. I'm sort of caught in the middle . . . Polly's probably given you some idea. It's—it's difficult. But I'm sure Sam's innocent and I want to help. We all can. I had an idea. Look, the hospital was pretty busy last night, and for almost half an hour, from about eight-fifteen to about a quarter of nine when you and Myra saw Graham, Sam was sleeping in his car. It stands to reason that someone must have seen him there. How can you miss somebody like him! If you could find out from the patients or the nurses who had visitors and who they were, we might find a witness to clear him. You'll have to check Emergency and Outpatient too. Maybe Polly can help. What do you think?"

"It's a good idea, Mom, and I think we'd better get started."

"Suppose some of them have left the island by now?" Kathy said doubtfully.

"Then we rack up a big phone bill, because probably some of them have. But between the patients they saw, or hospital records they filled out if they were patients, we can track them down. There's got to be someone out of all those people who saw that crazy guy snoring in his car."

"How do you know he snores?" Polly said huffily, opening the back door.

"Men snore. That's one way you can tell *la différence*. If you like, Kathy, I'll drive you down to your grandmother's and you can get your car. Unless you'd rather not." Maybe you'd better not, she thought, for the girl looked dangerously exhausted.

"Oh, I want to. Of course I want to. I'm sorry I'm so—slow, Kristin, but—Come on, Polly! Everything's piled up so fast that if we don't hurry up Sam will be tried and convicted before we know it." With a show of vigor she got into the car.

Saying something like "Not if *I* know it!" Polly got in beside her and slammed the door.

The trim white clapboard in which Sam Potter had grown up stood in a small clearing at the end of a short winding road. This was in as evil a state of repair as the long one up to the Barstow house, and the car steamed in complaint as it bounced off a half-buried rock.

"You'd better stop at a gas station first thing, Mom, and have them check under the hood. This wreck is running very hot. I think it's about to succumb at last."

"It wouldn't dare," Kristin said grimly. "All right, look. You get busy. I should be back in two hours and I'll help. The only thing is, we won't be able to do anything with Myra around. Where are we going to work?"

"We can't at the hospital, and I've got a three-party line. But we can use the phone here. Kristin, would you do me a favor?" Kathy said diffidently. "It'll mean a few extra steps but would you stay a minute and meet my grandmother and my aunt? They can't get over the way you treated Sam and they want to thank you. They're terribly worried about him. And they're so old. Grandma's seventy-nine and Aunt Faith is eighty-three."

Dr. Vernon would have snorted at this. "Nothing wrong with you," he had told Prudence Potter lately. "Nothing's ever wrong with you! Get out of here and stop wasting my time. You Todd sisters have the blood pressure of turtles. You'll live forever. Sometimes think you already have."

But his sphygmomanometer would have blasted off this morning:

The Todd sisters were a very Canaveral of indignation. Kathy and Sam, their sole and beloved connection with past and future, were in jeopardy because of the murder of a man old enough to have known better—about a lot of things.

And they were not about to thank Kristin either, not in so many words. With the ancient Yankee's unconscious arrogance and grace they merely remarked their approval of her cool head and good sense and invited her in for a cup of tea because she looked pea-kid.

There was no way out of it. But once inside the vast cheerful white and yellow kitchen, Kristin knew that she would go in again on bloody stumps. These old ladies, as like as two peas with their yards of white hair wound around their small shapely skulls, were affable and loyal to each other everywhere else, but they began to spark and bristle at each other in their clipped musical voices the moment they stepped onto their battleground. She could picture them during times of crisis like this one, eating back to back at their separate tables and lobbing lethal salvos at each other.

Genius! she saw, grasping the situation at once as she sat down at the table with the yellow cloth. For a moment she felt absurdly happy.

"Will you have pekoe or orange pekoe?" Prudence said, holding a can of each, like Justice.

"Green's better for the stomach," Faith said. "You know that, Prudence!"

"I'm sure you're right, Miss Todd, but I've never been able to like it," Kristin said apologetically. "That's what the school nurses swore by, but it always made me sicker."

"*Boil* the water at least, Prudence? You have to kill the germs."

"It need only be *hot!*" Prudence filled her tea kettle at the white sink and clapped it onto the white stove (bottled gas). "Boiled water is *flat*."

"I let it smile," Kristin said. "When it's smiling, just smiling, I pour it."

Faith put her kettle on the yellow stove (electric) and opened the yellow refrigerator. "Lemon and honey, Mrs. Weiden?"

Prudence headed for the white one. "Milk and sugar, of course."

"Nonsense! Sugar causes cancer, I read, and milk has fallout. And it kills the flavor too. Along with *warm water.*"

"I really like it with scotch. Otherwise I prefer it plain. And please call me Kristin."

Katherine smiled wanly and Polly began to splutter. "Mom, what's next on your agenda?"

"The supermarket, the vet, and the dump. Oh—and the plumbing. Perley Stokes said his son—"

"Not Toby," Prudence said. "I *shouldn't* have Toby Stokes, Kristin."

"Oh? Isn't he any good?"

"He's a very good plumber," said Faith, "but he abuses dogs, for one thing. Kicks them. We don't respect him. And then too, some people never learn the meaning of fidelity. We complained to the phone company and got a private line."

"I'm afraid I don't understand."

"We took exception," Prudence said, "to his language. It was vulgar. We can't think what Perley's done with that boy of his."

"Did he break into your conversations? Did he listen to them?"

"It was the other way about," said Faith. "Not deliberately, mind you, but you know how party lines are. You pick up the phone and you're thinking of the number you want to dial and you even begin to dial it before you realize someone's been talking all along. And what they're saying doesn't register until you've hung up. But the Stokeses use their telephone much more than we do, so it quite added up, you see. The kinds of things we heard." She sniffed.

"That young man has astonishing conversations with other women," Prudence said in disgust, "considering how he feels about you, Katherine."

"Oh Grandma! I've been turning Toby Stokes down since seventh grade. It's just a joke," she told Kristin. "A stupid joke. Every Fourth of July he proposes and I laugh at him and say yes and he laughs back. We're just friends, or at least we used to be. We don't see eye to eye on things anymore. Sam never liked him at all. But Grandma and Aunt Faith think that if he'd only lived like an anchorite, he'd have convinced me of his undying *fidelity* and then I'd have married him no matter how he talks on the phone or treats dogs. Because then I'd have been safe. Safe! They despise him because he let them down." She began to laugh hysterically.

"*Kathy!* Tell them Mom's plan about Sam. After all, it's their phone."

"Oh yes. I'm—I almost forgot." She took a deep quivering breath and told them. "It'll mean tying up your wire and getting under your feet, though."

Yankee bullheadedness is a poor creature next to hope based on logic. The old ladies smiled upon Kristin and expressed gratitude in their own way.

"You do looked pea-kid, Kristin," Prudence observed. "Drink pineapple juice. It's very good for the kidneys and bladder. Flushes out all the poisons."

"I have some. I love it."

"All the *doctors* recommend cranberry juice now." Faith was very firm about this. "Since you're going out, see that you get some."

"I will. I promise," she said, limping out to the car.

"Oh dear, you haven't seen Sam's paintings," Prudence said.

"I really must go but I'd love to see them some other time." She didn't want to. Fierce blobs of red and purple, probably. She wouldn't be able to bear her disappointment, or hide it.

"There's a plumber in the village. Near the market," Faith shouted over the Chevrolet's agony. "Don't forget."

"I won't, I won't," she shouted back, and drove away laughing.

But as she jounced, grunting from pain, all the way down the hill, she decided to call Toby Stokes whether the old ladies liked it or not since Myra would call him anyway sooner or later. Besides, I want to. It's a small world, she said to herself, and who knows? Maybe he's mixed up in this one way and another.

She dawdled in the village, possibly because her feet hurt too much to take her quickly through the crowds, possibly because it was a relief to be away from that house on the hilltop with its associations and its morbid odor, to be occupied with pleasant mindless errands, to mingle with people she did not know and need not speak to or be careful with if she did.

She passed the Women's Exchange, where Church Guild ladies

ticketed sad old clothes and with pathetic artistry arranged chipped china and tasteless gimcracks on dusty shelves and tables, and lingered at the window of the Attique (pronounced *attic*), shifting her weight from one foot to the other and admiring the extravagant mixture of antique and boutique in the window. The display was joyous and provocative, the markups outrageous, but even the costliest pieces remained hardly long enough for shoppers to read their price and provenance. A ship captain's desk (circa 1840, four hundred dollars) occupied the center of an exciting clutter, and she gazed at it delightedly.

A tiny woman next to her said, "Do you like it?" She had been there for some time, her face distorted with yearning for the little desk.

"It's marvelous. I've never seen anything like it. I love antiques —I'd like a whole houseful. A feeling of continuity with the past—"

"Really? *I* wouldn't," the woman said loftily. "I couldn't be happy with used furniture."

"Oh? I'm sorry to hear that. Because in that case your husband will never be able to be President of the United States, will he?" Kristin said solemnly. The woman glared at her and walked away.

Tomorrow I'll come back and see what the Guild ladies have in used swim wear. I can't afford another new suit, she thought as she went into the supermarket. I'd love to nail the creature who stole my thirty-dollar one. Why couldn't he have taken the new white dress instead! It still had tags on it too. *I* shouldn't have bought such a thing, of *all* people! It looks like a uniform.

She spent more time in the checkout line than she had collecting the things on her list, and the gallon jug of cranberry juice weighed a ton by the time she reached the car. She had bought it in deference to Miss Faith, to assuage her guilt in the matter of Toby Stokes. It was lunchtime. He might be home.

He was, and he gave her a startled look and a curt nod as he heaved a carton of equipment into a small van near the bulkhead of the silvery-shingled farmhouse. "With you in a minute," he called out, and ran down the cellar steps.

At least he doesn't look like his father, she thought, waiting impatiently for him. He isn't a patch on Graham but he and Kathy wouldn't make a bad-looking couple, not at all. And if he's as good a workman as they say, that's two things in his favor . . .

This place could be photographed for a travel poster of Ye Olde New England. They must really clean up on us summer people to keep it like this . . . That honeysuckle's like a trampoline the way the bees are bouncing on it . . .

She was watching them when Perley came out of the barn and walked hastily to the van as his son emerged from the cellar carrying the white German shepherd she had seen at the ferry. She got out of the car and limped over to them.

"Maw-nin', Miz Weiden," Perley said, touching his cap. He looked worriedly at his son. "Well?"

"He's finished. Too bad." Toby hesitated, glanced at Kristin, and told Perley to open the van door. "Not worth bothering with. White shepherds're weak anyway, not like the dark ones. He's had it. Can't even stand up." He put the dog on the front seat and shrugged as he closed the door.

She looked through the open window. "What's wrong with him?"

The dog was almost unconscious and panted weakly and irregularly. The dangling tongue was ulcerated and nearly white, the eyes glazed with fever. Where the bandage on the ribs had been was a jagged wound that bulged with infection out of a large patch of shaved inflamed skin.

"Poor boy," she murmured, blinking rapidly. "Poor thing." She turned sadly away. "I just can't believe this happened overnight."

"Where'd you see him?" Toby said sharply.

"At the ferry. And if the man who brought him is a friend of yours, you're better off without him, the way he was pulling that poor creature along. What did you do for him? Why wasn't he taken to a hospital instead of on a boat ride? He's badly dehydrated and he's in shock or close to it. Didn't you even give him any water last night? Or this morning?"

"Did the best I could but I had other things to do, ma'am. And I have other things to do now. Five customers waitin'."

"Sorry. I didn't mean to hold you up. I only stopped by to ask you to have another look at the Barstows' hall bathroom. It's almost unusable and I don't want to use hers. Whatever we can do to make things easier for her now should be done."

"I'll try to get up there sometime today. Can't promise, though. I'm pretty jammed up."

"If it will help, I'll take the dog to the vet for you. I'm going there now." She looked at the dog again. "What's his name? I ought to know his name."

"Dog," he said tersely. "Just—dog. I'll take care of it. Thanks anyway." He gave her another curt nod and got into the van and drove rapidly away.

"Bad biz-ness, Miz Weiden, that murder," Perley said in his insinuating way.

Twister! Did you ever manage to say anything straight in your whole life, you bucolic Uriah Heep? she thought, moving away from him.

"Yes," she said. "Very."

She had to force herself to go into the animal hospital, and she put off the moment by stopping to wonder why Toby Stokes's van was not yet there, as she had expected it to be. His dog was plainly dying. Why had he waited so long?

And why was she waiting so long? Because it would be more painful to walk up that crushed-shell path and get Frey's collar and the container of his ashes than to take off her shoes and socks and bandages and tread a mile of broken glass. Very slowly she got out of the car.

It was some time before the doctor ushered her into the examining room. A short dark compact man with hair like a black shoebrush and such vigor that he generally bounced up and down on tiptoe as he spoke, he sank onto a stool and lit a cigarette, exhaling smoke and exhaustion. "Sorry to keep you waiting but I've been in surgery since seven o'clock—alone! Someday I'll have to get a robot. The only assistant I trust has salmonella or a busted leg or both." He rubbed his eyes. "I'm very sorry, Mrs. Weiden," he went on gently, touching a brown paper bag at his elbow. "I'm really very sorry. I've seen hundreds of animals die over the years, plenty of them my own. In fact I'm about to lose another one.

After eighteen years. Nothing more I can do. It always hurts." His strong hands rose and fell helplessly.

"I think people like us are absolutely crazy, Dr. Amaral," she said shakily, wiping her eyes.

"I don't agree. People have to love and be loved, and I never knew anyone including myself so blessed and lucky they could afford to pass up love no matter where it came from or who they could've given it to. Even plants—why, do you know what I heard recently? That plants react to people with responses that are measurable. They're like emotional or psychological storms. Sounds crazy but I'm told the experimental evidence is impressive. They're connected up to a lie detector—"

"A *what?*"

"That's right, a lie detector. Weird, isn't it? If someone with bad vibes so much as comes into the room they turn away and the needle goes all over the graph. But those same plants respond like loving children to other people. Their responses are actually observable on a lie detector."

"I can believe it, I guess. Look at Myra Barstow and *her* plants."

"Dreadful thing, that situation. In fact this whole weekend was one of the worst I can remember. I saw Mrs. Barstow last night. Nice dog, Dandie. Bit too nervous for a collie, though, even allowing for what's happened. I had to give her a tranquilizer on top of everything else I shot into her. Here, have a cigarette. You look all in."

"I've reformed."

"Doesn't seem to have done you much good."

"I guess not, but Dandie's a lot better. That's one small thing."

"Glad to hear it. The way things're going, it'll be all I can do to give her another dose. Damn nuisance the way my supplies are disappearing. But the dogs are too, so I don't know what difference it makes after all. But syringes and things are expensive."

"Don't you use disposable ones?"

"Sure. Everybody does. But I keep the big ones; it's cheaper to sterilize them. The ten-cc. ones, and larger. But all I could find last night was a fifty-cc. one, and now that's gone."

She laughed. "They're mainliners, all those dogs and cats, sneaking needles when your back is turned. Seriously, though, every animal hospital I've been in has all the goodies in easy reach. Look at your own cabinets. Easy pickin's, Doctor. When you get that robot, program it and put a club in its hands." She got up to leave, her eye on the brown paper bag. "We loved him so much."

"That's all the eulogy *I'll* ever want," he said quietly, handing it to her.

"Yes," she whispered. "Yes," and stumbled blindly out.

One more stop, the dump, and then home to rest, fix her feet, put hot packs on her leg which was itching again, have lunch, and maybe a nap. By then Kathy and Polly might have some news. And there would be Myra, of course . . . And I've got to see Dr. Vernon. If he doesn't come across, I'll explode!

The old car exploded first, blowing off the radiator cap, and steam curled out from under the hood.

"Dammit to hell!" she yelled, pulling over to the side of the road. She flung open the door.

There were some greasy rags in the back of the car and she covered her hands with them before raising the hood. Little wreaths of steam were twirling out of the overheated radiator and she regarded them with rage and despair.

A vehicle approached rapidly behind her and she turned, waving frantically. The driver slowed down. And then as they recognized each other, Toby Stokes stepped on the gas and callously whizzed by.

"Why you miserable—!" she shouted, staring at the van until it disappeared around a curve. "Now what am I going to do!"

There was only one thing to do.

She opened the jug of cranberry juice and poised it over the radiator. "If it's good enough for my pipes, it's good enough for yours. Cheers!"

She did not bother to look for the radiator cap. It might have fallen to the road or only lodged on the engine, but it was not worth searching for and she could safely drive ten or fifteen miles without it. She put the jug into the car and with some misgivings started the motor. It coughed and sputtered, gaining strength, and presently she drove on with an eye on the temperature gauge.

No fires, whether deliberately set or caused, as they frequently were, by spontaneous combustion, were fouling the air with heavy smoke, but the dump stank and Kristin breathed through her mouth as she entered the littered grounds and stopped, leaving the motor running, near the edge of a trench. It was a new one some hundred feet long, twenty feet wide, and fifteen feet deep, its sides and one end as sharply perpendicular as if the ground had been cut with a knife. The nearer end, however, might have served as a ramp for a monster crawling out of the bowels of the earth. For half its length it was almost empty yet waste of every description, which could so easily have been thrown into it, was scattered every place else. From the look of things maintenance had been given up until the summer people left.

No one else was there, and hundreds of sea gulls wheeled and screeched above the violated ground, stabbed the filth with their strong yellow beaks, stumbled and lurched and fought over the bottom of the trench like drunken miners disputing a lode. They erupted like a geyser when she tossed down her trash bags, but settled quickly in a greedy scramble to investigate this new wealth.

Revolted, fascinated, she watched them flutter and land and flutter and land up and down the trench. Suddenly she cried out in anger and wrenching pity at the sight of a limp white body lying at the bottom, surrounded by birds.

She bent over and vomited.

Chapter X

The gulls were already fighting over her vomit when she put the car into reverse, and she might have vomited again had she noticed. But she was looking over her shoulder and zigzagging toward the sloping end of the trench.

And then she was out of the car and plunging recklessly down, slipping and sliding in the loose sandy soil, heedless of her lacerated feet, choked by the cloud of dust, unaware of leaving a sneaker in her frantic wake when she stumbled over a stone.

The greedy birds flew off as she dropped panting on hands and knees beside the abandoned animal. "Oh god, oh god," she whispered.

Gently she stroked him, telling him that it was all right, that he was not alone, that he would not die alone with dirt in his mouth, that she would not leave him in that filthy place to be pecked to death. His eyelids flickered and his tail twitched as he roused a little.

The tiny response heartened her. "Oh god, don't let me hurt him," she prayed, and gathered him up and staggered back sobbing in grief and outrage.

She was just putting him down on the front seat when a state police cruiser drew up and Lieutenant Amaral called her name. She turned and stared dazedly at him and the trooper beside him, her breast heaving, her eyes enormous in her dirty tear-streaked face.

She smiled tremulously. "Take*courage—men—I*hear*—thecava*lry *—com*ing!" she mocked, and tottered away retching.

"Lee," Amaral said after a comprehensive look, "get him to my brother—no, don't move him! And for crissake take it easy! I'll call you there. There's no rush now, so give Joe a hand."

He caught her before she fell on her face, and held her by the waist while the spasms twisted her thin body. Then he picked her up and carried her back to the cruiser, relinquishing her reluctantly so that she could rest on the back seat with her feet up. Hunching in beside her, he took out a clean handkerchief and tenderly wiped her face. "What happened?" he said. There were a dozen other things he would have liked to say.

"The radiator blew. Toby Stokes—that gutless conscienceless—! He knew who I was but he didn't stop. When I got here I saw the dog. He left it here!"

"*His* dog?"

"He said it was, that vicious swine. But I'm beginning to wonder. He called it *dog!* Some man brought him off the boat last night—the dog, I mean, and I saw him again this morning at Perley's farm.

Those sea gulls were just about to start on him. I'll never know how I did it. I couldn't lift a double scotch now, and I need one."

"Oh, I don't know. You seem to thrive on challenge."

"It certainly brings out the best in me," she said wryly. "If you hadn't come along I'd have managed but—How did you know I was here, anyway? Or did you?"

"We've been on your trail for quite a while. The robbery gave me an idea and I got a warrant after I brought Sam in. Lee Williams was going to take your statements while I searched the house, but no one was home. I checked in down at Sam's but you'd been and gone. Grandma told me what you were up to. I heard your car was about to break down and I was afraid you were stranded somewhere and would try walking home on those feet. You've lost a sneaker," he said softly, examining the bloodied filthy sock, and took off the other sneaker with the greatest care as if her foot were an egg that would break. "I think we'll leave this off too," he said, knocking the sand out of it and putting it on the floor. "I'll carry you. Hurt bad?"

She wiggled her toes and bit her lip. "Bad! Now I feel it! My throat hurts too. Did you say the vet was your brother? You said the hospital—did you mean the animal hospital?" I don't want him queering my pitch at the other one, she thought, hoping he had not seen Polly and Kathy. "And is Mrs. Potter your grandmother too?"

"Joe Amaral is my older brother. Mrs. Potter and my grandmother were close friends and so were Sam's father and my father. Joe and I have called her Grandma since we were born."

"Well I'll be! You're lucky having those crazy ladies around. Funny. I brought Frey to your brother two years ago—he didn't remember me—but I didn't connect him with you. This place is really a small world."

"It has its advantages."

"No wonder you're so—so kind. I can see it runs in the family. Forgive me, but at first I thought you were just being a clever cop." She did not notice that he had not answered all of her questions. "You seem to know a lot about dogs. And you care about them."

"I help Joe a lot when I'm free. As a matter of fact it was a toss-

101

up which one of us would study veterinary medicine, but money was tight and Joe was older . . . And luckier," he added after a moment during which he wondered what had happened to him since morning.

"Luckier? Aren't you happy in your work, Lieutenant?"

"I meant, because he met you first. In his line of work he'd stand a better chance to. But I'm smarter."

"Oh? How so?"

"I would never have forgotten you."

His quiet sincerity was obscurely alarming. She said lightly, "Well, of course. In *your* line of work—"

She still didn't understand him. Or wouldn't. "I was a man first, Mrs. Weiden. I always will be that first." He hesitated, watching her smile fade at his rebuke. Troubled, he climbed out and resolutely put the door between them. "I'm taking you to Vernon," he said in his official voice. But first he went down the slope of the trench to retrieve her sneaker. He slapped it against the heel of his hand to empty it of sand—or perhaps to chastise himself—and handed it to her through the open window. She took it without thanking him, and they did not speak to each other during the twenty-minute ride back.

He did not trust himself to carry her, or even to support her into the hospital. But he would not allow her to walk. "Stay there," he said brusquely. "I'll get a wheelchair," and stalked away.

She was grateful for this respite from the tension between them but set her lips firmly as though unwilling to discuss it even with herself. I'm a mess, she thought, remembering with annoyance that her handbag was still in the Chevrolet. She was vigorously finger-combing her dusty hair when he came back.

Aloof now, he steadied the wheel chair with a casual hand and looked away, but once she had settled herself in it his gaze fixed on her head. With a certain anger he pushed her into the hospital.

"Goddammit!" Dr. Vernon bellowed. "Who do you think you are, a rescue service? Look at those feet! Dirt, blood, mess!" He rattled a basin in the sink, filled it with warm water and antiseptic solution, and slopped it down in front of her. "Let 'em soak. Jesus

Christ! Some day off! Well well. Poison ivy too. Is *this* a time for gardening?"

"I wasn't. I got it on the beach path, I guess, before I saw you yesterday."

"Any more of that scotch in your desk, Doc?"

"Yes. Go get it! Best twelve-year-old scotch on the island—and *you* don't deserve any, young lady. Now turn over and lie down." But the whiskey took the edge off his temper and he worked so calmly and patiently over her feet that she decided to ask him about Graham Barstow.

"Forgive me for bothering you this morning," she began demurely. "I called at a very bad time." She was lying on her stomach now and could not see the police lieutenant's admiring smile or the expression in his brilliant eyes.

"Wouldn't've mattered when you called. Damn near everybody else has. Came in, too." He sighed gustily. "Including Myra Barstow. With all due respect she's sore as a boil. Well bred and quiet, but I got the message."

"Oh? I haven't seen her since about nine-thirty. What can I look forward to?"

"God knows. When she heard about the autopsy we did last night, she hit the roof. All upset over what he was going to look like. What the hell does she think we do at an autopsy, hack a body to pieces? Pathologists may be frustrated surgeons but they aren't butchers! She wants the body immediately for cremation and funeral services. Well, I'm not ready to release it."

"Why? What's so special about it? You said something last night—"

"I remember. And that was before the autopsy. Well, we did it after you took her home and I still feel the same way. I told you, Kris, I'm no medical sleuth but something's got me bugged. Maybe I'm too tired and too old to think straight anymore, but till I do, Barstow gets cooled instead of cooked."

"I thought you said you don't perform autopsies."

"Don't. I watch 'em. Usually call Ralph Perkins the funeral director as one witness, and Matt here is often my second. They were both here last night. Steve Black does the job when the state pathologists can't make it. He's a good hospital pathologist but he'll never be a forensic genius. I trust him. No choice anyway. All four state guys were tied up, and none of 'em anywhere near here. And something told me not to wait. But till Steve and I agree, till I'm sure, I won't sign the death certificate and release the body. *No*sir! Barstow gets froze instead of fried. Since midnight I've had calls from the D.A. and two of Barstow's relatives—brothers—practically ordering me to give it up. Press have called *and* come. They would've anyway, guy like Barstow, but now they're really sniffing around. Damn pack of vultures. What's so mysterious about a stabbing death, they want to know."

"For goodness' sake, Doctor, what's hanging you up? I'd call this a nice clean deliberate murder. Isn't it?"

"Looks like it."

"*Well* then!" One bandaged foot flew up in exasperation, almost knocking off his glasses. He banged the leg down onto the table. "Sorry, Doctor, but you've gotten so cryptic you're hardly human anymore."

"What I *meant* was," he snapped, "there wasn't very much bleeding. If the internal mammary artery'd been cut, I'd be happier."

"I wish you were. But would Graham Barstow be any deader?"

Amaral laughed.

"I'm serious, Dr. Vernon."

"So'm I. *I* didn't laugh."

"Well, I'm no anatomist or physiologist so I can't appreciate the fine points. But how can you and Steve Black disagree on something like *that?*"

"We don't."

"Oh god!"

Amaral laughed again.

"It isn't what we saw. It's what we didn't see."

"Could I have some more scotch, please?" she said piteously, and flushed when Amaral instantly took her cup, filled it, and gave it back, his big brown hand shaking slightly.

"It's that expression Myra said she saw on his face," the doctor said, finishing with the other foot. He tapped her lightly and she sat up.

"I wondered about that too. So?"

"So, Kathy Field didn't see it."

She stared at him in growing consternation. "What do you mean?"

"People don't die with a grimace on their face unless they've been fatally burned. Or had strychnine poisoning, or tetanus. Or epilepsy, maybe. Convulsive-type things that cause muscle spasm. Also heart attacks, or the bends."

"But I thought—"

"That's what everybody thinks. Fantasy of all those lousy movies people see. You should've heard Ralph Perkins on that last night, right, Matt? Between the two of us Perk 'n' I have seen thousands of bodies, some of them dead from the most horrible vicious abuses, but with the exceptions I mentioned muscles relax when people die and that's that. But Myra said she saw a grimace and Kathy says she didn't. She *says* she only got a quick look before she ran off. But you can see most patients clearly from the door if they're on their back, as he was. And—she says she didn't see any grimace."

"What are you hinting at? What do you mean, she *says*? Do you think Kathy—or Myra—? I'm sure they're—They couldn't have—!"

"We don't think *they* killed him. Only, Steve says to hell with that grimace, Myra was too upset to see anything straight and Kathy was too. But I'm still bugged. And until I'm sure—"

"You won't release the body?"

"I won't release the body."

"You'll have a hard time holding out, Doc," Amaral said. "Mrs. Barstow isn't the only one who's screaming."

"I know that! Been fielding the calls, for crissake!" He wiped his face on his sleeve. "Prominent family like Barstow's can make things hot for an old country doc like me. Damn good thing we moved so fast on that autopsy, Matt, or they'd've tried to stop that too. If Barstow'd been famous in politics instead of education, they probably would've."

The telephone rang and he groaned. "I'm not here," he said as Amaral reached for it.

"Relax, it's for me. What's up, Lee? . . . God! Any chance? . . . That's a hell of a lot. Tell Joe I'll be over soon as I can. . . . Take your time. . . . Oh? No kidding! Very resourceful of her. Right. Do what has to be done, but I doubt if you'll have to leave it. . . . Yeah, make them do it right away. . . . No, I will. I'll wait for you there."

"How is he?" Kristin said fearfully. "What's wrong with him?"

"Dogs!" the doctor grumbled, but he listened eagerly.

"What isn't! Uremic poisoning, diarrhea, vomiting, dehydration, shock, bad infection from that mess on his ribs. Generally the temperature's subnormal with uremic poisoning but his is high because of the infection. Joe doesn't know what to make of that yet, Lee said, but he was afraid to take time to x-ray. First thing he did was hook up an I.V. Then a shot of antibiotics. Then dialysis—homemade variety. Don't worry, Mrs. Weiden, that dog's getting the red carpet treatment. Lee said Joe went into high gear after one look and one sniff of the breath, and he hasn't stopped yet."

"Urine odor," the doctor said. "Ulcers on the tongue and gums too, I suppose."

"Nasty ones. I saw them. Joe's praying, Lee said, and he's mad as hell. So am I. He's going to start cleaning out that wound soon."

"What chance does he have, Lieutenant? Did your brother say?"

"Fifty-fifty. Maybe. The kidneys would have shut down in four or five days without care. In ordinary circumstances," he added grimly.

"What are you going to do to Toby Stokes?"

"I'll think of something."

"Make it good, Matt. That fella never went over big with me," the doctor said angrily, and stood up. "No driving, Kris."

"I couldn't if I wanted to. My car's at the animal hospital."

"Lee's driving it back for you, Mrs. Weiden. He's going to stop at a gas station first," Amaral said. "He wanted to know if what you put in that radiator is what he thinks you put in it."

"Probably. The only thing I had around was cranberry juice. Miss Faith says it's good for the plumbing." She grinned and got up shakily.

"In that case they'll have to do a little dialysis on your car, Kris." The doctor looked more cheerful. "Just as well it's out of your reach. I don't trust you. Take 'er home, Matt, 'n' put 'er to bed."

Amaral turned red and then pale but Kristin, calm and lightheaded from exhaustion and several ounces of straight whiskey on an empty stomach, accepted his help unself-consciously. She was asleep in the back of the cruiser long before they reached the Barstow house.

No one was there, but the door had been left open. Surprised but relieved, he carried her inside without waking her, and stood undecided for a moment at the end of the hall. Where would Myra be least likely to bother her? Where could she rest undisturbed?

He wandered from room to room, cradling her long light body possessively while he scrupulously weighed the question. Finally, unwillingly, he put her down on the couch in Graham's study. She stirred and murmured something as he covered her with a thin blanket, but it was plain that she would sleep for hours.

He hesitated, looking down at her, marveling at the delicate veined eyelids and their long black fringes, at the level brows so fitting to her candor and courage, at the lips firmly set but sweetly curved and full, at her breast rising and falling quietly and peacefully, at the slender fingers still dirty from the rescue at the dump.

He looked, and shook his head wonderingly, as though he had never seen any of these things before, and whispered, *"Cada vez mais!"**—a shattering truth that brought him to his knees beside her, weak and joyful and almost afraid. Very close to her now, he looked again, and kissed her dusty hair.

And then he went outside to wait on the back step for Lee Williams, and to psychoanalyze himself.

Chapter XI

Thunder rolled in long waves over the house and woke Kristin at six-thirty. She began to stretch luxuriously, and groaned. Sleep and good whiskey had vanquished fatigue and even quieted the rash on her leg, but she ached from her throat to the soles of her feet. She got up stiffly and shuffled out into the kitchen, where Myra and Polly were eating supper.

"We didn't want to disturb you, Kris," Myra said as the girl jumped up to set another place.

* Portuguese: More and more. [i.e., Each time (I see you) I care more.]

She laughed. "It took a clap of thunder to do that. Just listen to that rain!"

It was falling heavily now and gusts of wind flung it against the big window. Myra shivered. "The storm came out of nowhere. It's getting colder."

"Hungry, Mom?" Polly said, and shook her head slightly at Kristin's inquiring eyebrow.

"No, not very." But disappointed, she thought, although I didn't really expect them to get anywhere so soon. There must be at least a hundred people to check on . . . I wonder how Sam is.

"We made the hot dogs and beans and salad you bought," Myra said. "But you shouldn't have bothered with shopping, let alone anything else. I'm afraid to thank you—it might encourage you too much, and goodness knows what you'd do next."

"I'm all right. Did Toby Stokes come?"

"No, and we really shouldn't use that bathroom anymore," Polly said, putting a steaming plate in front of her. "But from what the police told me, I wouldn't want him if he were the only plumber on the island."

"You called them? What for?"

"Lieutenant Amaral called here a little while ago to ask if you were okay. He said he'd be here around seven. He still wants your statements and a complete list of the things that were stolen. I wrote down what Myra thinks she's missing."

"But the dog? How is he?"

"Dr. Amaral thinks he'll pull through," Myra said. "He told me all about it when I took Dandie back this afternoon. I'm sure I don't know which of us was angrier. I'll never let Toby Stokes set foot in this house again, never. Or his father! I stopped there on the way home and got my key and discharged them both. It was a monstrous thing to do to a helpless creature."

"If the dog makes it, Mom, the vet will give him to you. Isn't that what he told you, Myra?"

Kristin put down her fork and pushed the plate away. "No," she said softly, "no," and stood up.

"Mom, please. Tell me what you want and I'll do it."

"Thanks very much, darling, but there are some things you can't do for me. I'll get you a sweater, Myra, while I'm at it."

"Thank you, dear. In the bottom drawer."

Impulse moved her—fortunately, as she discovered a few minutes later—to look quickly but carefully through the drawer in which John had found the black lace panties. They were not there, nor were they in the others.

Well, she said to herself as she took out a sweater, our burglar has catholic taste, at any rate. Clothes, books, antiques, jewelry . . . Thoughtfully she limped into the bathroom.

She was innocently drying her hands and face when Myra looked in worriedly and said, "You were so long, I wondered if you were all right. You left the table so suddenly."

"I'm sorry, Myra. I didn't mean to spoil your supper. I guess I'm too tired to eat, after all. I won't be much good to you at this rate."

She sat on the bed while Myra put on her sweater, and her eyes fell on the large family tree. "So many Barstows," she said sadly, "and not one here to help you now."

"Graham's oldest brother is coming, Kris. I didn't have a chance to tell you. He's flying home from Europe on Wednesday, thank heaven."

"The one in the diplomatic corps? Your favorite?"

"Yes. Jonathan. I spoke to him this morning after I left the police station. With his credentials he'll take care of Dr. Vernon, that dreadful stubborn man! *And* Mr. Trueblood. No matter what they say, Graham will be cremated Wednesday evening. On Friday when everyone's had time to make arrangements, we'll have the services in Christ Church. Will you come?"

"Of course we will."

Myra drifted over to the family tree and touched it lovingly, reverently. "You know, I wondered sometimes what would happen to me if we'd been divorced. It would have been . . . difficult, the position of a childless divorced woman in her husband's family. But now . . ." She sighed and turned away.

"They would never have let you go. After all these years. A woman like you."

"Perhaps. Perhaps. But you don't know the Barstow pride."

"But it was Graham after all who—"

"Yes, Kris. But he *was* a Barstow. They would have overlooked everything else. It may seem odd to you, but I've been part of them for so long that I revel in that pedigree as much as they do. So if it had happened, if he'd divorced me or let me—*forced* me to divorce him, I would have taken myself off to spare them the embarrassment of doing it. Of dropping me. And they would have. It sounds fantastic in this day and age, doesn't it. Oh god! I would have done anything . . . I would have given anything—!" She stood there, hopeless, desolate, bereft even of tears.

And then the telephone rang and someone knocked loudly on the kitchen door. Dad was calling, Polly said, and Lieutenant Amaral was dripping all over the floor. Myra went out of the room.

"Tell your father I'll call him back," Kristin said. She had not thought of him since last night. He had no place in what was happening here. Was there really no place for him in her life at home anymore? I'm getting very mixed up suddenly . . . Does it have anything to do with—with *him*? What's happening to me? I know I'm glad he's here. I shouldn't be . . . isn't it rather *too* soon for a rebound . . . the classic reaction . . . ?

She tried to distance him at once with cool formality. "Thank you for all your help, Lieutenant. I regret your having to make an extra trip in this weather."

He made a production of finding a place for his coat. "I didn't want to wet that hardwood floor, Mrs. Barstow, so I came around the side."

"It doesn't matter," Myra said listlessly.

"Look, Mrs. Barstow," he said in that kind way of his, "why don't you go and rest. Miss Weiden—"

"Oh, call me Polly," the girl said impatiently. "And here's the list you wanted."

It was not a long one. "Thanks, Polly. Now all I'll need is whatever Mrs. Weiden can add, plus her statements. You needn't sit through that, Mrs. Barstow."

"I'd really rather not. It's been a very difficult day. No doubt Mr. Trueblood would insist on my staying. I'm very grateful that he didn't come back."

"You won't have to see him again except in court. Don't worry about it."

"Good night, then. Come, Dandie. Kris, I think I'll need one of your sleeping pills, if you can spare it. Mine ran out."

"In the hall bathroom, Myra. Help yourself."

Polly talked about the weather until Myra had shut herself into her bedroom, and then said casually, "If you don't need me either, Lieutenant—"

"My friends call me Matt."

She appraised him swiftly and smiled. "I think you are a friend. If you really don't need me, I'd like to go out for a while."

"Kathy's waiting for you down the hill," he said blandly, then grinned. "And for godsake keep at it. You're saving us a lot of work. And by the way, I've told them at the jail to admit you any time. Up to eleven, anyway. Sam needs his rest."

She blushed and laughed. "You're a pretty smart cop, Matt. I really do thank you. We're getting there, Kathy and I." She kissed Kristin's cheek. "I don't know when I'll be back, Mom, so don't wait up."

"I wish I could go with you, Polly. Tell Sam I— Lieutenant, do you think he's guilty?"

With those gray eyes on him he could not lie, nor did he want to. "No," he said, shaking his head. "No, I don't think he's guilty."

"Then why—?"

"Pressure." He sat down and rubbed his forehead wearily as though it were all inside his skull. "Barstow pressure from far and near. But don't kid yourself—there's plenty of probable cause. I may have hunches, I may have feelings for Sam, but I have no proof. Of anything. Not yet. But the D.A. *has* a case and he isn't standing still while I run around this island helping ladies in distress. I want your word that you won't quote me. It could jeopardize Sam, for one thing. So, no hints, no knowing looks, not to him or Grandma or Kathy or anybody, is that clear?" They nodded gravely. "Don't worry, we have time. Sam will be arraigned in the morning, but the trial is weeks away. Keep at it, Polly. You're on the right track."

"It was my mother's idea. But I suppose you knew that too."

"Yes, I knew." He regarded her almost with dread as she went up the steps, leaving them alone again. Taking refuge in relating another bit of news, he said briskly, "You've got company, Mrs. Weiden," and waved the sheet of paper Polly had given him. "Toby Stokes says his van was stolen late this afternoon while he was working on a job."

"I'm glad to hear it. I wish I'd thought of doing it myself. But you sound as if you don't believe him."

"I don't, but I don't know why. Wishful thinking, I guess."

"If I were going to think wishfully about Toby Stokes, I'd wish he'd get tagged for the robbery or the murder. Preferably the murder. Maybe he sold his van and lied. For the insurance."

"No, he paid more than four thousand in cash for it but never bothered with insurance against theft. Said he didn't believe in it. So he'll lose a lot and he won't get a nickel. It was almost new, too, and full of valuable supplies and tools. Now, in view of all the robberies and stolen vehicles this past year alone, it's hard to understand how he could be so trusting. And we don't have anything on him, so I don't know what he'd have to lie about."

"It's a shame you have to be so damn legal, Lieutenant."

"I often think so. But what did you have in mind?"

"Oh, it came to me how nice and easy it would be, getting something on Toby *via* the phone. The old ladies shared a party line with him and Perley, but he shocked their sensibilities and they got a private line. I'd love to listen in on him. Couldn't you tap his phone?"

"No, not at this point." He leaned on his elbows and rubbed his eyes with the heels of his hands. His fingers were well formed and long, the nails clean and trimmed. "What a day. What a night! That autopsy took four hours. The younger the pathologist, the slower he works. And then we argued about it and didn't get anywhere, not even to sleep. And then I had to see Kathy. And then I met Phil Trueblood here."

"It must be hard on your family too, the hours you keep."

"I don't. Have a family, I mean."

"You've no children?"

What remained of the circle of pale skin on her ring finger was a shadow now. He had worn one like it many years ago. Suddenly he wanted her to know about it. He sensed that it was time to tell her about himself. "I'm not married. I was. Happily married. At least I thought I was. After high school I spent two years in the service. And two more on the force under Trueblood. Then I got restless, I wanted an education. I went up to Boston and got a B.A. and an M.A. in sociology and criminology. I met Anne when I was a senior. She was in advertising. Things were good until I went to the State Police Academy . . . I was twenty-nine then. It seems a long time ago . . . Anyway, the work fascinated me but she never liked it. It depressed and upset her and she resented the hours I had to be away. And then one day she was gone. A policeman's lot—" He shrugged. "I came back to the island three years ago."

"Oh. I'm—very sorry." *Am I?* she thought. *Am I? Yes, because someone he loved caused him pain, but . . .*

"I was sorry too. Once. But after a while I wasn't, I didn't care anymore. I even began to think marriage was for other people until—" His eyes met hers and his ears turned scarlet. "Well, about this list," he went on in a businesslike way. "Anything you want to add to it?"

Her heart was pounding as she read it through. "Myra didn't include the names of any of the books."

"Would she be able to? Apart from everything else, she has several hundred of them."

"I guess not. Still, I read most of the titles yesterday morning before I went to the beach, and I'd given them a good look when we came on Friday. I'm sure there are a few fairly new novels gone —*Airport, Herzog,* things like that, and that fifty- or seventy-five-dollar volume of Wyeth paintings, and some law and psychology tomes, of all things. Even *Lassie,* if you can believe it."

"You're very observant," he said, writing everything down.

"Not really. I'm much more apt to observe things—emotional atmospheres and that sort of thing—through my pores than with my eyes. I told Polly last night that Graham's closet in the back bedroom looked different. Less crowded. He slept in that room, you see. All his things were there. But I can't remember . . ." She closed her eyes. "We came in to unpack, my husband and I. And he opened the closet and I opened the drawers . . . Oh, I know! He took out a gray suit with a little blue stripe and a belted back. And flaps on the pockets. Anyway, we never did unpack, there wasn't any room, so the only other time I took a good look at that closet was last night after we put Myra to bed. There must be other things missing from it. One suit wouldn't make the difference. You know, Toby Stokes is about Graham's size. Why don't you search his place?"

"I wish it were that simple. Did you ever see a warrant? It has to specify what we're looking for, and where we want to look for it, and why. And I mean exactly where, what, and why. For instance, a house—gray shingle cottage, two stories, with a trumpet vine on the piazza. Or, what. A box. Seven inches by ten inches by eight inches, gray metal, with a hasp, and so on, containing x, y, and z. And unless we have probable cause, the *why,* something to go on, we can't look for it, even if we know what to look for and where to look. People think the police can just walk in and search till they find something that looks suspicious. No way."

"What were you going to search for here? You said you got a warrant."

"You'll never guess. Nope! *You* probably will." He grinned at her and she laughed, thinking in relief that they were talking now as friends.

"Graham's book. The galleys, I bet."

"Right. I've got Sam's papers in the car now."

"But I thought you said the warrant had to do with the robbery."

"One thing led to another so fast that I wasn't thinking when I said that. After the autopsy I saw Kathy. At approximately the same time you saw Sam." He smiled, then grew serious, even worried, and she put a hand to her mouth in dismay. "You told me this morning about Mrs. Barstow's silver mirror being missing. And the jewel box, remember? Well, for a minute there I thought Kathy had taken them—and your things. The kinds of things a woman might take as a blind for something else. Letters she'd written Barstow, for instance."

"But why? Even if Myra had found them, they'd be more damaging against Graham than against Kathy. But Myra wasn't going to divorce him, she told me so. And from what she said before you came, she would have died herself to keep scandal and embarrassment from the noble Barstow line."

"Well, yes, but . . . He and Kathy had a fight. In the cave yesterday afternoon, Kathy said. He'd changed his plans somewhat, and his offer. He couldn't budge Myra, so he was going to maintain her as his wife, in Cambridge. Keep up the family name and all that. He asked Kathy to live here with him as his mistress. Myra say anything about that? Or Kathy?"

"No. Kathy didn't even tell me his name yesterday. Or hers. Oh god, what a mess! But what did they tell Graham?"

"Myra turned him down. He quoted her to Kathy as saying that without children her life had been hollow enough. That she wasn't going to have more of the shadow and less of the substance than she'd already had."

"And Kathy?"

"She told him virtually the same thing. She wanted kids, a name for them, a proper home. Which she never could have had here. Too many people know her, and Barstow was too prominent. And he wouldn't live anyplace else but here. This place meant more to him than all the others, and he'd been all over the world. They argued, she cried, she told him to think it over, and she left him sitting there."

"You said you don't think Sam's guilty. Do you think Myra is, or Kathy?"

"Myra didn't have to kill him. He couldn't divorce her, no matter how hard Kathy held out for marriage. She knew that if *she* held out, though, sooner or later he'd forget his drive toward youth and act like what he was, an elderly man. No, Myra didn't kill him. She held all the aces—except his love.

"But when she got to his room with her coffee, Kathy was standing at his open door, holding onto the knob. She could have been coming out after checking that I.V. bottle—and killing him too. *She* said she was just going in. So there's her opportunity. And motive? She had everything to lose. She didn't want any Back Street setup and she was hurt and angry. But I don't think she's guilty. Not Kathy. And apart from the fact that she was running herself ragged during that half hour, she's still in a safe position because no one knew about her and Barstow except Myra, you and I, Polly and Doc Vernon and Sam and the old ladies. Which sounds like a lot, but Myra won't say a damn thing to discredit Barstow and everyone else is protecting Kathy."

"And, to get back to where we started, she *was* on duty last night so she wasn't here, breaking and entering. It would have been better if she had."

"Yeah. I wish they'd both been here watching the place burn down, she and Sam. But that small fact, her being on duty, didn't hit me till this afternoon, long after I'd spoken to her and Sam and you. I guess I'm just too tired. By the way, Sam said that out of consideration for your position here he didn't tell you about Barstow's new offers to Kathy and his wife. He thought you'd feel even worse about Myra's situation if you knew all the sordid details. But he didn't hold anything back from me, which is why I got a warrant for Barstow's galleys. The only thing is, if I find them and they indicate plagiarism, I've got to give it in evidence, and the D.A. will say, 'Q.E.D., Sam's motive for murder!' and then we'll be in the soup for real. That's why I don't want you to say anything about Sam. What I think, I mean."

"I can't understand why you've told me anything at all. You were pretty cagey this morning."

"Because I trust you and I need your help, Mrs. Weiden. The principals in this mess are in a tight little knot. You're one of them and so am I. I know Sam, I know Kathy. It's lucky in a way that I was off-island for so many years. It helps me look detached about this whole case. If I can avoid being publicly discredited—and how the press would love to do it!—I'll be able to keep working. I don't want them to reassign me. You see?"

"Yes, I see. Don't worry. We'll be careful. About those galleys, do you want me to look for them?"

"No. You can't. I realize I'm contradicting myself, because I've said I need your help. But this is police business, like it or not. Sam knows that, of course. Besides, you'd better keep clear when you can. Now. Is there anything else?"

"Just my statements. Graham and the robbery." She dictated several economical sentences and signed her name to them. "This sounds crazy, but there is something else missing, I think." She told him about the black lace panties. "I can't imagine why in the world Myra would have such stuff in her wardrobe, but she did."

He made another note and sat back studying the list at arm's length, but distance gave it no significance. He put it away and yawned. "Make some coffee, will you, Mrs. Weiden, while I take a quiet shot at Barstow's desk. I have the chance now. I don't want to bother Mrs. Barstow any more than I can help."

He was back with a mailing carton before the water had come to a boil. "Here it is. No trouble at all," he said unhappily. "And what a hell of a job I've got in front of me. You should see Sam's stuff. An encyclopedia, on one small project!"

"I'm not surprised," she laughed, limping to the stove. "Look, why don't you bring it in and I'll help you. Myra won't come out, I'm sure of that, so there's time. Let's shoot for, say, a dozen close and crucial parallels, assuming there are any, between the two works and then you can relax with your duty done. And if—*when* Sam's exonerated, the university will reinstate him, so we'll be killing two birds with one stone. God, what a hideous expression!"

He laughed. "I accept your offer, your sentiment, and the coffee. Let's go!"

Two hours later, when they had found what they were looking for, and more, they sat back and regarded each other wearily.

"Why?" she said. "What was he thinking of? Why would he do a thing like this to Sam? To anyone? Money certainly wasn't the issue."

"No, I don't think it was. But put this in context and it seems to fit. He drove that yellow Porsche. A toy. And toys are for the young. He loved a beautiful young gal. He was as fit as a man her age or younger. He gave up a long honorable career to start over someplace else, not quite from scratch, but still—a beginning. I think Sam was right. He wasn't retiring, he couldn't retire. The old retire. As Sam put it, he was leaving in a burst of glory, a kind of birth: That book. Who knows? He must have hypnotized himself into thinking all the work was his. But the heart of it is Sam's. Sam's journals and dates and professors' remarks show that. But it's easy to understand, I guess, in the larger context of the world we're living in. The youth cult, and so on."

"Yes. The all-American fear of death. I was thinking about that on the beach yesterday. The more we fear death, the more we struggle to go back the other way. Toward youth and the illusion of unlimited time that kids always have. I had it once myself. You know, Lieutenant, in a sense Graham was as much his own victim as the murderer's victim."

"Victim of his own tangle, maybe. But that sort of tangle doesn't always take a man as far as murder. What you say is true provided his death *is* connected to Kathy or Myra or Sam. And we've ruled them out, although we have no evidence! All in all, I'm not sure where all our philosophizing can take us. And I'm not satisfied with it anyway. I feel there's something missing. You're so close to this that maybe you can pick up whatever it is that I don't have."

"I almost think the wrong person was killed, if it comes to theorizing. It would make more sense for Graham to have killed Myra. My god—or even Kathy!"

"And how do we know he wasn't killed for half a dozen other reasons that had nothing to do with them at all?"

"We don't," she said. "But we've been impressively profound, anyway. Any sophomore would let us into an all-night bull session." They laughed comfortably at each other, and for a little while longer there was simplicity and peace between them.

"When did you start coming here?" he said, getting up and gathering the papers into a neat pile.

"Ten years ago. The accommodations were never so grand but we had happy times . . . once. Wait a minute. I'll get you some bags for all that stuff."

"You don't like this house, do you."

"No. Not from the minute I walked in. I wouldn't be surprised if some of those plants suddenly grew huge and horrible. Man-eaters. Strangler vines." She shuddered. "You know, Lieutenant, there weren't any plants in Graham's bedroom or his study."

"Yes. I heard. I saw. You could call it his statement. Kathy said he came to hate them."

"That poor gal. She looked like coming apart at the seams this morning."

"She'll manage in time. People do." He put on his wet coat and picked up the bags, and she opened the door for him. "They lose things—love, security—but most manage."

"Sometimes I think it's almost harder to lose something you never had, never possessed. Something you glimpsed and reached out for —and couldn't grasp."

"I know." He looked at her steadily and would have said more, but she raised her hand palm out as if to ward off threat.

"Please," she whispered, trembling. "Don't."

"I'd better get out of here," he muttered.

In a moment he was gone, and she stared into the darkness as rain spattered her face and rolled down her hot cheeks, like tears.

Chapter XII

The weather on Tuesday morning was as cranky as Kristin's temper, the sky as changeable. Rain followed by clearing followed by sun showers followed by dark low clouds chased by a stiff breeze out of the west that, perversely, dropped more rain.

Well, it's appropriate, she thought miserably, putting the phone back on the wall. I'm just glad that Polly and Myra didn't have to hear that conversation. It's dreadfully embarrassing to watch a marriage break up. I would have had to watch Graham and Myra Sunday night . . .

John had said he was having a great time, although the heat and humidity were terrible and he was working twelve hours a day. Shocking news about Barstow—Polly had given him a rundown last night—and they were right in standing by Myra. He was glad he wasn't there, though—damned sticky situation what with their mutual connection with the university—and he hoped she'd be careful with the press if by some chance she had to make a statement. Naturally he'd come back if there were something he could do to help . . .

Only thing was, and he knew she'd understand, the team was moving up to San Francisco for another week's work, maybe two, and he didn't see how he could get away. He was due at a meeting right now, in fact, but if anything critical came up, if she really needed him . . .

She had almost told him then that she did not need him anymore, but she only said no, everything was under control . . . There would be time enough to tell him. When she was absolutely sure . . .

How much, she asked herself, did Matt Amaral have to do with it? Did she really feel any different about John now than she had thirty hours ago? Could you weigh and measure that kind of thing so that you knew without any shadow of uncertainty whether you did or you didn't? She had spent half the night trying to answer that question.

She sat brooding on the little steps, chilled by the unheated house, depressed by the weather, angry at herself and everyone else. But nothing could grow in such an environment—except Myra's plants, it seemed. This insight being all too welcome, she got up and went into the bathroom to examine her feet.

"They're much better," she told Myra a few minutes later in the big bedroom. "Not so raw."

"No infection?"

"Nope. Clean as a whistle. But I've got to get some more bandages and things. I forgot to ask Polly." The girl had gone down the hill before breakfast to meet Katherine Field and go to the County Courthouse, where Sam was being arraigned. "I just used up the last of what Dr. Vernon gave me. Is there anything I can do for you while I'm out?"

"There is, dear, if you're sure you're in condition." Myra put down the tiny shears with which she had been snipping plants and took an empty vial from her handbag. "I used the last of these sleeping pills too, so have the chemist fill this prescription, will you, dear? And here's a list of a few more things—face cream is the most important. And Dandie needs another shot. Could you take her for me? Dr. Amaral said I could come anytime in the morning and not have to sit with people in the waiting room. They were—staring at me yesterday. But I'm expecting another call from overseas and I just can't risk going out now. Do you mind? Is it too much for you?"

"No, of course not. I'd be glad to." But I'm not, she thought with resentment. I don't want to take care of Dandie or any other dog.

"Take my car, Kris, do. You'll love driving it."

"I couldn't stand the luxury, thanks. I don't know what I'd do if we won that car raffle. Anyway, if you should have to go out after all, you wouldn't love driving mine." Or Graham's. "Come, Dandie."

Dr. Amaral quickly attended to the collie and nodded in satisfaction. "She's a lot better, Mrs. Weiden. Eyes pretty clear now, temperature about normal. Much coughing? Any more vomiting? Good, good. Put her in the car, will you, and give me a hand for a minute. I've dropped one bottle, I don't want to drop any more."

He was mopping up the floor and grumbling about salmonella and the labor market when she limped back inside. "Guess I'm just plain losing my grip," he said, dumping shards into a wastebasket. "I was adding up the hours I slept this past week—don't ask me why—and that bottle fell right out of my hand. How's Mrs. Barstow?"

"Waiting for a call from her brother-in-law in France. She's amazing, although I don't think she's done much sleeping either, pills or no pills. None of us has."

"It's a wild one, all right. Here, hold this," thrusting a bottle into her hand, "and follow me. He needs company along with everything else. He's in my infectious ward all by his lone."

The big white shepherd lay on a thin floor mat by the side of a rumpled cot. Behind him stood a ladder-back chair with an alarm clock on the seat. A clean bandage covered the wound on his ribs and a strip of adhesive tape on one foreleg kept a venous catheter in place. Still holding the bottle, Kristin lowered herself cautiously to the floor. "He's breathing a lot better," she said, lightly stroking the cream-white coat. His stiff ears twitched and his eyes, clearer now, brightened in recognition. "I'm glad he isn't in a cage."

"Didn't have to be. He isn't going anywhere. I'm getting housemaid's knee but it's easier on him not to be moved around." The doctor took out of his pocket a long transparent tube with fittings at both ends. "I'll have that flask now," he said. Holding it upright, he pushed the spike quickly into the bull's-eye and inverted it immediately to check the vacuum and the fluid level in the dripmeter. Satisfied, he hung it on the knob of the chair and reached across the dog to give Kristin the other end of the tube. He fetched cotton and alcohol from a cabinet, then put a hand on her shoulder and knelt creakily.

"How's the big boy, hey? Feeling better? That's a good fella. You'll do, you'll do. He's nicely rehydrated now. Been filling him up for twenty hours. Slept here with him. My wife set up the cot and kissed us both good night! But this guy has been through the mill and if he's going to be any good to himself and anybody else, he needs a lot of lovin'. Yes indeedy, a lo-o-o-t of TLC."

He went on talking softly to the dog while he cleared the tube of air and clamped it, removed the adhesive and the hub from the catheter, and connected the tube to the catheter. Then he wiped off the drop or two of blood that had come out in the process, put fresh adhesive over the catheter, and timed the rate of the flow. "Good. There we are, young man. A little snack for you."

He got up again and measured the flask with a practiced eye, then fixed a strip of adhesive to the middle. "We'll give him fifteen minutes' worth and then I'll check him again. Doesn't do to load him up too fast although the kidneys are beginning to shape up now, thank god. That bastard was feeding him meat and never mind all the nitrogen wastes he couldn't handle! We had a little diarrhea and vomiting around here yesterday to slow things up, didn't we, boy."

"Those ulcers seem to be healing."

"Yep, they're healing, all right. Breath odor's better too. It was touch and go for a while there but I think we're out of the woods now."

"Are white shepherds really weaker than dark ones?"

"No, not necessarily. I had one for ten years. Lightning. That was his name. Lightning."

"How old is this one?"

"Oh, seven or eight months. Teeth're all in now. Ears nice 'n' perky. Great big eyes, too—not like some shepherds I've seen. Had some rotten shepherds in here. Bad breeding. Not this one, though. He'll be a big 'un when he's reached his growth—look at those *feet!*

—hundred 'n' twenty pounds, maybe. He's eighty pounds now, at *least*, for godsake! And his hips'll carry him, thank god. I x-rayed them too while I was at it. He's yours if you want him."

"I don't think so. Thank you, Doctor, but I'm—I'm just not ready yet. I don't think I'll ever be."

"Understandable. But the way dogs have been treated around here, I'll be damned if I give him to just anybody. He's a fine animal and I'll keep him myself till I find the right home for him."

"Why don't you just keep him?"

"Got two unclaimed cats and four dogs already. Bastards find their pets are sick and just leave 'em here. Summer people mainly. I had one dog—saw the driver throw him out of the car and take off like a bat out of hell. Leg broken. What's done with the other unwanted ones I'll never know. Thrown in the dump too, I suspect. They sure as hell aren't in the county pound. I used to check over three-four a week during the season, but it's been about empty for a long time." He knelt again to examine the wound. "Just hold his leg steady, Mrs. Weiden. He's beginning to feel his oats ju-u-u-st a little bit. A vet doesn't need a degree for this job, he needs four hands and that's a fact."

"What caused that mess, Doctor? Barbed wire, maybe?"

"Thought so at first. But I x-rayed it at one o'clock this morning. Matt—my brother—helped me out. *He's* in a mood, I can tell you," he added parenthetically, sitting back on his heels to think about it.

"He must be exhausted," she said, her cheeks burning. "This is a crazy case."

"Sure is. He told me about it. I thought he was worried about Kathy Field. We've known her for years—guess you knew that—and I kind of hoped he'd marry her some day. I asked him last night was that what was bothering him, but it isn't. He never loved Kathy Field and he never will, not that way. He said there were some people you loved and some you didn't. Which makes sense, all right, but he damn near snapped my head off. You'd've thought I was arguing with him. I guess it's this damned case."

"What did the x-ray show," she said, breathless.

"Oh yes. It's like a pocket in there. Probably a cyst was removed —I don't know. Some butcher who calls himself a vet pierced the muscle badly while he was at it and then infection set in all over the place. So, nephritis. And that plus a meat diet and no care brought on uremic poisoning. I'd've liked to do a tissue study but I just haven't the time. Had one helluva job cleaning that out."

"How did you manage? If it was sutured and closed—"

"Sutured! There weren't any sutures! And it wasn't closed, not much, anyway. Too full of pus, for crissake!" He was quietly furious about this. "Had to risk opening it up to drain it and flush it out. Bastard! I'd like to take his diploma and ram it down his throat!"

"If you ever find him," she said, giving the dog a final pat, "let me know and I'll hold him for you too. I'd better get going now. I've got a few things to pick up. Myra can sleep if she takes a pill, though maybe not all that well, but they don't work on me. I took two the night before last and—nothing. But I'll get some more and try again."

"Get some cranberry juice too, while you're at it." His dark eyes twinkled. "And if you see my brother give him some of each. He needs them both."

"I will," she said, and limped out, her heart pounding.

Having gotten what she needed at the village pharmacy, she went slowly down the street to the Clothing Exchange. Dreary and dingy as it was, its business was as brisk as the Attique's now, and a crowd of stubborn impatient arm-laden women blocked the narrow passage between the cash register and a wall of books behind the door. She wedged herself through just as stubbornly and poked among the forlorn clothing on the racks at the back, wondering if she would be lucky enough to find a decent bathing suit. Perhaps the burglar had sold hers to the Guild.

But that was unlikely. For one thing, the Guild ladies would not have entered it so soon on their voluminous books. For another, they took all but donated articles on consignment, and why would anyone have stolen the suit or anything else except for ready cash? Third, no one so clever and persistent would leave stolen articles so close to home. Fourth, he could have given that bathing suit to his girl friend—if the burglar were a man and he had a girl friend and she were as tall as I am, Kristin reminded herself. And the same goes for those black lace panties. Not everything stolen was fenced, even unwittingly by dealers of good faith. She smiled briefly, picturing the Guild ladies carrying on a sinister operation under the dust, fencing her bathing suit and Myra's black lace panties, gloating over their ill-gotten gains.

She did not find her suit, of course, but, reviewing the stolen articles and thinking once again how out of place the panties were in company with such a discriminating selection, she decided that the burglar might well have discarded them here. Simply dropped them on a clothes counter and walked away.

My god, she thought, suppose Myra saw them! What would she think?

You're an idiot, I've told you that before. She buys her clothes in Bonwit's, her books at Hathaway's—everything at the finest shops. She wouldn't come in here in a million years, and if she did, and if by some chance she happened to see those panties, she wouldn't buy them in this place from those ladies any more than she'd read Kathy's letters to Graham at town meeting. You'd better take a pill, you fool, and go to bed. The whole idea of coming here was ridiculous. Nevertheless she spent some time looking for the bits of cheap black lace.

And found them under a pile of underwear and sweaters. They were not ticketed and, after a hasty look around, she put a pair into her handbag, though she was not sure why.

The only things worth mention were the books, and she stopped at the shelves behind the door to look at them. The passage was clear now and she took her time, enjoying this most special kind of freedom. And then she saw, bright among a dusty row of old volumes, the familiar book jacket of *Lassie*.

She stared at it as if it were a treasure she had spent years searching for, as if to touch it would cause it to crumble into dust. Slowly she put out her hand to it.

Inside the cover were the remains of a bookplate. Blue and white, like the Barstows'. Yes, and thousands of other people's, she cautioned herself, patient possessive types who feel compelled to paste them into thousands of volumes.

But there can't be anything coincidental about this, she thought, scanning the shelves. I know this is Myra's book. The others must be here. I guess I'll just have to go through every one of them. She started at the top shelf and touched each title to make sure that she missed none.

Ten minutes later there were five heavy books on her arm and a stack on the floor. She dropped one, and the large brown hand she had come to know so well picked it up and took the others from the crook of her arm.

"At it again," he said. The words were a caress. He had been watching her for almost as long as she had been there.

She blushed. "This was an accident. Really. But I think I have them all. Most of them, anyway. We'd never be sure short of checking them *all* out in a card catalogue! The Barstows ought to have made one. Anyway, I'm almost done. Do you have a minute? Can you stay?"

He had a lifetime. "Yes, I can stay. Carry on."

At length, when another book had been added to the pile, she leaned next to him against the counter and wiped her grubby hands on her jeans. "What a job! I'm a wreck. It's a good thing you came by, Lieutenant. I would have had to lug them out of here one by one."

"We serve the people, ma'am. Now, what's the tab?"

There were no prices in any of the books, and the old Guild lady at the cash register looked at them in bewilderment. "I can't understand it," she said, opening each of them again. "We don't put anything out, even books, until they're priced first. Except paperbacks, and they're either ten cents or twenty cents automatically, depending if they're old or new. I don't think I can charge for them. It wouldn't be right." Her voice was sweet but faded, as if she had been in the shop since the day she was born.

"Oh no. I couldn't just take them. Would ten dollars cover them?" Kristin said, impatient to leave.

"Oh my, that's very generous but—" Unbusinesslike, too, that was plain.

"A donation to the Guild," Kristin said persuasively, taking a crisp bill from her wallet.

"Oh, my, how lovely! We do appreciate it. I hope you enjoy them. Such a lot of reading, though, for summer. Do be careful." She accepted the money with a delicate reluctance as if she might be held responsible for the consequences.

Kristin laughed as they went out and walked slowly away. "That nice old gal is very worried my vacation will be spoiled, Lieutenant."

"A lot of it's heavy stuff, that's for sure. But what did you have in mind, restoring them to Mrs. Barstow?"

"Now I come to think about it, I really don't know. It just struck me as a weird collection and I thought I'd take a look at them." A few paces further she added, "I'm thinking now," and said no more until they had walked almost aimlessly for two blocks. A sudden shower sent them under an awning, and she shivered.

"Come on, I'll buy you a drink," he said, and led the way to a little eating place mischievously called The Joint.

The pungency of hot cheese and garlic almost floored her.

"Oh boy, that's better than oxygen," she said, sniffing delightedly.

"Or anaesthesia. The kids may raise hell everyplace else but they seem to be comatose in here. The worst they can find to do is ruin poetry. Let's go in the back."

"Hey, man, whaddyuh know?" said the youth behind the counter as they sat down in the last booth. A pizza disc whirled above his Afro and he caught it and spun it deftly.

"Nothing much, Giggy. What's the word?"

"Weather," disgustedly. "Oughta sold a million a these by now, but you're the seventh dude in here since I opened, is all. What'll yuh have?"

"Coffee and a coupla slices. Okay?" he said to Kristin.

"I'd be happy with the smell alone, it's so thick. I've never been in here." She looked about.

"It's new. Best pizza on the island. The décor is something else, but the kids keep it clean."

The walls were a shiny stark white with a dado-high spatter print of tomato sauce that was squeegeed off weekly. Peace and Love were celebrated psychedelically at casual intervals, and bad paintings and poetry (the latter unbearably earnest and moving) were hung or pasted in between. The tables and booths were mere slabs of pine slapped together and covered with red and white paint as tough as the vinyl on the floor.

"They do a land office business as a rule. At night you can't get in," he said.

"That boy looks familiar. I can't think where I've seen him . . . Anyway, I'm glad nobody else is here. I have to improve my mind, and for that job I need all the peace and quiet I can get."

"Where were you planning to get it? Home?"

"No, not really. Myra—everything—is too much *there*. The little beach would have been a good place except that it's raining, and I don't know how I'd have carried these tomes down there and back anyway. And the library isn't open yet. I guess I'd have just sat in the car—and frozen to death. But you're always coming along at the right time."

They were friends now, colleagues, and his response was simple and direct. "It's practically a full-time job keeping track of you, the way you operate. For godsake take it easy."

"Why do you say that? What could happen to *me?*"

"I don't know. That's the trouble, dammit, I don't know—anything. I just have a feeling something has to give, and I don't want you in the middle when it does."

"I've been in the middle from the beginning, unfortunately. But it's all so—so shapeless that I don't really know where the boundaries are anymore. Oh wow! That looks terrific," she said as the youth put the food on the table.

She watched him walk away and then leaned over and said in a low voice, "Now I remember him. I saw him at his booth at the fair on Saturday. With another boy—he called him Jack when I saw them again at the ferry landing Sunday night. There are plenty of Afros around, but he's the only boy I've ever seen with an Afro *and* a missing index finger."

"Firecracker last year. He's lucky he didn't lose all five. What was he doing?"

"Annoying Frey. I told him he'd lose another finger if he didn't stop. The two of them were waiting for the man who brought the dog off the boat. They were very impatient. Nervous and sweating."

"Did they say anything?"

"Oh, something about making money with a dog like Frey. I wasn't paying much attention. Why?"

"I'm learning that where you are things happen. There's a pattern somewhere in all this and I have a hunch you're the catalyst. Come on, let's eat this before it gets cold."

But nothing could have spoiled it, and without asking her he ordered more.

"I was at the arraignment," he said while they waited. "Sam looked—dimmed, like all the filaments weren't working. The girls tried to buck him up but—" He shrugged and stopped when the pizza and coffee came.

"You won't believe it but I haven't talked to either of them about what they're doing. Polly was up and gone before Myra and I woke up, and I was—asleep last night when she came back." She had not been, but she had not wanted to talk about anything to anyone. She bit her lip, thinking of what had kept her awake. "But I suppose if she had any news—" She questioned him with an eyebrow as she dealt with long strings of cheese.

"Nothing yet. You won't believe this either, but those two have been through about seventy names and there aren't many left. They said they may go back to the hospital and make sure. I convinced Trueblood to hire them as special clerks, so it'd be legal, and Kathy introduces herself as 'Miss Weiden of the Police Department' when she takes over, for anonymity. Grandma and Aunt Faith have been giving them coffee with and Sanka without and all other combinations pertaining thereto." He shook his head and laughed. "What a pair! I apologized for having to take Sam in, and they said, 'Don't worry, Mattie, we know you don't mean it.' They'd love to make a few calls themselves."

"But won't the girls scare people off, saying they're from the police? People hate to get involved."

"It's a risk either way, but they haven't had any trouble so far. Only, no one has seen a redhead snoring in a car! It's a long shot, but you never know. Cases break in the damndest ways sometimes when they do break." He pushed the plates away and put a large book on the table. "Now what have we here?"

"Wait a minute. I want to show you something." She took the lace panties out of her handbag and spread them on the table.

"Hmph! Very smart. Latest in fine underclothing for high-class ladies. You found these in the Exchange?"

"Yes. No price on them either."

"Well, we'll file them away for later. Now. *Sexual Offenders and Their Offenses.* Hot stuff, Karpman. I read him in graduate school. Hmmmm. Looks well used." He opened it in the middle and watched the pages waver, then cocked his head at the binding. "It's rarely conclusive and it's usually hindsight when it is, but sometimes you can tell from the loosening of the signatures, especially in reference works, where a person did most of his reading. Let's try another one. Albert Ellis, hey? He's an aggressive type."

"There's a Havelock Ellis too." She put it on the table. "Anything?"

"Nope."

They flipped through the pages of each book looking for marginal notes or underlined passages but saw none. "Maybe bookplate types don't mark books up," he said, closing the last psychology book.

They went through the assortment of novels in the same way and with the same results, and then she handed over the last volume. It was a brand-new family legal encyclopedia and clearly showed that someone had cracked the stiff binding somewhere past the middle, loosening a signature. It opened of itself at a subtitle regarding the search of the home and the person. "Looks as if he took a quick look at this and got rid of it," he said.

There was something between two pages near the front of the book, as they saw when they looked at it sideways, and he opened to it and took out a small faded envelope addressed to Mrs. Graham Barstow. The date on the canceled stamp was dim but legible.

"Thirty-four years ago," he said, drawing out a flimsy bit of notepaper. He read it and gave it to her.

" 'My dear,' " she read, " 'there is no one in the world who can or ever will equal your infinite capacity for love, compassion, understanding, grace. There are no words to express my infinite gratitude to the Almighty for giving me such a wife. On this our first anniversary I have no other gift to give you but my deepest thanks and my love. God bless you. Always, your Graham.' "

"How old-fashioned he was at twenty-one," she said, putting it back into the envelope. "And what a place to find it in."

"Yeah. Cheek to cheek with grounds for divorce in fifty states.

Christ! The question is, though, did Myra leave it there or did Graham? Myra, undoubtedly, but it's never safe to make an assumption till after you have the facts," at which they both laughed. "We know, though, that she wasn't going to divorce him. Maybe he was the one who was doing the checking . . ." He slapped the books into a pile and frowned at them. "That's some collection, but where are we now? I don't get it. And I've read most of them too." His voice was flat with frustration and weariness.

"I don't get it either . . . but here's another piece of wishful thinking. Maybe Toby Stokes is a homosexual and he's trying to fathom himself. Breaking and entering being merely the symbolic outward form of the inward struggle for insight, for bursting out of his binding chains."

He laughed. "It's possible simply because anything is possible. I'll think it over. And if I have occasion to arrest Toby, I'll be sure to haul him in for the symbolic outward activities. The other isn't criminal as far as I'm concerned." But he added seriously, "Toby does make plenty of money even for a plumber. Between him and Perley they live very well. Now, where are you going to stash these?"

"In the car, I guess. There are so many books in that house, Lieutenant, but whoever was there took these and not others. There must be a reason and I'm going to find it if it kills me."

"Please," he said, laughing. "There has to be a better way. How about one more coffee for the road?"

"I'd love it. Where are you off to now?"

"My office first. I have to catch up on paper work."

"Your brother told me to tell you to catch up on sleep."

"He should talk. He was up all night soaking the dog in sugar water."

"Sam is the one I'm worried about, even more than Myra. How is he making out on a prison cot?"

"Don't worry, he's being treated well. He's trimming everyone at poker. They're losing gladly, to keep his morale up. If the bed he sleeps on were his worst problem, I'd be a happy cop. I forgot to tell you something else last night. He told Barstow at the fair that he was going to nail him to the wall. That he was going to blast this dissertation thing wide open and discredit the hell out of him. The D.A.

has a witness who can hardly wait to testify that flames were coming out of Sam's ears. This circumstantial case is getting tighter all the time. I couldn't sleep now if someone pounded on my head for an hour."

He insisted on carrying the books to her car and stopped at the supermarket on the way to get a carton for them. "The safest place to keep them and read them is Grandma's," he told her as he put the carton on the back seat. "Use Sam's room. Even if all you get out of it is a nap, you'll still be ahead. What's your next stop?"

"The hospital, I think. If the girls are there, I'd like to talk to them before getting back. Even though Graham was murdered there, it's still more neutral ground for me to talk in than Sam's house or Myra's, I'm not sure why."

She got into the car and he closed the door and leaned on it. "How're the feet?"

"Better, thanks."

"I'm glad."

"And thank you for lunch."

"You're welcome."

"I enjoyed it."

"So did I."

"We didn't get far with the books. I'm afraid I held you up for nothing."

"No."

"If I do find something, or think of something—"

"You're tired," he said, touching the dark circles under her eyes.

"Yes, I—everyone is."

"Please be careful."

"Yes. I will."

" 'By."

" 'By."

"Get some rest."

"You too."

Why did he have to spoil it? she asked herself as she drove away. But—if he hadn't? I've got to be careful. I can't leap into something *now*. It isn't time yet . . . I have to be sure . . . I have to be fair—to *him*. He's a very fine person, and he's been badly hurt himself . . .

Furious again, she honked the horn, crossed a double yellow line and flew by three cars. But the discomfiting thoughts remained with her, and she dragged herself into the hospital as if they hung from her neck like an albatross.

The girls had gone through the records again and left only five minutes ago. Try Admitting, Emergency said, eying her with avid interest. She nodded and went back upstairs, having already found that they had left that office twenty minutes before.

She limped across the lobby to the big glass doors, and as she pushed against one, backing out wearily, a violent shove from behind knocked her off balance. On hands and knees, she turned to see a small boy of five or six regarding her through the glass with scientific curiosity. She scowled at him and picked herself up as an irate mother—who clearly had been irate for five or six years—charged up the steps, grabbed the child by the ear, and buried him under an avalanche of abuse. She was the woman who had spoken to Kristin at the Attique, and Kristin, who had disliked her then, despised her now.

"This child will be my death," she said as Kristin came out. "I don't know what to do with him. Are you all right? Did he hurt you? I don't know what to say, I'm so mortified. Don't you know better than that, you bad boy?" A shake and a slap. "What am I going to tell your father, and him so sick in there! Three times a day I come here to see my husband and three times a day I tell this little monster to sit in the lobby and behave while I go upstairs. And do you sit like a good boy?" Another slap. "No! You run all over the place like a wild Indian! I'm sorry, but I just don't know what to do with him!" She let go of the ear and the child ran off again.

She doesn't recognize me, Kristin thought, or she wouldn't bother to apologize. "Well," she said, going slowly by, "I never fancied prolonged torture myself. Why don't you shoot him and get it over with? After all, you're bigger than he is. And I'd suggest," she added as she went down the steps, "I'd suggest you do it now, because pretty soon he'll be big enough to get you first."

"If I had known," she told Matt Amaral later, "that that poor little brat was the witness we were looking for, I'd have gotten a gun and shot her myself, out of gratitude. On Sam's behalf, of course."

Chapter XIII

At the sound of the Chevrolet's cracked blast Polly and Kathy came running out of the house and scrambled into the car out of the rain, anxious for news.

"I haven't got any," Kristin said, showing them the books. "Or if I do, I don't know what it is yet. Lieutenant Amaral looked them over but he didn't have anything to suggest except that we hide them in Sam's room."

"This is some collection, Mom," Polly said. She handed a few volumes to Kathy to lighten the load and picked up the carton. "We read about perversion in almost all my abnormal psych classes, but why would anybody who's into Karpman *et al* read *Lassie* too?"

"Who knows?" Kristin said crankily as she followed them in through a heavy downpour. "The only connection I can make is that Lassie is played by a laddie. I remember feeling gypped when I found that out. Male chauvinism seems to have no limits. Men stoop to any low trick. Or maybe it's just a throwback to Elizabethan theater."

"What are you saying, Mom? That our burglar's a fouled-up epicene type? Or just plain queer?"

"Well, now that you mention it, it's certainly a possibility either way. Now, who fits the bill?"

"How about we hang it on Toby Stokes?"

"I'd be satisfied to hang him. I saw the dog this morning."

"Let's have something good and hot," Kathy said as they dried off in the warm kitchen. "What would you like?" She was looking better now after hours in Polly's sturdy company.

Kristin grinned. "Hot chocolate's a safe bet."

"Not in this house! Aunt Faith won't have anything but real cocoa as bitter as gall, and Grandma loves the sweet mixes." She took a kettle from the nearest stove, filled it, and set it on the burner, laughing. "You had them so buffaloed this morning, Kristin, they've gone upstairs to rest. What'll you do if they invite you to dinner?"

"I don't know but I wish one of them would. I like this house. I like the people in it. Their kind of craziness makes sense. Which table do I sit at?" She chose the one with the yellow cloth and put her feet up on another of the yellow chairs.

"Do you think Sam's crazy?" Polly said carefully.

"Everybody's crazy and Sam's the craziest person I ever met. I can't imagine what he paints."

"Want to see?"

"I'm not up to that yet, Pol, I don't think. Purple blobs—"

The girls burst out laughing, took her by the hand, and led her into the living room. Paintings and sketches covered the walls, and she stopped in her tracks, then turned slowly from one work to another, limp with incredulity at the slow groping development of an extraordinary talent.

"I don't believe it," she murmured. "I . . . just . . . don't . . . believe it . . . Look at that deer—he's in a morning mist . . . those birch trees and a deer floating in a mist . . . a dozen lines— He *must* be crazy! What does he want to teach for!"

"He likes kids," Polly said happily.

"Goya-esque, this one," Kristin went on, paying no attention as she studied two boys fighting over a dying fish. "All kinds of vigor busting out of that canvas . . ."

She laughed delightedly at a cartoon of a town meeting pontificator with a face like a largemouthed bass. "Oh, right on, Sam, right on." The teakettle whistled a cheerful emphasis and Kathy went to attend to it.

At length, when Kristin had seen everything a second time, she turned and looked at her glowing daughter. "Well, how about that!"

"You don't know how crazy he is," the girl said tremulously. "That maniac proposed to me last night."

"And?"

"After two days? Mom! I'm a *psych* major! I'd've been even crazier to say yes." She smiled. "Although I don't think I'll feel any different about him after two months or two years, except more so.

But until this thing is over, it's silly to think seriously about anything else. Come on, let's go in and compare notes. Kathy's pretty down."

"So is everyone else, one way and another, although I must say I'm feeling a bit better now. And she looks better. Has she said anything about anything?"

"There actually hasn't been time. Except for that short break at the jail last night—" She shook her head. "I guess I'm fading. Sorry about that." They went into the kitchen arm in arm.

"I think I'll go see Sam tonight. If I can get away," Kristin said, sitting down and putting her feet up again.

"He'd like it if you could. He was asking for you," Kathy said, setting cups of steaming hot chocolate on the yellow cloth. "You're walking better, I think."

"Lots better. But how are you? I feel I haven't seen you—either of you—in weeks."

"We've been so busy and caught up, I haven't had time to really think, thank god," Kathy said. "I don't try and prevent it, but it's all like a bad dream now. Real but receding as fast as everything else that's happened. It doesn't hurt so much now." The lovely face was sad but strangely peaceful, as if grief had been experienced fully and laid away in memory.

She'll manage, Kristin thought, remembering what Matt Amaral had said. Yes, she'll manage. "Would you mind telling me what happened? Sam told me what he knew. I couldn't ask Myra."

"Of course you couldn't. No, I don't mind. When we saw her go upstairs, Sam and I, I suddenly got scared. I knew there wasn't anyone else she'd been seeing. She had no friends on the island. Not that she wasn't sociable, according to Graham, but when they were here she spent most of her time gardening. I don't think she ever went to a beach. So I told Sam I'd better go up, and when I got on the floor and saw the list of patients and then read Graham's chart, I couldn't believe my eyes. I'd left him in the cave at about three-thirty, I'm not exactly sure, and an hour or so later he's brought back with a skull fracture! It was simply unbelievable!"

"How did he seem when you were with him? Dr. Vernon was upset because he'd left the hospital too soon after that horse show business."

"I was too, but he insisted on meeting me there, and he really seemed all right. A little tired, of course. He did slip on a rock but so did I. Most of the barnacles are further down where the water comes in. I guess I was bothered by my own carelessness. I'm a nurse, I shouldn't have missed his condition. He must have been shakier than he looked. I should have known . . . But if he'd been clubbed by someone, well . . .

"Anyway, I read the charts, and the instructions on his were to check his blood pressure. If it was still low, his medication was to stay the same. Otherwise I was supposed to switch from a saline solution to dextrose and water. I was torn between wanting to see him and wanting to spare Myra's feelings and my own, but Nora—Nora Silva, the other floor nurse—was tied up with a patient and wouldn't leave her, and she was so nasty about it that I had no choice. So I got a sphyg and a new flask in case I had to change it and I went into his room. And—it was awful!

"There was Myra sitting there holding his hand on one side of the bed. She looked so beautiful but—naked, almost. I mean, you could see how much she loved him, how miserable she was. And I was on his other side, being a nurse, being very professional, and loving him just as much. Only, she had his past. I had—I thought I had—his future.

"Maybe it would've been all right, but he wasn't unconscious, not way under. And I had to change the flask after all, after taking his blood pressure, touching him, and he said—he said, 'Kathy. Kathy.' Very low, very low. I almost didn't hear the first time.

"I didn't say anything. I just finished what had to be done and said I'd be back in half an hour to check the I.V., and she said thank you. I saw her kiss his hand as I went to the door. That poor woman! None of us asked for this!

"Anyway, just as I put my hand on the knob, somebody knocked and I opened the door and there was Sam. Asking to see Myra. I was in a state of shock, I guess, but I said no, of course. She'd had enough. He told me later that I looked at him as if I'd never seen him before, and at that minute I felt I never had. He went away—I saw him go through the swinging doors and down the steps but the police said he came back, of course—and then I just went on working. But I had my eye on the clock and at eight forty-five I went back to Graham's room and opened the door—" She stopped, her eyes wide and blank as she remembered.

"And I saw something—a knife handle—something dark—sticking out of his breast. I'd never seen it before. His mouth hung open a little. That's what Myra must have meant by the distorted look on his face. I didn't have to take another step inside to know he was dead, but I would have, of course, just because it was my job and I was doing everything mechanically—except that just then Myra came up beside me and *she* looked in. And she said, 'What have you done, what have you done?' Do you know, I never told Matt that part of it!

"Anyway, I just let go of the knob and I ran. I should have been doing my job—disconnecting the I.V., looking at my watch and noting down the death on the chart, getting a doctor, giving comfort, all those things. But I didn't think. I couldn't think. I just ran. Sam found me down in Steve's lab. And—that's all."

"That's about what I got from Dr. Vernon and Sam. Except that Myra didn't tell the police or Dr. Vernon what she said to you, did she."

"No, otherwise I might be in a cell next to Sam as an accessory or something. Myra wouldn't say anything unless she really thought I'd killed him. Obviously she doesn't. And anyway, I was pretty busy for that half hour until I went to his room again, as my additions to the other charts show."

"To say nothing of the fact that you had no reason to think she'd leave his room for a good while, or that if she had, she wouldn't see you either *in* the act or just leaving as she got back. That's about what did happen, by accident, after all," Polly said loyally. "If you were planning to do it, you'd have had the rest of the night. So it makes no sense to suspect you even if you had a motive."

"That's what Matt said. He came to my apartment after Sam had left. But it's funny—I never even thought of defending myself with such an argument. I never even thought of it at all until he said it. In any case Myra was the hindrance, not Graham. If I'd been unwilling to accept that—that offer to go on as we were—if I'd insisted on marriage, and murder were the only way to get it, Myra would be dead now, not Graham. But I never thought of that either."

"Sam said you left Graham thinking in the cave, Kathy. What did you tell him?"

"I told him . . . that it *would* have to be marriage or nothing. That what we had wasn't right for any of us. That I'd go away from here if I had to and not tell him where or when, because I had to live with myself before anyone else. And I couldn't live with this. No one should have to. And I also asked him," she added, putting a hand on Polly's, "to give Sam a break no matter what else happened. He just nodded. I went out to West Beach and drove home."

"You didn't see Sam on the beach again?"

"No. But if he'd been there, where he always was, near the rocks, he'd have seen me and stopped me. But he'd gone at least an hour before I did. The police can't let him go—not yet—but even Phil Trueblood knows Sam never lied about anything or did a mean cruel thing to anyone. You're lucky, Polly," she said fondly. "You can trust him till the end of your life."

"I hope we all get that chance," Kristin said thoughtfully. "But you haven't come up with our missing witness yet, and short of the murderer's confession, that's all we have to hope for. I wouldn't want to count on an acquittal on reasonable doubt. Sam was seen at every place where Graham had trouble. It may be circumstantial but it's too strong for comfort."

"Can't we pin something on Toby Stokes?" Polly said longingly.

"Kathy, you said Sam didn't like him and you didn't see eye to eye with him anymore," Kristin said. "Why?"

"Sam just didn't like him. Toby's older, of course, so they didn't know each other all that well, but I don't know that Sam was ever more specific about it than that. You could ask him. But Toby and I went through school together. We dated in high school, we were usually the romantic leads in the drama club, we went to the senior prom together. The gang took it for granted we'd be married someday, and for a while I did too.

"We had a class party after graduation, a big clambake on the beach on the Fourth of July. The summer I left for Rhode Island to study nursing. And everyone was teasing us, and Toby got down on one knee and proposed. 'Will you be mine, I can't live without you, promise you'll return to me'—that sort of nonsense from our senior play—and I said yes, and I really thought it was settled. He kissed me in front of all of them just the way he'd done in the play, and they cheered and clapped. Everybody had a *great* time.

"But for the rest of that summer it was different when we were alone. He never touched me, never tried to kiss me . . .

"I was disappointed, of course, but I put it down to the pain of parting. He was withdrawn, irritable . . . I'd take his hand and he'd pull away . . . We were both eighteen . . . I was even intrigued by his moods, they seemed—romantic!

"Well, the day I left, he went with me to the ferry, and when it was time to say good-by he grabbed me and hugged me hard and said, 'I'm afraid. If you go—' I thought he meant I'd find someone else. But it wasn't that. It wasn't that at all. But I don't know what it was.

"I don't know as much psychology as you do, Polly. We didn't have much in school. But every time I came back, and especially at the clambakes every Fourth, the gang got going again, teasing and nagging, and Toby would get down and propose and I'd say yes, and it was all words. Because he never so much as took my hand or put his arm around me when we were alone. One night when he was walking me home from a movie I asked him point-blank when we were going to get married, and he said, 'I don't think I'll ever marry. I don't have—enough.' He wouldn't say what he meant and I never asked him again.

"So we fooled around for the gang's benefit, but we were only friends. And after a while we weren't even that. He started grubbing for money, pouring everything into that farm, and the joy and fun we'd had through school just—faded away. That's all. Except that I met Graham a year ago, and nobody I'd ever known was anything like him. At least I was spared the misery of a broken marriage. If I'd married Toby, or anyone else, he and Myra would've been in the same boat sooner or later. That's how quick and right it was, with Graham."

"And the phone conversations Toby had with other girls, the ones that upset your grandmother and your aunt, what about them? Was he interested in other women?"

"I honestly don't know. Oh, he dates other girls now and then. But I never heard any of those evil conversations myself." She laughed. "The Todd sisters are kind of strait-laced about some things, the darlings. They don't hold with free and easy language like damn and hell. Poor Sam has to watch his mouth when he's home."

Kristin grinned. "Like putting a cork in a bomb." She put her feet down and sighed. "I think I'd better be off, Kathy, or the way that rain is coming down, I might have to leave the car here and swim back. And Dr. Vernon doesn't want me to get my feet wet."

"Maybe you'll win the car raffle, Mom. Kathy took me to see that gorgeous thing. I bought two tickets myself."

"Well, you shouldn't have bothered, darling. Winning it wouldn't be congruent with the rest of this vacation of ours, which is why we aren't going to win it."

She was right, and they didn't, but by the end of the week, it no longer mattered.

"I'm on duty tonight so I'd better go too," Kathy said. "I've been neglecting my laundry and stuff."

"Want to wash these cups first? It'll just take a minute," Polly said, stacking them.

"Thanks, but we can't deprive Grandma and Aunt Faith of the chance for another skirmish," Kathy said, laughing merrily as she unstacked them. "When they see white cups on the yellow cloth with sweet chocolate in them, they'll be so busy arguing and keeping score they won't have time to worry."

Their cheerfulness, relative though it was in the circumstances, was thoroughly doused by the rain, and they went into the house on the hilltop feeling as beaten as the flowers in Myra's garden. Nothing promising had developed out of the talk at the table with the yellow cloth; nothing but depression could arise from another meal at the antiseptic butcher-block table which had never yet witnessed a happy gathering. In the dreary interim Kristin napped, Polly read, and Myra wrote letters, and after supper the girl suggested going to a movie.

"I knew Myra wouldn't go, storm or no storm," she said as

they drove to the jail. "But I've seen that show, so here's a rundown in case she asks."

She drove carefully through the worsening storm, interrupting the story briefly to find a weather report on the radio. "Hurricanes are all we need," she said as Kristin turned the radio off with an irritable snap. "We'd better make this fast, Mom, and if we get back before the show lets out, the storm's our alibi."

"I really don't think Myra cares. And I don't either. All I want is something that'll spring Sam. All the way, without any doubts. If we can just do that I won't even care if they never find the murderer."

"Not much you won't," the girl said as they reached the little county jail. "A compulsive lady like you? You'll gnaw at it and gnaw at it until you find him and bring him in yourself." Kristin hesitated, seeing the state police shield on the car beside them. "Come on, Mom, let's make a run for it."

The wind blew them inside and, when with some difficulty they shut it out, it raged around the old building like a savage beast robbed of its prey. The only warmth immediately within was Lee Williams' smile as he spun on the chair at the desk and jerked his thumb toward the cells in the back. "I wouldn't go near him if I were you. He took four bucks off me last night. I told Phil I'd rather mind his store than play poker with that shark."

They came laughing like partygoers to the open door of Sam's cell and found the suspect playing poker on the floor with Dr. Vernon, Matt Amaral, Chief Trueblood, and Steve and Charlotte Black. The young couple, all eyeglasses and long hair, greeted Kristin with warm interest. Chief Trueblood, who had not enjoyed himself so much in years, was elaborately genial, Amaral elaborately casual, Sam clearly dizzy over his luck in cards and in love. The old doctor paid no attention to anything but his cards, at which he frowned in concentration. Everyone was drinking beer and eating pizza, and a boxful of the fragrant pies was keeping warm on a hot plate just outside the door.

"My god. If the D.A., the judge, and the jury were here now," Kristin said, "you'd be acquitted on the spot, Sam."

"I will be anyway, so why rush it?" he said happily. "I've won twenty-two bucks less beer and food since I checked in. And Phil says all my paintings sold at the fair! There's nothing frivolous about this either. I'm shooting for enough to buy Polly a ring." He paused, then added with that odd shyness, "With your blessing, that is."

"You have that already, Sam. For what it's worth."

Matt Amaral's face, momentarily unguarded, mirrored his estimate of that, but everyone was looking at Sam, who had jumped up and was kissing Polly soundly. "Hey!" she protested laughingly. "I feel like royalty. Everything publicly arranged."

"Then you *will!*"

"I'll tell you in six months. Six months after you're released—or after the trial," the girl said seriously. "Let's let the dust settle a bit."

Trueblood looks disappointed, Kristin thought. I bet he'd like to have the wedding and the honeymoon here too. And for real drama, a verdict of guilty and death in the chair. But she knew that the thought was inaccurate and ungenerous: It was plain that Trueblood considered Sam no more guilty than himself. The Barstows must be a powerful clan, she thought uneasily, and shivered in sudden fear.

"You're cold," Amaral said instantly. "Here, wrap yourself around this. Best on the island." He put a wedge of hot pizza into her hand and turned away like a good host to help the others, and she ate conscientiously because in her confusion there was nothing else to do.

"I'm holding onto this hand," Dr. Vernon announced, putting his cards carefully into his pocket and accepting the pizza with relish. "Let's have a quiet powwow, bring things down to earth a bit. Then I'm gonna beat the pants off you, Sam. And then I'm going home to bed. Polly, what's the score with you and Kathy on those calls?"

"Zilch. And we didn't have as many people to call as *you* thought, Matt. Most of them were island calls, by the way, so long distance won't be too much. But we sure put out more than we got back."

"Anybody sound suspicious?"

"No, Mr. Trueblood, unless it was suspicious of our mental state. Some of them thought at first that we were playing a prank. But all of them had seen the papers so they realized we were leveling. Besides, our style improved. By the time we finished we were hoarse. We sounded like the FBI."

"Well, just this once I'm glad you did and I wish you were," Vernon said. "Anybody ask any interesting questions?"

"No. It went very smoothly and very fast. We didn't get a clue."

"Hmph! Kris, how about those books? Anything there?"

"Not yet, Dr. Vernon. But I slept all afternoon. The way my mind works, something's sure to pop out if I back off a bit. We'd love to tag Toby Stokes, I'm sure of that."

"Perversionwise? I don't know," Vernon said. "What's your thinking on him so far?"

"We don't have much. Kathy says he avoided physical contact with her, but that doesn't mean anything. Also, he's a money-grubber—puts it all back into the farm. His new van isn't insured against theft, and it's been stolen. He maltreats animals. And his temper's very raw."

"Hmph! Not much there either. Sam, you've had *some* time alone. Got anything?"

"About Toby? No. I didn't know him well and I didn't like what I knew. No reason, just a feeling. And nothing special. Some people you just don't like."

"Sam, did anything or anyone disturb you while you were in your car?" Kristin said slowly.

"Everybody's asked me that but you, and the answer's still no. I did hear some gal calling someone, but I wouldn't have seen her unless she stuck her head in my window. I was lying down."

"Did you hear what she said? A name?" said Charlotte Black, pushing her heavy eyeglasses back onto the bridge of her nose.

"No. Wish I could oblige."

"You're not holding out on us till you've made your pile, Sam?" Steve joked.

Sam grinned. "Can you think of any better reason why I'd want to? No, I'm not fooling around now. I've tried to remember but the damn thing is that I was thinking, not concentrating on outside sounds. I heard her voice peripherally, so to speak. Subliminally, almost."

144

"Well, but enough to have gotten an emotional impression?" Kristin persisted. "I mean, was she—did she sound mad?"

"You've got onto something, Kris," Steve said.

"Yes, I just remembered. It's one of those things that popped out. I didn't think anything of it at the time and I don't know if it means anything now." She told them about the child who had knocked her down and the woman who called herself a mother. "She visits her husband three times a day, she said. You must have called her too, Polly."

"We probably did, Mom. But a mother like that isn't likely to ask a mischievous kid what he was up to or where he'd been, or tell us if she knew. She'd just grab him when she found him and pound the living daylights out of him again."

"Well, but look, Pol," Charlotte said. "If she visits three times a day, her husband's probably in a private room and there aren't many of them. Go through the register again, why don't you, and—"

"Right on!" and the girl shot out before Kristin could stop her.

"I may need a ride," she said worriedly. "We weren't planning to stay long. Myra's alone. She thinks we've gone to the movies."

"No problem," Amaral said, and quickly asked another question. "Anybody happen to know who's backing The Joint? I found out when I got this stuff tonight."

"Toby Stokes, I'll bet," Dr. Vernon said. "His dog, the fellas at the ferry, et cetera."

"Yeah. I didn't want to shake up our nine-fingered pizza genius at this stage of the game but he didn't quiver when he told me, so maybe there's nothing fishy after all. But that and that van of Toby's bother hell out of me. Where does Toby get all his money? From plumbing? I'm going to his bank in the morning. You never know." He took another bite of pizza and chewed it glumly.

"Camels," Kristin said, staring into space.

He perked up immediately. "What?"

"Camels . . ."

"Want a cigarette?" Sam said. "I've got Larks. Some joke."

Steve offered her a Pall Mall. "This do?"

She shook her head. "No. Thanks. That isn't what I meant."

Amaral looked at her intently. "What did you mean?"

She met his gaze blankly. "I don't know. I don't know what I meant."

"Oh yes you do. Give."

"Well . . . something your brother said. It was something he said . . . about the dog. . . ."

They watched, breathless, as if she were a seer in a trance pursuing a thought as tenuous as smoke.

"It was about that wound on his ribs. Like a pocket, Dr. Amaral said. Where a cyst might have been removed. So then I naturally thought of camels."

"Naturally!" Vernon snorted.

Her eyes focused. "No, really. They use camels for smuggling. I read about it. They sew things—diamonds, usually—under the skin and take off with a whole caravan. Then they step over the border somewhere and unload the poor beasts and let them die . . . let them finish dying. And then they get some more. You mentioned drugs, Lieutenant, and Toby throws away a dog with an infected pocket under the loose skin. And that boy with a finger missing was pulling at the loose skin on Frey's back. And he said something to the other boy about making money with a dog like Frey . . . And your brother said there aren't many unclaimed dogs around these days. Do you see what I mean?"

His eyes were large and brilliant with excitement. "Yes, I see. Crude implants would lead to uremic poisoning, wouldn't they, Steve? Doc?"

"Sure," Vernon said. "Infection. Wildfire! Plastic wrapping, probably. Rejected in a week. Bastard!"

Charlotte laughed, breaking the tension. "Doc, if you don't relax you'll be speaking shorthand in a minute."

"Matt, did Joe do a tissue study?" Steve said. "Did he say anything about that?"

"He wanted to but he didn't have time. He's been working alone the past few days and the dog was in a bad way. If there was anything in that wound it's gone now, damn it to hell. But even if he'd found something, how do we connect it to Barstow?"

"His brother—Graham's oldest brother—is coming tomorrow," Kristin said. "Myra's planning to have the cremation tomorrow night."

"No way. Not in this storm. Our blueblood isn't going to make it here tomorrow," Steve said. "Anyway, Doc and I have our notes and he can't snatch them and the body too. We put down everything we saw, every goddam thing. You might say Barstow's been reduced to a stack of paper."

"But why?" Kristin said. "I thought you were satisfied with the cause of death. What's going on here?"

"We're waitin' on Doc," Trueblood said. "If he ain't satisfied, then I ain't satisfied."

"Well, I'm not either," she said, exasperated. "If one of you medical gents would stand by and translate, I'd read those notes myself. Here's a nice neat murder, weapon and all. More than lots of other people get to go on. What more do you want!"

"If we knew, you'd know," Vernon grumbled, and gulped down half a can of warm beer.

"This is the thing," Steve said. "Sam didn't kill Barstow. Neither did Kathy. Sure, she could've popped in and done the deed and popped out again, but she didn't know when Myra was leaving that room. But—Myra knew when Kathy would be back."

"Oh sure!" Kristin cried. "Myra stuck that flint right through him and then she sat around killing *time* for as much as fifteen minutes if she did it right after Kathy left. Then she left at eight-thirty and made it her business to be back at eight forty-five sharp just when Kathy was to be back there again. And then she doesn't tell you she thinks Kathy was the murderer! Suppose someone had come in just before she left? Since when was a closed door in a hospital sacred to anybody! Suppose someone—Kathy especially—saw her leave, and went in and found him dead as a mackerel? And in turn said nothing about it to you! You're crazy! Even if Myra wanted to kill him, can you see her taking a chance like that?"

"Somebody did take that chance, Kris," Steve said reasonably. "And of the three people on the scene, we've eliminated two."

"By popular vote, yes, and *I'm* not demanding a recount! But Myra? You're out of your mind! And anyway, an autopsy is just

147

an autopsy, it isn't a coroner's inquest. We don't even have that kind of thing in Massachusetts, I understand. All you have to do is chop him up and take a look around! So what's holding you up? Don't tell me you don't know!"

"We don't, but we won't." Vernon took the cards out of his pocket. "We're gonna finish this game now. Talk's over. Better go to bed, Kris."

"I think I'll do just that!" she said furiously, and stormed out without realizing that she couldn't unless she walked all the way home.

"Be right back, Lee," Amaral said to the dozing trooper, and propelled Kristin out into the rain and into the cruiser before she recognized his voice or even felt his hand on her arm. Silently he took his place behind the wheel, and waited.

"Thanks. Again," she said softly. "I'm sorry I blew my stack. It was a childish thing to do."

"They don't mind. Even Sam says you've been having the roughest time of anybody except Myra."

"And now it'll be worse although I don't believe it for a minute. Do you really think she's a—a murderer?"

"It's more a matter of going logically from one thing to another. I'm not saying we believe it, but let's face it. She was on the scene and she had a motive, even if it makes more sense to believe Barstow was better alive than dead, considering her mode of life, her love of family and all the rest of it. A woman scorned doesn't always commit murder. But it has to be kicked around. We just didn't want to mention it in front of you."

"Well, I guess I can see why. But I'm sorry anyway. I had no business losing my temper."

He grasped the wheel with both hands before allowing himself to look at her. "I'm very glad you did," he said pointedly. "But the last place I'd like to take you to is that house, and the last company I'd like to see you in is Myra Barstow's."

"I—guess I'd better get back."

"Yes."

He turned on the ignition. It was one of the most difficult things he had ever had to force himself to do.

Chapter XIV

The hurricane, now well to the northeast early Wednesday morning, was slowly corkscrewing itself into the ocean and seemed fiercely intent on dragging the island down with it. Fortunately there were no big trees on the hilltop to endanger the house, but the wind scattered small debris everywhere and drove slashing rain through the putty and under the kitchen door. The beautiful garden was in ruins, the power lines were down, the telephone dead, the wires in Myra's station wagon and Graham's yellow bug sodden and unresponsive.

Polly had called from the hospital late the night before to tell Kristin that she was going to stay there since, storm or no storm, she had discovered from the register of patients and the floor nurse the father of the little boy. "The nurse says he's in no hurry to go home, by the way," she had said, laughing. "His temperature hits the gong every time that shrew of his leaves. The poor guy says they'd be doing him a favor to do a lobotomy on him. She doesn't answer her phone, but if she should show up in the morning I'll be on the spot, otherwise I'll go to her when it's safe to drive out to where she's staying. I'm going to sleep in the nurses' quarters, and the cafeteria's staying open all night, so I'm probably better off than you are."

Better off than you know, Kristin thought, miserable and nervous, as she helped Myra mop up the leaks while Dandie followed them around. We're marooned up here, and I'm watching her, and wondering, and there she is, as simple and normal as any other housewife, doing what everybody else is doing, with those strong beautiful hands of hers.

Those men are crazy! Methodical, logical, yes. A good policeman, a good doctor, covers all the bets. My god, I thought of it myself, who wouldn't? But if Myra killed Graham, then I stood by and helped. *No.* There's no way in the world that I'd ever believe she killed him. I don't care what *he* says, he's way off base.

He was Matt Amaral, and the morsel of language caused her pulse to pound frantically. Her great need for caution now was no impregnable bulwark against such a man. Even a good marriage was no guarantee that all desire had been fulfilled, or could be, that every corner of the heart was forever tenanted by countless intimacies shared with one person and one person only.

I'll stay until Jonathan Barstow comes and Graham's cremated, she told herself, and then I'll leave immediately. I can't drag *him* into my mess, not even casually. It isn't fair to him, he's too fine . . . And he's ready . . . And so am I . . .

A wet cold nose nudged her hand and automatically she stroked the collie's long sleek head.

"What's the matter, Kris?"

"What? Oh, nothing. I was just listening to the wind. I don't see how your brother-in-law can get here today. He must have been blown up to Gander. And that's no place to be stranded in, I'm told."

"He'll probably be here tomorrow. It will surely be over by then. I wish we could hear a weather report. Oh well, it will be over when it's over no matter what the weatherman says. Isn't this a mess! These towels are soaked already and we can't even dry anything out with a fire. I never thought to bring some wood in last night. It would have been dry by now."

She sighed and bent to wring out a towel over the bucket and put it on the floor again.

Could those hands have felt for the vulnerable spot and held the ancient knife and, with cold deliberate anger, plunged it into the heart of a helpless man just because he had found someone else to love?

Yes, if you overlooked the fact that Myra had not found the missing flint. It was possible in that it was not utterly impossible. But logical? No, and that's that, Kristin decided, and felt relieved of the lesser burden of her thoughts.

"What I'm really worried about is my garden," Myra said. "All the attention it got after our trip down two weeks ago was the few minutes I had on Monday before the police came. Since then—" She shrugged. "And we'll probably leave the island tomorrow night, Jonathan and I. I don't know when I'll be back. I was thinking of going away somewhere for a while."

"Then you'll be coming back here? Are you going to keep the house?"

"I don't know, dear. It's hard to give up anything of Graham's. He loved it so. And of course our nieces and nephews and their children spent time with us here . . . Maybe they won't ever want to again. But I don't have to decide anything yet. I can't. If there hadn't been any storm it'd be easier for me to think and plan. That's when I do my best thinking, when I'm gardening."

"Well, you'll be able to do that in Cambridge, anyway."

"Oh, but we don't have grounds there, Kris. I thought you knew. That's why this house meant so much to us. It's a huge penthouse duplex, it overlooks the Charles, you know, and it's lovely, but all I have is a small greenhouse on the patio. I only grow potted plants. And some fruits. We traveled so much, we didn't want a house. We rented a summer place for years in New Hampshire until we happened to see this property. We knew it was time to— settle down . . ."

Kristin put an arm around her. "Come on, Myra, come into the kitchen and let's have something to drink, some brandy. It's so cold in here and you're so pale. How about it? It will do you good. Do us both good."

"I don't know what I'd have done without you, Kristin dear. All right, we'll have some. Too bad we can't have it in a cup of tea, but the water heater's all cold now."

"Better today than yesterday. At least my rash is drying up. I can get along without the hot packs now. How's yours?" She brought glasses and a bottle to the table and poured generously.

"Better too. How's Josh's? Didn't you get a letter from him yesterday? I thought I saw one in that pile of mail I brought back."

"Yes, but I wouldn't dignify it with the name. 'Dear Mom and Dad. Home in ten days. Can you spare ten more bucks for ointment? How's Pollycracker? Love, J.' What do you think of that?"

Myra laughed. "About what I've gotten for years from all the children. They're all the same, the darlings, they don't mean anything by it."

Brandy and reminiscence warmed her and she chatted comfortably, exchanging stories with Kristin while the storm shook the house and rattled the windows. But soon the faint color drained out of her cheeks and she stared at her limp hands, her memories shriveled up by one so terrible that she could not talk anymore. "I'm sorry, dear. I'm exhausted, I guess. If you don't mind, I'll lie down for an hour. Don't worry about the leaks. Come, Dandie."

Kristin followed her into the living room. "That's all right. I'll keep an eye on them. I'll read on the couch if I can find a flashlight. It's as dark as a March afternoon."

Myra trailed a hand along the books as she went by. "I'll have to get another *Lassie* one of these days. It's the kind of book I get a lot of comfort from. Graham said it was silly sentimentality, reading certain stories every year, and I expect it was silly, to him. He only read the important books. They absolutely terrified me."

She went into her room with the collie at her heels and closed the door as she had done so often these past three days, shutting herself off to court relief. When she had found enough she would be able to come out again.

The flashlight Kristin had found in a kitchen drawer was too dim to read by. She closed her book and got up to see to the leaks, then lay down again and stared at the shelves.

How did Myra know that book was missing? she asked herself. I don't think I was ever specific. In fact I remember being as vague as possible, because after Monday morning's interview I was wondering what she would say. She's certainly left out some interesting items since finding Graham dead, and she never said anything about the robbery, just shrugged it off . . .

Maybe Polly told her. No, I'm sure she didn't. I guess she was just ready for her *n*th reading and couldn't find it, and that's *that*. Why are you making such a big thing of it?

To avoid the subject altogether, she fell asleep, and it was past noon when the telephone roused her.

"Progress report, Mom. I've been calling and calling, hoping it'd go through sometime."

"Now if the electricity would just turn on again, I'd be almost content. What's up?"

"Nothing. I mean, our subjects didn't show this morning. I guess the storm's just too bad. The name's Savage, by the way. Good name for her, from what you told me. Miriam Savage. Mrs. Henry. She doesn't answer her phone—they're staying at that apartment motel out near East Beach—but not because it's dead. I checked. She just isn't home, and her husband doesn't know where she might be. The nurse said he does but he won't tell. *He* doesn't want to see her or talk to her."

"Well, I do. What's the weather report?"

"By late afternoon we'll be out of the woods. Rain's supposed to stop sometime tonight. Those who haven't been washed away by now will see the sun rise tomorrow. How about I stick around here and see who shows up during the early afternoon. Then I'll come home and you take over. Do you good to get out."

"Thank you, darling. But don't drive if it's too bad out."

"It sounds much worse than it is if you're inside. I was over to see Sam, so I know. *Ciao.*"

Mrs. Savage and her son had not been among the few visitors at the hospital at any time up to five o'clock. "And a good thing too," the floor nurse told Kristin. "That poor man is feeling better than he has in days. He might even recover provided they never come back. The last time she was here, she showed him all the bills that had been piling up. I had to put her out finally, scrawny little bitch. If you find her she's all yours. But she won't be much loss to anyone if you don't."

"That's what you think," Kristin said, and went to a phone booth to call Chief Trueblood and ask for his help.

"She'll turn up sooner or later," he said casually, and rang off complaining of a press of work. He might have added that he was in no hurry to see Mrs. Savage either. The jail was a very different place these days. No point spoiling a good thing.

Nor was there any help at the state police barracks. Lieutenant Amaral had not been heard from all day, said the trooper on the desk, and it was anybody's guess where he was.

She was now very hungry, but after a day of cold canned food in a cheerless house she would not eat anything on the hospital cafeteria's bland limited menu. She stopped there long enough for a cup of hot coffee and then drove to the sprawling motel near the beach. The wind here almost lifted her off her feet.

"We've got our hands full," the room clerk said, rubbing his bald head wearily. "We get the brunt of every storm, and this one's a lulu. I don't know where the Savage woman is—someone else was asking for her this morning, I can't think why. She's a nasty-tongued bitch. Hasn't stopped complaining since they got here the first of July. After a week I told her to take the brat and go someplace else, but they'd paid two full months' rent in advance so we're stuck with her until Mr. S. gets out of the hospital. Say, you're not a nurse, are you? That dress a uniform?"

"No." She had put on the new white dress to cheer herself up and defy the weather. A mistake, obviously.

"Thought you were one of that poor bastard's nurses. Well, I don't wish him any hard luck but I'll be glad when he's well enough to leave and get her the hell out of my hair. And I don't have much so you can just about imagine!"

"I don't blame you. I've had a few run-ins with her myself. But it's very important that I locate her and the boy. I don't suppose you could—uh—call all the apartments here and—uh—no, I guess you can't."

"Lady, even if I could I wouldn't. With all due respect you sound like trouble and I've got enough of that. All I can say is, they're around. Maybe they'll wash up on the beach in a few days. I hope."

She laughed herself back into the car and drove to the village supermarket. I'll get some of those synthetic logs, she thought, and we can heat a can of soup or something in the fireplace. And even if the power's on by now, it'll be cheerful having a little fire.

But the market had closed promptly at six (and the logs were sold out anyway). Thoroughly frustrated, she huddled into her raincoat and walked as quickly as she could to The Joint.

Its sharp spicy fragrance immediately fortified and solaced her. "Oh boy, I'd like one of everything you've got," she said happily to the nine-fingered youth behind the counter. "And a box to take home." She put her wet coat over a chair and studied the menu cards on the wall.

"Anything you say, sister. How's about a meat-ball sub while yuh wait? I gotta coupla pies in the oven ain't all done yet. Say, you the lieutenant's chick was in here yesterday?"

She blushed. "You must be kidding." Inspired by intuition, she added, "I may know a lot of different people but—" and shrugged. "He's a little too interested in what I've got in my head, is all." And *I'm a master at equivocating,* she thought. *I haven't said one word that isn't all too true* . . .

"Huh! You 'n' everybody else! Yuh wanna sub?"

"Sure. And four pies to go. No hurry. How's business? How come I'm the only one here at this time of day?"

"Business is lousy. Place been practically empty all day. Dunno why people stop eatin' in a storm. What the hell, *I'm* here!" His great puff of hair swelled with hurt pride. He poured sauce generously on the bread and set it before her with the flourish of a Cordon Bleu graduate.

She bit into the savory mess and hummed delightedly through her nose. "Mmmmmmm! You're a genius! That's what the lieutenant said, and for once he's right!"

"He really say that? Hey, whaddyuh know! 'Bout time somebody around here appreciated my work."

"Everybody does, don't worry about that."

"Coffee?"

"Please. Say, why are you wasting yourself in a place like this? With that name and the food you'd make a fortune in Harvard Square. Not that they don't need you here, but—" she fished, although she meant exactly what she said.

"Right on, sister! We're savin' our bread every way we can—see our booth at the fair?—'n' Cambridge is where we're headin'. Me 'n' Jack—he's my partner—we like class, 'n' Harvard's where it's at. 'N' it'll be *our* place."

"You mean this one isn't yours?" Her eyes were very wide and clear.

He was about to reply when angry frightened barking issued from the kitchen, and Jack stuck his head through the swinging doors. "Hey, gimme a hand, Giggy, will yuh?"

"Now? Crissake, man, I'm cookin' now, not vettin'."

"Today's the day 'n' it's worth five bucks saved, ain't it?"

"Somebody has to watch the front, 'n' I gotta coupla—"

"What's the matter," Kristin said, putting down the sub.

"Gotta dog out back needs his stitches out," Giggy said. "Hey, sister, you're a nurse. A stitch is a stitch irregardless. You do the job, sub's on the house."

"Fair enough." Her pulse roared in her ears but she got up and went behind the counter as calmly as Edith Cavell. "Let's see him."

"Say, d'y'mind goin' out back? Board o' Health walked in here now 'n' saw him near the food, it'd be worth our license," Giggy said apologetically, opening the door for her.

"No, I don't mind." Relieved that neither of them remembered seeing her at the ferry, she marched into the kitchen with the aplomb of an R.N. She had looked very different on Sunday night, and they had been very nervous, of course. "Where's the patient?" she said briskly.

"He's in the john, ma'am. Sorry about that, but Gig does things by the book 'n' so do I. Against the rules t' have animals in victualin' places."

The lavatory was as clean as the rest of the place, she saw, impressed, as Jack dragged out from under the sink a rangy golden retriever with anxious eyes and furrowed brow and a shaven patch just below the back of his neck. He panted with fear and shied as her hand went out to him.

"Here, lemme get him down 'n' hold him," Jack said. He grabbed the dog's paws and flung him on his side, and the frightened animal instantly scrambled back under the sink. "Goddam!"

"You'll never make it with that approach," she said with professional scorn. "We want his co-operation, not a bloody arm. Leave him alone. Got a scissors? Tweezers? Good. Hold *them*. Now." She knelt and said softly, "Hello, ol' sweetie. How's my pretty boy? Come on out and say hello. A-a-attaboy, that's a sweetie. What's his name, Jack?"

"Scamp. Scamper. But I call him Scamp."

"Doesn't fit. This is a gentleman, aren't you, Scamp." She stroked his shining head, talking quietly, saying his name over and over until he was tranquil and trusting. "Would you like to lie down now, Scamp?" she asked him, sitting back on her heels and folding her hands in her lap.

The dog lay down and rolled over onto his back, tongue hanging out of his open jaws and an expression of adoration in his liquid eyes.

"Attaboy. But I really think it would be better to roll over, Scamp."

The dog arched his back and rolled over and was under the sink again, head on paws and a grin on his face.

"Hey, you scamp, you're laughing at me, aren't you, boy," she said, moving closer and holding up a hand. "Scissors! Tweezers! Okay, here we go."

He quivered when she touched the sutured wound but lay still as she snipped the threads and gently pulled them out. "Hmmmm," she said in a cool medical tone, palpating the bare skin. "Still a little puffy but it seems to be healing nicely. How did he get this, and when?"

A pause. "Barbed wire. Bad scene. About ten days ago. Hey, you're all right! Nice job, ma'am, thanks a lot."

"You like this dog?"

"Yeah."

"Then don't ever yell at him again, or manhandle him. And watch that—barbed wire. You want him to trust you, so take better care of him. How would you like to be treated this way? Hear?"

"Yeah."

"I mean it," she said severely, getting up.

"Me too, ma'am, honest. You're pretty cool." He was patting the dog lovingly as she left.

"No trouble," she told Giggy, and sat down to finish the rest of the sub.

"Want I should hot that up a little?"

"Nope. Just fine. If food is any good at all, it's just as good cold as hot. This is, anyway." She wiped her hands and sighed with satisfaction. "Giggy, you've made my day. Now if I can get that pizza back home without the rain drowning it out—"

"I wrapped the box up real good for yuh. Rain's lettin' up anyway so it'll be okay. Sausage, pepper, onion, 'n' mushrooms. All fresh, too, none a that canned or frozen crap. Buck sixty-five apiece, 'n' the sub's on me, like I said. Thanks, sister. Peace."

"Peace," she said, smiling, giving the salute, and went out into the rain. But her face was grim as she walked back to the car.

You're taking a lot for granted, she told herself as she drove home. One, that those nice kids are in the drug traffic. Two, that the golden and that white shepherd are two of their canine couriers. Three, that all the missing dogs Dr. Amaral talked about were used for the same purpose. Four, that Toby Stokes is the local mastermind of an organization on the mainland. Five, that Graham Barstow is plugged into this somehow. And six, that you're by way of becoming an ace medical dick.

Well, forget that part of it, it isn't your line of country. You should have called Dr. Amaral before you left the village.

Nevertheless she knew that no barbed wire had torn that golden's back. A trained hand had shaved off a patch of silky red hair and made a neat incision with a surgical knife, then with a forceps carefully separated skin from connective tissue to make a little pocket.

Chapter XV

Myra was so nervous on Thursday morning, awaiting word from her brother-in-law, that Kristin insisted on attending to the errands and taking Dandie to the vet. "She missed her medication yesterday, remember, when it was so cold in the house, and now isn't a time to take chances, Myra. I'll ask Dr. Amaral if he can switch her to pills. My feet really are better and I don't mind at all. Come, Dandie."

And I'll be able to get going again, she thought in relief as she drove carefully down the hill with the big collie in the back seat. The road was worse than ever now. There was not much litter on it, but it was deeply gullied wherever the water's flow had been diverted by large stones. She steered skillfully, holding her breath and sitting forward stiffly as if to lighten the car's burden.

"Whew!" she said, breathing hard as they got to the bottom, and sat for a moment enjoying her first good look at the new day.

The sky seemed vast, as though the hours of rain and buffeting winds had stretched it, and a peculiar pellucid chartreuse light lay over Perley Stokes's meadow, which rolled like a green sea away from the county road. A bright yellow earth-mover, a toy at this distance, moved slowly over a brown spot between two clumps of tiny trees. The air was clean and sweet and filled with bird song, and flocks of birds flew through it drying out in the tender sunlight. The world was serene and busy again.

"Oh Frey, it's beautiful!" she said, forgetting. Tears pricked her eyes as she drove down the road.

Dr. Amaral was clearing debris from his little parking lot. He waved cheerfully and brushed off his hands. "Small payment, that Bella, for a day like this. Come on in."

"You men! Why does a hurricane have to be female! Why couldn't it be Bertram or Blake or Brock?"

"I'll speak to the Met' Department in D.C. You've got a point there. Now, how's this young lady?"

"Much better. And if she hadn't been, I'd have invented something just to get myself out of that house. If we're—lucky, we'll leave tomorrow. I've got news for you and it's been killing me that I couldn't call you. Not with Myra around all last night. Where's the lieutenant, by the way? I can't seem to get any attention from anybody, even Trueblood."

"I'm not sure where Matt is at the moment. Last he said, he was on his way to the mainland yesterday morning in a chopper. He got a lead from Toby Stokes's bank Tuesday night—too restless to wait till morning—and went off in a hell of a rush. He must've made it okay or I'd've heard. What've you got?"

She told him about the golden. "You didn't happen to treat him, I suppose."

"Not that one. No wounds like that on any of my patients—except the shepherd. I could call the vets from here to Boston, but even if I had the time, no one involved with drugs would tell me anything."

"No, of course not. How's the dog?"

"Come see for yourself."

"I don't know . . . I'm feeling a bit low at the moment. I called Dandie 'Frey' just now . . . by mistake."

"Par. But don't hang onto that forever. Come on in. He's been asking for you. Do him some good to see a friend. Stay put, Dandie."

The white shepherd was still on the mat near the cot, which was still rumpled. "I've been sleeping with him through all this," the doctor said. "He's coming along nicely but we were a bi-i-t skittish what with all that noise and storm, weren't we, ol' fella."

The dog was greatly improved after three days of intensive care and made an attempt to stand. His tail waved frantically as Kristin approached, and when she sat down beside him he rested his big head on her lap and heaved a great sigh.

"He's eating from a dish now. Be on his feet tomorrow. We ought to celebrate by giving him a name," the doctor said quietly.

"About time, too. What did you have in mind?"

"Couldn't decide. He's special."

"Yes." For so many reasons. She stroked the white fur thoughtfully. "How about—how about Capo? The Chief. The Head. Capo."

The doctor's flat *a* almost destroyed it, but he did not seem to notice. He nodded approvingly. "That's it. Capo. Got a kind of druggy Mafioso sound to it, but it fits, any way you look at it. Hey, Capo, how about that, boy! New life, new name— Now all we have to do is find you a new home." He sighed dramatically and went out, leaving them alone.

"Very clever, Dr. Machiavelli," she said a few minutes later as she came out wiping her eyes. "But I'm not going to take him."

"What? What's that?" He looked around, immensely abstracted

by the task of counting pills into a vial. "For Dandie. Instructions on the label. You say something?"

"You know perfectly well what I said. Never mind fussing with those pills. Just forget it, Doctor. And keep your fingers crossed that nothing else happens. If we have to stay on for any reason, what excuse will I have to get away from there?"

"You don't need any excuse. Just go. Let her brother-in-law take over. American foreign policy doesn't rest on him. He should've been here three days ago, the self-important bastard. Glad he wasn't, though, in a way. It's been nice having you around. We'll miss you."

She blushed furiously. "There's one thing I'd like to do before I go home, and that's wring the money out of Stokes and Son to pay your bill. They shouldn't be allowed to get away with this."

"Don't worry, they won't. I don't give a damn about the money, though. Matt'll be back soon, by noon maybe, and then by god! I'll sic my little brother on those sons of bitches. We'll let you know what happens."

"Please do. By the way, I left a message for him at the office, but if he should call you first, tell him I think we've found our missing witness. In a manner of speaking, anyway," she said, and explained. "Got a piece of paper? I'll write down the name and address for you. If our Savage lady's home now, though, I'll bring her and the boy to Chief Trueblood myself. Bodily!"

"Here, call first. Save you a trip if she's out."

She was. There was still no answer at the motel apartment out at East Beach.

"She's probably shopping like everybody else," Kristin said, "but she'll certainly be at the hospital sooner or later. As long as her husband's flat on his back she won't go far. And neither will Sam, poor guy. Come on, Dandie, let's go shopping."

"Doc Vernon still sweating that autopsy?"

"He was as of Tuesday night. I don't know what's the matter with that stubborn old guy. Next thing you know, he and Steve Black will be arguing whether there was even a knife in Graham Barstow's ribs, let alone an expression on his face!"

"You never know," the doctor said, laughing, as he opened the door for her. "There's lots of ways to skin a cat and Doc usually finds them sooner or later."

Almost two more hours passed before she loaded her groceries into the car and inched out of the village, but for once she was not chafing with impatience. There was a contagious holiday air about the place and a new surge of interest in the fair, which was ending Saturday night with square dancing in the Grange Hall and a lamb barbecue in the field. I wish I could go, she thought. It would be such fun . . . I wish it were all over, finished cleanly, that I were —free . . .

"I wish I weren't such a fool," she told the collie, and once away from the traffic she drove rapidly to Perley's farm.

"Sit tight," she said, and leaned on the horn until Perley came running out of the barn. He stopped when he recognized her, and ambled over with his head on one side in that provoking way that made her want to smack him. If she had been incensed before, she was recklessly angry now, and whatever control she might have mustered up at the last minute exploded at sight of the straw in the corner of his mouth.

She jumped out of the car. "Where's that miserable son of yours!" she yelled when he was a dozen feet away. He came on slowly, a half smile on his weasel face.

"How's that?" he said, cupping an ear, his bad teeth working leisurely on the straw. "How's that you say?"

"I *said where's Toby?*"

" 'Round and about."

"Well, I want to see him. And I want to see him now!"

"What fer?"

"You know what for."

" 'Fraid I don't, Miz Weiden. Don't hold with guessin' 'n' dern foolishness. No time. I'm a busy man." He grinned and pushed his cap back to scratch his dirty hair.

"You'd better take time, you little swine. You and that son of yours. Time enough to put your hand in your wallet and pay for the dog you threw on the trash. He's getting better now. A state policeman's brother has been working on him since Monday morning, in case you're interested."

His eyes narrowed in brief alarm, but he shrugged and shook his head. "I ain't. No business a yours. Nobody asked yuh t' butt in. Dog was dyin'. No sense throwin' good money after bad."

"In another week that dog will be ready to chew you up and spit you out, both of you. You know the police dog's reputation."

"Ain't worried."

"You may not be now. You will be soon. I can promise you that. If the dog isn't ready, the police are."

"F' throwin' a dog in a dump?"

"That and much more."

He spit out the straw, saying sharply, "What're yuh talkin' about?" He was worried now and she laughed at him.

"Take a guess, Mr. Stokes. I guarantee you'll be right the first time."

"What d' y' know?"

"Just what you think I know," she said incautiously. "What's more to the point, the police do too. But that's between them and you and that vicious creature you call son. They'll be by eventually. What I want is money. A hundred dollars ought to do it."

"You're bluffin'."

"No."

He was silent for a moment, then shook his head. "Toby's out in the medder—you'll have to talk to him. I ain't in charge a money in this outfit."

"Where is he? What meadow?"

"Foller me in a minute. May be we can work somethin' out." He touched his cap respectfully this time and went back to the barn at a brisk pace.

"Dandie," she said, getting back into the car, "does he really think a hundred dollars will buy me off and the police too?"

Do you think he thinks so? said intuition.

She shivered apprehensively but when Perley drove a battered pickup truck full of equipment out of the other end of the barn and honked his horn, she promptly followed him down a muddy wagon track through several acres of storm-bent corn and out into the great meadow she had stopped to view with such pleasure. Some distance away was the bright yellow toy moving over the spot of freshly turned earth between the trees. They were huge spreading oaks, she saw now.

Braking behind Perley, she saw too that the toy was a large backhoe and the brown spot as big as an acre, its surface lumpy with stones and clots of damp soil. She walked over to the truck as Toby jumped down from the backhoe, reached up for what looked like a big canteen, and slung its strap over his shoulder.

"Seems a strange place for planting," she said. "I don't know what that son of yours needs sunglasses and a cap for. Not much sun at high noon what with all those oaks."

"What we plant here don't need much, right, Son?"

"Right, Pa. Now, what's all this?" Toby said pleasantly, adjusting the strap.

Seeing what hung from it, she said, "I'm sure you know already. A walkie-talkie's a practical thing to have around on a place as big as this."

"I think so. But Pa just said you were coming. He didn't go into details."

"There aren't many. About a hundred is all."

"A hundred what?"

"Dollars. To pay the vet bill for that dog you threw away."

"Balls."

"You could use a couple. The vet needs the money. He earned it."

"Who asked him to?"

"I did."

"Go to hell."

"Possibly. Anger's a deadly sin, I'm told. What circle they'll put you on is something else again. Between violence and fraud you'll have a lot to suffer for."

"What's she talkin' about, Pa?"

"She *knows*."

"Knows? Knows what?"

"Stop playing games, Toby Stokes. You know what I mean. And

you know a hundred dollars doesn't begin to cover what you stole from me but—"

"Stole! You're out of your tree!"

"No doubt. But fingerprints—" She shrugged, improvising boldly.

"No way, lady! I wore gloves—" He stopped, clenching his fists, then took a menacing step forward. "Why, you bitch!"

"Call me anything you like. I want a hundred dollars for the vet and then I'll go."

He considered her thoughtfully. "And then what?" he said very quietly.

Her mouth suddenly went dry from fright. "And then I'm packing up and going home. I've had enough of your island hospitality one way and another."

"What else do you know?"

"Enough. The one thing I'm not sure of is how Graham Barstow fitted into your scheme. And why you took those books of his, and the black lace panties, and then dumped them in the Clothing Exchange."

"Barstow had plenty of grief. Just look in his desk. But books?" He was plainly puzzled. "I didn't take any books. Or pants. My women have better taste. And books don't sell. Not the kind he had, anyway."

"No, I don't suppose they would. But why didn't you burglarize the house when they weren't around? I'm sure you had plenty of chances off-season." He shrugged and she added shrewdly, "Or did you suddenly realize you needed more convertible goods to pay for that shipment you got off the boat Sunday night?"

He took another step forward and stopped again, smiling crookedly. "Tell you what," he said, reaching for his wallet. "I'll give you two hundred. Give the vet a hundred and keep the rest, or keep it all, I don't care, just so long as—"

There was just time to see his big fist flash out before she fell unconscious to the broken ground.

Something was making a very loud noise, and the ground trembled. And someone was holding her. Her face hurt, and someone was holding her and rocking her and saying something. The words were soft, crooning, and came from a far distance. Something brushed over her cheeks—a handkerchief, light, feathery. A gentle hand smoothed her forehead, pushing the curls away, and then the arms tightened around her. Her eyelids fluttered and warm lips kissed them closed.

"Rest, rest, my darling," a voice whispered hoarsely. "I'll kill the son of a bitch. You crazy fool, you fool. Oh god, he came close, the bastard. I love you, I love you." The rocking was faster now.

She stirred and opened her eyes, focusing with difficulty in the circle of his arms. She recognized his smooth gray jacket and brushed some dirt off the lapel. He released her just enough to study her face intently. She blinked up at him with a faint mocking smile.

He smiled back. "Glass jaw. Next time pick on someone your own size, at least. How do you feel?"

"Dizzy. And it hurts," she whispered.

"I'm glad. Teach you a lesson."

"How long have I been out?"

"Long enough. No, not long enough!" He pressed her close again so that she heard the rapid beating of his heart. "Rest. Take your time. There's no hurry, no hurry now."

She closed her eyes contentedly, listening, thinking how strange it was that the roaring noise could not drown out the sound of his powerful heartbeat under her ear. "What's that?" she said groggily.

"Backhoe."

"Why?"

"You'll see. Soon. Just rest."

"You ought to put me down. I'm heavy."

"No."

"I'm sorry."

"You should be."

"Forgive me."

"I'll try."

She slept in his arms on the tail gate of the car while the backhoe thundered behind them and the hole that Toby Stokes was digging at the point of a gun slowly grew larger. But it was not the noise that woke her.

"You shouldn't. You mustn't," she said, feeling his lips on hers.

"I didn't think you'd notice. I'm sorry."
"You should be."
"Forgive me."
"I'll try."
"It's—lousy."
"I know."
"I love you, Kristin."
"Yes."

His arms fell away from her and she sat up slowly and swung her legs over the tail gate.

"Feeling better?"

"Yes. And no." She put her hand in his. "Now tell me."

He shook his head. "It doesn't seem important anymore. Not now." His thumb stroked the back of her hand. And then he grinned suddenly. "But you can't stand not knowing, can you."

"Nope. Go ahead, put me out of my misery. We'll trade. I have something too, I think."

"Fair enough. Well, to begin at the end, they were about to bury you alive. How about that for a topic sentence?"

"I'm impressed. Go on."

"After I took you home Tuesday night I kept thinking about camels. Remember? It bugged hell out of me. I couldn't wait till morning so I roused the president of the bank, an old buddy of my brother's—I told you there were advantages to living here—and we found some interesting patterns in Toby's account over the past eight or nine years when things began looking up at Perley's farm. I won't go into details—they don't matter anyway at this point—except that the deposits kept getting bigger all the time but not big enough to account for all the money they were spending. The IRS will have a field day with those two. And there were a number of checks made out to a vet in New Bedford. Very large checks. I hopped over to the mainland in the morning and spent a good part of the day tracking that bastard down. Surprising how people move about in a hurricane."

"You should know."

He laughed. "It was one wild ride, I can tell you. But it was worth it. I got to Bud Finley—he's a special agent in Boston with the Bureau of Customs—and he came down fast, and from then on it was beautiful. That vet sang like a bird about the implants he'd been doing, among other things, and lots of things fell into place that Finley'd been working on. Toby's the island rep of a pretty big crowd and the feds are closing in. I don't know yet how he started or where—that's Finley's bag—but we think it was something very simple. He did some plumbing, probably, for a customer here, a guy with connections, and they clicked, and he was off and running. Knowing Perley, I'd say he balked for a while and then got used to spending money. The farm's his pride and joy. Besides, by the time he found out where all that cash was coming from, Toby was a user and pusher of years' standing and there was nothing he could do about it. Toby's got a load in him now—his eyes are dilated from here to next week. Anyway, I couldn't get back last night. It was too late and we were too tired and there were things to do there this morning anyway. Finley and I got a chopper back—landed at eleven—and went to the barracks. They gave me your message about Mrs. Savage and the boy, but I knew she'd keep, and Sam too. Toby was tops on the priority list. But Finley wanted something to eat first, so while he was having coffee I called Joe. And when he told me your crazy idea of reaming money out of Stokes and Son to pay his bill, I grabbed Finley by the hair and got Lee Williams and tore over here." His hand tightened on hers. "And there you were, out cold, and Toby was starting to dig a hole to put you in and Perley was standing over you with a crowbar. Only, I thought you were dead! Oh god, when I picked you up I thought you were dead! And I thought, How many times and how many ways was I going to have to lose you, Kristin! No, don't say anything! There's nothing to say. Except"—and he laughed shakily—"your jaw's all swollen. It'll be a nice shade in a few hours."

"And serve me right," she said, trying to smile as two large tears rolled down her dirty cheeks. "You make it very hard for me . . . Nothing like this ever happened to me before. None of it."

"Are you sorry?"

"Yes. No," she whispered, and looked at him directly. "How could I be? But—I can't. It would be—too easy."

"There's something wrong between you and Weiden, isn't there, Kristin."

"Not wrong. Over. Only—I keep thinking, should I try again? Would it help? Would it matter? I took my ring off on Saturday. I was very sure then. And then—then I met you, and although it sounds crazy, I wondered if you'd tipped me over the edge. Even though I was well over it long before . . . I want to be sure of one thing before—before I—before I—"

"And I've been making it harder for you. But as Sam said, you're something else . . . and everything happened so fast . . ." He raised her hand and looked at it carefully. "It's all dirty," he said, and kissed the palm and released it. "We'll talk about it later. Now trade. What have you got?"

"Toby—Toby was at the house Sunday night. I don't know why he was having trouble with the door, though. Perley had a key. But probably he told Toby the Barstows were off limits and he wouldn't give him the key. Anyway, I hinted that you had his fingerprints—a silly movie-type trap—and he blurted out that I was crazy, that he'd worn gloves. He said he didn't take the black lace panties or the books—any books—because they don't sell. That level of pornography's too high class, I suppose, Karpman, Krafft-Ebing, that lot. And his girl friends, he said, have better taste in underwear. Anyway, I asked where Graham Barstow was in all this, and he said, 'Barstow had plenty of grief. Just look in his desk.' Did you?"

"What, look in his desk? No. Galleys make a big package. I looked in the closet first and there they were on the shelf. Did you?"

"No. I assumed it wasn't necessary, and besides, you told me not to. I wonder what Toby meant. Did he have something on Graham? Was he trying on a bit of blackmail?"

"About Kathy? I don't know—he hasn't had time to do much talking yet—but I doubt it. Not because he hasn't leaked it anywhere but because he knew her and cared for her, after a fashion. And if he had threatened Barstow, it's probable Kathy would have known. And she would've told me. Maybe there is a scruple or two left in that bastard, who knows. We'll find out soon. But I guess I'll have to take another look. An illegal one, because this time I don't know what I'm going to look for. But if he didn't take those books and things, who did?"

"Well, I didn't. Polly wasn't here yet. Toby didn't. Perley didn't, by inference. Kathy and Sam didn't. The only person left is—Myra. But why? She didn't read heavy stuff, she told me so. She said it scared her."

"I'll have to go through his desk, that's all there is to it. When—and why—did Toby deck you?"

"Oh, I took a wild guess and hit a nerve. I asked him if the reason he robbed the house when he did was that he needed more money then he had on hand for the shipment Sunday. In the dog. He jumped, and then he got very nice, took out his wallet and offered me two hundred dollars to keep quiet—and pow!" She wiggled her jaw cautiously and groaned. "From head to toe I'm a wreck. But now I'm beginning to wonder if Toby was at the cave Sunday afternoon. Or Perley. They don't seem to have any scruples about hitting people on the head."

"I don't think they had anything to do with Barstow. Except for the robbery. And even if Toby didn't take the books, we're still ahead, we've got it narrowed down a little more. What else?"

"Did your brother tell you about Giggy and Jack and that golden retriever at The Joint?"

"My god, another one? No, he started off with Toby and you, and I got so scared I hung up on him and took off. Let's have it."

She told him and he laughed. "Nurse Kristin! Well, you handled it very nicely—no questions to scare them off."

"What's going to happen to them, Matt? They're good kids, they're working hard—they've got such pride. At first, when you said Toby was backing The Joint, I thought they were into drugs too. That boy Jack was so jumpy at the ferry. But last night I felt he was just scared and wanted out, even if it was a good way to make their pile and get their own place. It seems a shame to lock them up and destroy the valid part of their life. They wouldn't be much good when they got out."

"We'll see. Depends how far in they were. If all they did was handle a few dogs—a delivery service—if they didn't push or use the stuff themselves—we'll see. If that place is Toby's outlet—and it probably is—and if they were handling it, that'll be something else again. I'll do what I can, don't worry about it. Now. Want to go take a look? Still dizzy?"

"No, I'm all right now. Poor Dandie. She's been so good. What were they going to do, bury her too?" She got off the tail gate and he closed it.

"More than that. Did you see that acetylene torch in Perley's truck?"

"Is that what it is? I wondered. What's it for?"

"For cutting things up. Your car would've been put in alongside you. On the old principle of helping you on your long journey. All the comforts of home in the other world."

"They wouldn't have been doing me any favor," she said laughing. "Not this heap."

"That alone proves the Stokeses are no friends of yours. Come on."

The hole between the oaks was deep and wide now, and piles of wet soil were heaped around it. And, under the heavy police revolvers of Sergeant Lee Williams and Special Agent Finley, a nondescript man with hard eyes and a shapeless fedora on the back of his head, Stokes and Son were sweating and slipping in the rich earth, sullenly hauling up a small part of what they had buried in the past few years.

Pieces of Toby's van came first.

"Why?" Kristin said. "Why, Matt?"

"I told you you were a catalyst. It must've been because you'd seen the dog and made a fuss about it. I have a hunch Toby made a show of saying he'd take him to Joe when you offered to do it. He couldn't take him back down cellar—I think he froze a minute there and stopped thinking—not with you standing there. And he was afraid to hang around until you left, and then bring him out here. You might just come back. And then when you saw him coming from the dump when you weren't too far from Joe, he couldn't stop. And I don't think he did any plumbing later, either. I think we'll find he came right back here in a panic and took that van apart and planted it. Not necessarily because of what was in it—traces of drugs, maybe—but just to throw us off the track, be another victim. Things were getting too close for comfort. But all he's accomplished is to lose an uninsured van. Among other things."

Finley said, "This is only the beginning, Matt. Stokes says there's plenty more. We'll have our hands full doing lab work on this stuff. But unless they were very very careful, we'll probably find traces of this and that. If we're lucky, what with all that dirt! What a job."

"I think we'll turn up a few of my stolen cars as well," Matt said. "Keep them at it, Bud, we want it all. Why don't you go home, Kristin? Take a rest, a shower"—he grinned—"get something to eat. I'll be in touch. Are you up to driving?"

"Yes, I'm fine now. I don't especially want to go back there but Myra must be wondering where I've got to."

He walked her back to the car and opened the door for her. "If her brother-in-law's here by now, she's got other things to think about. Doc Vernon's going to try to delay a little longer releasing that body. I hope to Christ he does!"

"Why? Does it matter now?"

"I don't know, from a forensic viewpoint. From a purely personal one, I hope he holds out forever!" He tilted her swollen chin and looked at her searchingly. "Because the longer he keeps it, the longer you'll have to stay," he said huskily. He kissed her parted lips and walked rapidly away.

It was as well for another reason that she left when she did, because presently Toby began to dig again and the terrible stench that escaped from the hole heralded a veritable charnel pit of dogs.

They were falling to pieces, most of them, and crawling with worms and insects. Their eyes had been eaten out, and the soft linings of their mouths and nostrils.

And as Perley and his son lifted the poor bodies and carried them out of the hole and lay them on the ground, the rotting flesh came away in their hands.

Chapter XVI

She followed the new station wagon up the hill and parked behind it, watching a tall thin man get out and with a courtly manner open the door for Myra and escort her into the house.

"I guess we're just poor relations, Dandie, way below the salt. Come on, let's go in. And don't forget to curtsy." She struggled into the kitchen with the grocery bags and dumped them onto the table. Not a word from Myra, who was sitting on the couch, or from Jonathan Barstow, who turned away to gaze into the fireplace. After putting everything away she went silently into the little back bedroom to collect clean clothes, and locked herself in the hall bathroom. The basin and toilet were still almost unusable, but the shower drain was free and the water very hot. She soaped luxuriously, rinsed herself until the tank ran cool, and dried herself with two huge thick towels instead of one, to make up for the neglect and discourtesy of Myra and the diplomat. When her hair was shining and almost dry, she put on the white dress and a pair of high-heeled sandals, decided that despite her chin she looked eminently presentable, and went out to make her entrance.

"Good afternoon," she said in a tone worthy of a presentation at an embassy. Apparently the diplomat had been constrained to disregard her in her capacity of dirty disheveled servant, but he turned now and, with a well-bred lack of surprise at her elegant transformation, haughty bearing, and swollen jaw, advanced with his hand out. She ignored it long enough to discomfit him.

"I am Kristin Weiden," she said, as who should say, "I am the Queen of England."

"How do you do. I am Jonathan Barstow." He was physically very like his dead brother but austere, remote, lacking Graham's vital interest in everything about him, and his hand, like the rest of him, was bony and paper-dry. It was difficult to imagine that he had once been young enough to sire children and rear them, or that he was at any time responsive enough to the needs (as he saw them) of his country to associate with all comers and elsewhere than on Brattle Street. It was easy to picture him a small boy bending intently and with proud patience over a large parchment, charting the members of a self-made aristocracy. "You have been exceedingly generous to my sister," he said stiffly, even disinterestedly.

She inclined her head in like manner and sat down opposite them both, feeling that she was playing a game. What's wrong with Myra? she thought. She seems almost frightened. If he's an example of a favorite brother-in-law, she might as well have Perley Stokes. Well, it's their ball. I'll see where they throw it.

"Kris, what happened to your face!" Myra said.

"It's nothing, really. I—tripped. I'm sorry the storm delayed you, Mr. Barstow."

"Yes. A bad crossing."

"Have you dined?" I'll fix his little red Rolls-Royce, she thought, disliking him.

"We haven't yet," Myra said, and almost jumped off the couch. "Let me get you something, Jonathan."

"Thank you, my dear. One of your omelets would be very welcome."

"I'll help you, Myra."

"No, dear. Stay and talk with Jonathan. Besides, you know I love to cook. Come, Dandie. How's my little girl? My, you were away a long time, weren't you, Dandie girl." She vanished in relief and Kristin began to grow seriously alarmed.

"When did you arrive, Mr. Barstow?"

"At noon. I flew down from Logan in a private plane a short while ago."

"Permit me to say how very grieved I am for you."

"Thank you."

"How long are you planning to stay?" Absurd question, but then this interview was as absurd as a garden-party exchange during a cataclysm.

But the question had been properly phrased and timed. The diplomat looked at her with a certain respect for her discretion. "Will you come and sit here?" he said in a low voice, pointing to the couch. "I'd like to talk to you."

She got up immediately and crossed the room. Wary but very curious, she watched him as he went around the coffee table and sat down close beside her.

"What do you know about this Dr. Vernon?" he said.

She blinked at him. "I'm afraid I don't understand what you mean."

"What is your estimate of him? I understand that you are a patient of his."

"Then that should be enough of an answer. He's a fine man, a good doctor, a good friend. And, like you, a dedicated public servant. Why do you ask?"

"He is suspiciously unavailable. His secretary at the hospital says that he is indisposed. His wife says that he is not at home."

"Indeed?"

"Yes. And the village police are equally at a loss to account for his whereabouts."

"I'm sorry I can't help you, Mr. Barstow. I haven't seen or spoken with him since Tuesday night. Is it something urgent?"

"It is indeed. You may not know that he is responsible for releasing my brother's body. Until he signs the necessary documents we cannot make arrangements for cremation and memorial services. My sister didn't mention this?"

"She must have done. Oh yes, she said something about it on Monday. The storm drove it out of my head. What are you going to do?"

"I have already done it. The State Department has issued an order to the doctor releasing the body to me."

"And he will comply immediately he receives it, I'm sure. Why shouldn't he? No doubt he was waiting for you, Mr. Barstow. Myra was hardly in condition—"

"My sister was and is in most excellent case, Mrs. Weiden," he said sharply. "I spoke with her on Tuesday."

"Well, possibly it seemed different to me. I was here, in the thick of things. From the beginning," she snapped, suddenly fed up with him.

"Yes, I'm aware of that. It must have been very difficult for you, a total stranger, to be thrust into this—ghastly scandal." Only the last two words had conviction.

"I'm hardly a stranger now, Mr. Barstow, and I wish you wouldn't treat me like one."

His icy reticence suddenly dropped off like a shell. "You're quite right, my dear. But you were not in it quite from the beginning. To someone as old as I am, and in my position, the news was an inexpressible shock. And to be prevented by a self-important country doctor from burying my dead in prescribed fashion—!"

"I can appreciate that."

"I wonder if you can. Graham was my youngest brother. The baby of the family. My mother's pride. To end his life the victim of a sordid murder—" He made it sound as though Graham had made another poor choice—again. "Perhaps we spoiled him. He was in many ways a fool. What do you know about him? About them both?"

"Very little. He was an intelligent attractive charming man. They weren't happy together, that was obvious. If they could have had children perhaps—"

"Oh, they could have. They did, in point of fact. But after five months Myra lost the child."

"Then why—couldn't they have had others?"

"I've never been certain. Graham had a breakdown shortly afterward. He was hospitalized for the rest of that year. The first year of their marriage. Myra was magnificent, of course. She has never been anything else. But he seemed changed. Strained. Naturally we never discussed it, nor have I ever mentioned it to anyone until now."

And probably he never would again, because at that moment Myra called them and Kristin saw him retreat once more into his shell as plainly as if he had walked inside and slammed it shut.

"Shall we go in?" he said, coldly formal, and offered her his arm.

The phone rang at five o'clock, when she had begun to shiver on the sun deck.

"Mom? It's me. Guess what."

"Sam's home free."

"How'd you guess?"

"I'm a good guesser. How is he?"

"Fine. Mrs. Savage and the boy came through beautifully. She's so pleased with the publicity she actually kissed him. You'd've cried to see it—that poor kid jumped a mile, it was such a surprise. But Chief Trueblood's in spasms. We had one last beer together. He hated seeing Sam leave. Said he'd miss him! Where are Myra and the diplomat? He came, I assume."

"Yes, he came. I had a heavy time, as you'd put it. They're out trying to raise Doc Vernon—they're going to have that cremation tomorrow no matter what. I don't expect they'll be back for supper."

"Somehow I don't care. As long as Sam's all right, I don't care about anything. Well, I do care about Myra. But look, would you mind if we—if I don't come home either? The ladies are giving a dinner." She giggled and whispered, "Sam's having beef with Grandma, and Kathy and I are having chicken with Aunt Faith—it has less cholesterol, she says. Those two are going out of their minds in the kitchen. It's the only place they ever fight in."

"I know, I realized that right away. I can just about imagine what's going on there. What a great movie they'd make! No, of course I don't mind. I'm looking forward to complete privacy. For a little while at least. Take your time. Tell Sam I'm very happy for him. Tell him I said hi."

"I will. Say, Mom, you were right about that guy. He does snore. The boy was roaming around the parking lot and heard him and looked in. And the first thing he said when he saw Sam was, 'You snore and you have a pumpkin head!' Even in the dark he could tell!"

"Give that child ten silver dollars. Where were they all that time, anyway?"

"Next door huddling with her mother. No wonder poor Mr. Savage doesn't want to go home!"

Kristin hung up, laughing. She was feeding Dandie and I Chee when the phone rang again.

"Kris dear," Myra said anxiously, "do you mind if we don't join you for dinner?"

"Of course not. I didn't expect you to. I don't see why you should have to sit and look at my jaw. It's turning all colors. Take away anybody's appetite. Everything's under control so just relax. Where is Mr. Barstow sleeping? Shall I make up the couch in the study? No trouble. Fine. And, Myra, I know it sounds silly but—have a good time."

"You're such a comfort, dear. I know Jonathan doesn't show it, but he was very impressed with you."

"I'm glad."

"And, Kris, don't be surprised if that nice lieutenant comes. We just saw him at his office and he asked for permission to go through Graham's desk. Something to do with the Stokeses. He said he could get a warrant but asked if I'd be willing to waive it. I'd rather not be there, but I saw no reason to say no, and neither did Jonathan."

She replaced the receiver with an almost palsied hand. I've got to get out of here, she told herself. I'll go down the hill and invite myself to dinner with Sam and Grandma, to even things up.

But the kitchen doorbell rang and Matt let himself in. She moved, putting the table between them, and grasped the back of a chair.

He leaned against the door, amused. "What's that for?"

"Why did you come *now?*" she said unsteadily.

"One, police business. Two, I need your help. Three, for supper. Four, because I knew you'd be alone."

"Can't we—can't we just be friends?"

"No. Not just friends. I love you, Kristin. I think you love me. I don't intend to let you forget that."

"It isn't fair," she whispered.

"I know. But then, life isn't fair. It's just—life."

"I'm all mixed up, Matt. Nothing like this ever happened to me before. Even in the last three years I haven't looked at anyone else. I just kept on trying by myself until I couldn't try anymore. And now, in spite of everything that's happened *here,* I'm happier than I've been in three years. Longer than that, if I look back further and don't try to fool myself. My life seems centered here, grounded on this island. I've been glad John wasn't here. Even before I met you, I was glad. But I told him—last week—that I'd stay if he were willing to try, to get help together. After twenty-three years I thought we ought to try."

"Yes. I guess you should. But *I* don't know if *I* should give up or try harder! I'm no wife stealer. Nothing like this ever happened to me before either. All I know is that I love you, everything about you—even your lousy temper. And I also think you're as sure as you're ever going to be about divorcing Weiden. That what's bugging you is the way you feel for me, not him. It's happened pretty fast."

"I'm—scared, Matt."

"Yes. I know. Who wouldn't be? I am too. I don't take things for granted. And I want to be just as sure as you want to be. I like things to be clean and orderly too. We're both compulsive people, Kristin—that's partly why I'm a cop and why you want to do what you want to do. Well, there's one thing we can be certain of—that I love you. I won't say it again. For a while. Now, how about something to eat? I haven't had a thing all day. Finley stuffed himself to the gills, I don't know how, after what we saw in that hole Toby opened up. And by the way, before I go into that, I've got a piece of news I think will please you, darling. Toby opened up a lot of things besides that hole. Giggy and Jack were only involved with Jack's golden and the shepherd. They got a good dog for free, Toby said, with just one trip. And all they did where the shepherd was concerned was to meet the guy who brought him, and take him to Toby's house. And they only rent the space from Toby. He bought it a couple of years ago, thinking to use it as his base, but he couldn't get those two to go along with him. They may not look it or act it to most people, but those kids are as straight as a wall. They don't use the stuff, they don't push it—and not only do they not push it, they disapprove of it as strongly as if they were charter members of the Temperance League! They come from the dregs, Kristin, and they want out. Only, not that way. The little bit they tried was too much for them. Toby said they told him off but good! Even made him come down on the rent—or else!"

Only now did he come away from the door and sit down, and the balance between them was instantly and magically restored. She set about making supper, saying like a member of the team, "What did I miss?"

"Nothing you'd have thanked me for letting you stay and see. I don't know how many dogs those bastards buried. Christ, it was a canine Auschwitz. I can't get the stench out of my nose even yet. We had to shower and change before anybody'd talk to us."

"They must have been horribly decomposed, but could you see whether they had the same wound as Capo's? That's what we named him, by the way. Capo. I saw him this morning."

"I know. Good name. I didn't look too closely, Kristin, I couldn't. I mean it was physically impossible without a gas mask. I got one for Joe, though. He's doing some work on them now. I wish he didn't have to. But as far as I'm concerned Perley and Toby earned some time off in advance for handling the bodies as well as they did. I almost felt sorry for them. I did for Phil. What a swap! Sam and Polly kiss him good-by and leave in a beery haze, and Stokes and Son come in snarling and the place has to be fumigated. Phil marched them right out back and made them strip and wash under the hose and wrap up in blankets from the cells they're in. Finley and I took off for a hot shower and a double scotch. Do you have any around?"

"In the cabinet next to the fridge. Me too."

"Joe's going to call me here," he said, handing her a glass of whiskey. "Here's to him!"

"Couldn't anyone else do it? Finley's people?"

"No, those bodies are too far gone to be moved." He shuddered. "It has to be done, for the record, but it's open and shut. Finley's with him, that's something."

They were almost through cleaning up the dishes in companionable silence when the phone rang and he answered it. "How was it, Joe?" He listened for some time and turned pale. "Christ! Uh-huh. Uh-huh. Uh-huh. Glad it helped. Finley holding up? . . . Good. 'By."

He laughed and came back to the sink. "That Finley's an iron man. No gas mask for him! But he can't smell spicebush anymore, his nose is shot. He's also quite a lab tech, Joe said, but he wouldn't have cared if he wasn't. It was nice just to have the company."

"What did they find?"

"Camels! Just like Capo's wound, and that golden. They aren't sure yet what crystals and things are in the tissues but they made a batch of slides and Finley will take them to Boston. It's hard stuff, though, Finley's pretty sure of that. From the number of dogs Toby had there, he must've made a packet. There's a lot of work to do—all the kids he sold to, for one thing."

"Will you be in on that?"

"Yes, but there's Barstow's murder to finish up first. And I'm pretty sure the two aren't connected. Which makes it harder."

"Not necessarily. As you said, Matt, it wasn't a total loss, the Stokes business. Toby told us one big thing, maybe two. I've been thinking about it most of the afternoon since Myra and her brother-in-law left."

"And?"

"And I don't like where I'm heading."

He hung up the dish towel. "Want to talk about it, or get to Barstow's desk first?"

"Let's try the desk. If I don't think about it, I can think about it. If you know what I mean."

"Sure. Best way. The trouble with this job is, when things are happening you're so close to it you don't have time or room to back off."

"Don't you ever get any time off?"

"Theoretically we work a five-day week, like normal people. In practice—" He shrugged. "But tomorrow I'm taking a rest, I don't give a damn what happens or doesn't happen. Let's go."

Graham Barstow's desk was a massive and very old roll-top, and every part of it was stuffed with papers, documents, letters, the accumulation of years.

"We've got our work cut out for us on this deal," he said. "I meant what I said, darling. I need your help." He pulled over a small chair for her, put the contents of a cubbyhole into her lap, and took another for himself. "Let's do this carefully. Put everything back as it was."

"I bet this part will be the fastest. It's probably the most recent stuff—yes, it is," she said, looking at a postmark. "It's what he saved from way back that may be an awful hodgepodge. But I have a feeling that if there is anything here for us, it *is* way back. Matt, why do you think she waived a warrant?"

"Because she didn't call my bluff, mainly." He laughed. "I told you—I couldn't get a warrant this time because I don't know what I'm looking for this time except 'plenty of grief,' to quote Toby. Fortunately she and the diplomat didn't press me on it. But really, it's because she doesn't expect we'll find anything. Maybe we won't," he added soberly, and went silently to work.

An hour later they had drawn nothing but blood from paper cuts. In the dozens of cards, letters, clippings, bills that filled the top of the desk, there was nothing in the least suggestive, nothing on drugs or Toby Stokes or Kathy Field or anyone else including Myra.

"Oh boy," she said, massaging her neck. "Want some coffee?"

"Good thinking. We need a break and a stretch. The worst is yet to come." He followed her into the kitchen. "What did you think of Jonathan Barstow?"

"I'm not sure. Funny. I can see him more easily in an embassy or at a peace conference, where I've never seen him and never will, than I could when he was a foot away on the couch. He opened up and closed up in a flash. How terrible to live that way for seventy-two years. But he said some interesting things before he knew it. He called Myra his sister. Not his sister-in-law. Talk about family loyalty and solidarity! She's been sort of subsumed, if that's the word. Become part of a whole. But she calls him brother-*in-law*. It's as though she's part of them as they see it, but they aren't part of her, not entirely. Or am I not making myself perfectly clear?"

"I follow. What else?"

"Well, Myra had a miscarriage and then Graham had a breakdown, all in the first year of their marriage."

"That might explain the letter we found. Is that all?"

She told him the rest. "They never discussed it, 'naturally,' he said. Naturally! My god, Matt, how can a man who shares so little communication with intimates expect to deal with representatives of other nations and get anywhere! All that's at stake is world peace!"

"I don't know, darling. Most of the time I try not to think about it. We're being run by paranoids of the worst type. The kind who're doing what they're doing for God and Country. Maybe we'll all luck out. Anything else?"

"No, I don't think so . . . One thing, though. Myra seemed —almost afraid of him. Although she sounded perfectly fine when she called. She said Jonathan was impressed by me. And she'd wanted me to stay and talk with him, so maybe that was on her mind. I needed his stamp of approval, I guess. How did they seem to you?"

"About the same. Ready?"

They went back to the desk, opened the first drawer, and looked at each other in dismay.

"It looks like it was poured in! Well, here goes." He worked loose a part of the tight pack and handed it to her. "Let's try to keep it in order, an inch slice at a time."

They bent to the task again and found with some surprise that it grew easier as their eyes grew more selective, their hands more economical of movement. They discovered also that Graham Barstow had methodically stored up his past in geological fashion, the months and years being separated by rubber bands or bits of string, and in descending order.

"Matt, why don't we take a sampling from the very bottom," she said, leaning back and massaging her neck again. "Let's see if there's something more from that first year of their marriage. By now you should be able to put your hand on a day of a month!"

"Mmmmm . . . just a minute . . . This one's from Kathy . . . Here, read it. Tell me what hits you," he said tensely.

She took the letter reluctantly, read it, read it again, and frowned. "I don't know. One sentence, maybe. 'Your passion almost frightens me.' In the context she makes him sound like a starving man."

"That's just what I thought. Poor bastard, I know how he felt," he muttered, his hands clumsy as he put the letter into its envelope. He took a deep breath to recover himself. "I think you're right. Let's try the bottom drawer. Give me that stuff, I'll put it back first." He wedged the thick wad into place and closed the drawer. "That's another one done. What time is it? Eight-thirty. God, I hope they don't come back till tomorrow. We need time."

Her cheeks grew hot, but he had referred only to their unfinished task. He pulled out the bottom drawer and presently they were immersed in its contents.

"Paper's in pretty good shape," he commented. "Not much air could make its way in here."

"I'm relieved. I was afraid it would fall apart all over the place. It's bad enough being involved in this but I don't want it to show. I feel like a peeping Tom."

"So do I but it can't be helped," he said, and continued reading.

"Matt! Look!" she said a few minutes later. "Oh my god, it's so—"

"What've you got?"

"Something else I'd rather not know about," she said shakily, handing him a sheaf of papers tinged with brown. "It's so—so sad. Poor Myra, what a life she's had, and how gallantly she handled it."

She sat back staring at the blank wall on which Graham's pegboard had hung, and thought of the limb on the family tree that had withered so many years ago. And why.

"Yes," he said, folding the papers and returning them to the drawer with all the others. "Let's not talk about it now. I think I got what I came for—what Toby meant. If I need it I know where it is. If they ask you what I found, say I'm satisfied that Toby had nothing to do with the murder. Okay?"

"Okay. I'm glad it's done. I'm—I feel more as if Toby hit me in the stomach."

"I wish he had." He took her hands and pulled her to her feet. "You look terrible. Blue and yellow and swollen."

"Now that's what a girl likes to hear."

He kissed the place tenderly, and laughed.

She pulled away. "Oh Matt, don't spoil it. Please don't spoil it. We were working so well together."

"I know," he said softly, pulling her back again. "It's what I've been trying to tell you."

Chapter XVII

At nine o'clock on Friday morning Dr. Vernon signed the death certificate releasing the body to the surviving spouse, and a disgruntled Ralph Perkins bore the closed coffin away to his funeral parlor.

"Perk's pissed," the old doctor told Kristin over the phone. "No chance to embalm, no fancy flowers, no fancy cosmetics job, no viewing, no organ, no nothin'!"

She giggled.

"This is serious, young lady. Bodies are Perk's bread and butter."

She collapsed on the little kitchen steps, laughing helplessly. The doctor began to bark like a seal choking on a herring, and for some moments they clung to one another electronically and shook with mirth that they might not cry with anger and fear.

"If you're ready to pay at*ten*tion," he said at last, "get over to my office right away."

"What for?"

"Powwow. Matt thinks you've got something up your sleeve. May be right. Nice work pulling that Savage gal out of your hat."

More and more she admired his mode of expression. She laughed again. "I'll be along in a bit."

She delayed only to call Grandma Potter and leave word of her whereabouts, in case Polly wanted to know, and agreed with the old lady that nothing was less likely. And then she locked the house and drove down the hill, her heart beating wildly, her head spinning with apprehension.

He was waiting for her outside the hospital. "I thought you'd never come! Chin's looking better. God, I missed you. Let's walk up—it takes longer."

"Was this your idea?"

"Not exactly. Yes, it was. I need your help. We work well together. And I need you. Didn't you want to come?" He opened the door to the stairway.

"Yes, I did. You were right last night about my scruples. I think I *ought* to do this in a certain way. As much for your sake as for John's. Maybe more. Yes, I wanted to come, but I shouldn't have. Doc ought to tie me up in a strait jacket."

He took her hand and held it tightly as they walked up the steps. "When did they get back?"

She blushed. "Before I did. And Polly never did come home. I wish she had. Breakfast was a grim business without her. The embassy's under fire, it seems. The common herd is at the gates. Between feeling sorry for him and disliking him, I'm—torn. The way I am about—everything else."

His brilliant eyes clouded with pain. *"Why,* Kristin? This is no casual illicit thing between us. Your marriage ended a long time ago. You told me enough last night to let me see what's what. What are you trying to prove? How much more time do we have to lose? Life goes fast, *too* fast! Listen, Kristin, I'm going to fight for you. I've made up my mind. No, don't say anything." He let go of her hand. "Let's just concentrate, let's get this business over with. I know you're vulnerable. Weiden isn't here and you've begun to wonder, to tear yourself apart and assess your motives from *a* to *z*. It's understandable—you're tired and everything's been happening fast with you in the middle of it, so you've begun to doubt your judgment not only about Weiden but about me—about everything. Well, I'm going to keep pushing as hard as I can. I'm not going to let you get away. But let's go to work now and get this damned business finished and done. When you can rest, you'll be able to see things more clearly. You'll be able to separate us from all the rest." He opened the door at the top of the stairs and they went down the hall to Dr. Vernon's office. "Tell me, did they say anything?"

She was beginning to get used to his rapid shift from love to work—and back again. "No, not much. I told them what you said I should, and they accepted it and went on with plans for the cremation. I didn't stay with them very long. I said I'd clean up the kitchen and I excused myself and went to fix my feet. They're expecting to leave tomorrow afternoon, which surprised me, but Myra wants to get her plants back first, and Graham's pegboard. I wonder if she'll put the flint knife back on it." She shuddered at the thought. "Oh, Matt, I'm beginning to get so scared!"

"I know. But I'm here. Just take it easy, darling. Now let's see what we can accomplish. Doc's so upset he's had a few belts already."

The old doctor was slouched in his deep leather chair, scowling at a glass of scotch. Steve and Charlotte Black were drinking coffee and eating Danish pastry. "It's good and hot," Charlotte said, pouring a cup from the doctor's percolator. "Want a Danish? I've had three already and there's plenty more. Eating always helps me think."

"No, thanks. It works the other way with me." Kristin accepted coffee and laced it with whiskey.

"Hmph! Bag o' bones!" Vernon snorted. "Okay. The four of us—Perk, Matt, Steve, and I—didn't get far on Sunday night. I need a fresh pair of ears to bounce this off of. Hope things're beginning to pop out of that head of yours, Kris."

"About a nice clean deliberate murder?"

"That's the whole damn trouble, young lady. *Too* damn deliberate. Why does a person go into Barstow's room and stab him through the heart when he can easier cut his throat and slash his wrists?"

"Because there'd be blood all over the place," Steve said. "On the murderer and everything else."

"Exactly. Whereas there'd be very little from a wound like this. *But.* Even when a guy's lying flat on his back it's not so easy to stab through to the heart. Got to go in three or four inches—even five, to do a *good* job—*and* in the right place—to pierce the heart muscle. And as I said, it doesn't necessarily have to be lethal—specially if I get 'em fast enough. Heart acts as a seal even then, if no damn fool thinks he's doin' us a favor by pulling the weapon out. I've taken out knives 'n' ice picks right on the operating table and sewed the heart up and they're still walking around, some of them. But Barstow's internal mammary artery wasn't even touched."

"But the flint was in the heart, you said."

Steve nodded. "Oh yes, it was there, Kris. Right between the fourth and fifth ribs into the left ventricle. But there wasn't very much internal bleeding in the surrounding tissues. And there wasn't much blood in the *right* ventricle either, where there ought to've been."

"Was it—well, was it empty?"

"No, there was froth in it," Steve said. "I think I perforated the superior *vena cava* and a little air got sucked into the right ventricle when I squeezed the heart. Maybe that caused it. I took another look Monday night and I've checked our notes again, but I'm just not sure."

"Sure of what?"

"Whether it—the froth—was there before I started—or afterward."

"Or," Kristin said slowly, putting a hand on the top of her head, and stopped.

Charlotte laughed. "What's the matter, Kris? Did something pop? Don't let it get away."

"Shshsh!" Vernon hissed. "Or what?"

"Or," she said, "was Graham stabbed *after* he died?"

"That's what's bugging me!" Vernon said. "Was the stabbing the cause of death or was it a post-mortem mutilation? That and the expression on his face that Myra saw and Kathy didn't! Steve may be a pathologist but I've been around longer—but the damn thing is, neither of us knows enough together to know for sure."

"Are you saying that someone killed him and then stabbed him? For good measure? So *he'd* be sure?"

"No, Kristin," Matt said. "To implicate Sam. Remember, part of the case against him was his dispute with Barstow over that flint."

"But even so, all the murderer had to do was kill him with it. Right through the heart, just as you found it."

"Yes, and I'd say that's what he did," Steve said, "except for the discrepancy we've been arguing about. There ought to've been at least an ounce—a couple of ounces—of blood in the surrounding tissues in an ante-mortem injury, until the heart stopped pumping. Also, no major arteries were severed. And there's that froth in the right ventricle, although I think I was responsible for that. I haven't done all that many autopsies and I've never been involved in a homicide. At first I thought Doc was nuts—"

"Thanks a lot!" Vernon rumbled.

"—but now I'm beginning to wonder. Was he killed before or after he was stabbed?"

"But—there must be ways of determining that. The color of the blood, maybe?" Kristin said. "Or the composition of it? Couldn't you detect the sequence—I mean, stabbing before or after death—by examining the blood?"

"It depends on the circumstances," Steve said. "In some bodies there isn't any change. In others there's an immediate change. You can't pinpoint death that way. For example there was a body up in Toronto that'd been frozen for years, but when it was thawed out it looked as if it'd been only recently dead. Even the amount of aspirin a person took would have an effect. Or take death from carbon monoxide poisoning, or cyanide. The body turns cherry-red, but the color might show up immediately or not till two to five hours later. Even a high level of alcohol—"

"Never mind that, Steve. Don't get off the track," Vernon said. "Go on, Kris. Let's see what else you can come up with. Steve and I went through those notes so many times, nothing occurs to us anymore. We aren't medical sleuths, I told you, and we can't even hear what we're saying anymore. We were at it all day yesterday when the diplomat was looking for me."

"Well, I don't know . . . Let's— Why don't we assume Graham was stabbed *after* he died. Let's even say you saw that froth *before* you squeezed the heart, Steve. If we're talking about befores and afters, why not eliminate—examine, rather—those two points first. What would cause froth in the heart? What's it called, anyway? Just —froth?"

"Air embolism," Vernon said, giving himself more scotch.

"What causes air embolism?"

"Well," Steve said, "there's amniotic fluid embolism during pregnancy. They're very rare, of course."

Vernon snorted in disgust. "Very, in this case!"

Steve laughed. "Yeah. Well, there's fat embolism from the marrow of a broken bone—"

"And Graham had a skull fracture," Charlotte said.

"Even so, a fat embolus would go to the brain, not the heart. Block the respiratory center," Vernon said. "And there wouldn't be much damage to the lung either. But he didn't have *fat* embolism."

"Vascular clot? Pulmonary embolism?" Steve suggested.

"Sure, vascular clot goes through the right ventricle into the lung, stops the circulation, but Barstow didn't have a pulmonary embolus *ei*ther," Vernon pointed out.

"Yeah. Forgot that for a minute."

"What else, Steve?" Kristin said. "About air embolism, I mean. What else could cause the froth?"

"An embalmer's trocar," Vernon said. "But that's a post-mortem artifact, so that's out too. Poor ol' Perk. Most deprived man on this island! Only thing he's got to look forward to is cleaning out his retort and firing 'er up to 2200 degrees Fahrenheit or so. He'll be ready late this afternoon."

Kristin smiled but looked at Steve.

"Well, say a surgeon turns a bone flap. Then there's a venous channel open. Slight negative pressure causes air bubbles to pass in and through the venous system. Patient dies of asphyxiation. The froth of air bubbles effectively stops all blood flow and ultimately we get—"

"Anoxial asphyxia—and finish!" Vernon moved restlessly in his chair, exasperated by this long elementary medical review.

"The critical determinant between life and death," Charlotte murmured as if reading from a text, "is when the hypothalamus stops signaling the heart to pump."

"Well, but Graham didn't have brain surgery," Kristin said. "What else, Steve?"

"Oh, a patient could die suddenly after making what looked like a reasonable recovery from, say, a car accident, due to air having been sucked into an open venous channel that wasn't closed off soon enough. Or a suicide could cut his throat or slash his wrists but die in a matter of minutes from air embolism rather than from a slow steady loss of blood, as most people would expect. Same thing —air in an open vein. They're all natural causes of death but not common. Anoxic shock is momentarily very painful, though, like the bends. Heart goes into fibrillation, keeps on trying for two, three minutes, and then—all over! It can't pump froth because of the resistance."

"How about a heart attack? Did he—could he have had a heart attack—a coronary, I mean?" Kristin said. "From all that shock and concussion and everything—the horse show and all the rest?"

"No coronary," Steve said. "I looked. No thrombus in the coronary artery. The vessels were patent—open, that is—and showed little atherosclerosis and no thrombus. Coronary arteriosclerosis doesn't remotely resemble air embolism. And for a guy as old as Barstow, by the way, his arteries were in damn good shape. Very little narrowing of the arterial walls. He'd have had a good long life."

"So if—"

"Hold it, Kris, I just thought of something else," Steve said. "That open vein and negative pressure deal. When I was interning we had a hell of a case one time. Patient was being fed intravenously after surgery. It was winter and all the beds were full—some in the halls, too—and a lot of staff were out sick and everybody was being run into the ground. Jesus! Remember I told you about that, Charl? Something like what we've got here now. Well, the nurse drags in, cockeyed sleepy, pooped, to check the I.V. and she sees fluid in the tube and the dripmeter and she thinks the flask is pretty full and she goes out again. Well, it wasn't anywhere near full, it was almost empty, and when it ran out the patient died. Except it never got to court or even out of the hospital. Everybody passed the buck—'I was doing my job here' or 'I was working there'—and anyway the nurse took it hard. She killed herself, poor ol' gal. It was a lousy situation. Because to top it off, to make it really lousy, she'd come in later on to check the I.V., saw it was empty and connected a new one, and never even realized until she finished that the poor bastard was dead! Of air embolism, they found later, which is the point of this story. They couldn't understand why, and they went over that flask and tubing with a microscope, practically. There were pinpricks, very tiny pinpricks, in the tubing. They destroyed the vacuum—lethally. And when the flask was completely empty, more air got in."

"Oh, how awful!" Kristin said, picturing it. "But . . ." She blinked and stared into space, and Charlotte murmured through a mouthful of Danish, "She's off again!" and Vernon held up his hand. "Matt," she continued, "your brother did something to Capo's flask, his I.V. flask. He put a strip of adhesive on it to make sure not to overload him, he said, and he'd check it in fifteen minutes. I think that's what he said."

"We use the double strip method here," Steve said. "One for where the flow should be by hours, and one for where it should be in thirty minutes. God knows what that nurse saw. We used the single strip method there. I guess she saw what she expected to see, what she wanted to see. She was busy and ragged and she never looked at the strip—just saw solution in the dripmeter and the tubing and thought 'Thank god I don't have to do *that* now.' So she went out to do seventeen other things."

"Well, is it possible—is it conceivable—that Kathy could have made the kind of mistake she made, Steve? Was she so exhausted, physically and emotionally, that she connected a new flask too late? After the other one was empty?"

"Hardly," Vernon said. "It wasn't empty. She noted the amount on the chart. She also took his blood pressure and noted his breathing —in Myra's presence—before she connected a different solution according to my orders."

"Oh! Of course! How dumb of me."

"I don't know about that," Matt said quietly.

Her cheeks grew hot. "Well, where are we now? I seem to be fresh out of ideas . . . The only thing is . . ." Her eyes went blank again and then she caught her breath. "Could it have been . . . ? I mean—I mean, we've been talking about natural deaths from different kinds of embolism. But—if we go on with our line of thinking and the stabbing was *extra* and *afterward* and the froth was *before* and not accountable for by *natural* or accidental causes, then maybe it was—*un*natural." She paused and said again, *"Un*natural."

Steve snatched up a pile of notes and riffled through them. "Kris, you've just given me a thought. Doc was so twitchy after that autopsy that I dashed upstairs and got Barstow's chart and Xeroxed it in case it suddenly vanished because of Barstow pressure and pull. Here we are! Wait a sec!" He ran a fingertip down the copied sheet. "Here it is!" he said, as breathless as if he had just run a mile. And then he sat back and sighed angrily. "Goddammit, I forgot! Kathy didn't enter the death on the chart. She got there at eight forty-five, right, Matt? And she looked in and took off. Then Myra looked in. Then she *went* in. Then she went out screaming and Silva came in. And *she* was so flustered that she didn't disconnect the tube and note the chart until—let's see—eight fifty-three, after Doc got there and took over."

"What're you getting at?" Matt said.

"The time of death. The I.V. stops flowing when death occurs because of resistance in the vein."

"So the time of death was somewhere between eight-thirty and eight forty-five, so what?" Vernon said fretfully.

Steve struck himself on the forehead. "Doc, I'm getting soft and you are too. Now you can see why we needed someone else to help us get our heads together, Kris. Doc, remember that case in New Hampshire over twenty years ago?"

"You were in diapers then," Vernon grouched. "And you're still wet behind the ears."

"You're right. I admit it humbly. But remember? Saunders or Sanders or Sandler? Something like that. I remember reading about it."

"*So?* It was death by air injection. Euthanasia, he claimed. He was acquitted, too. So what's that have to do with the time of death? What I'm bugged by is the *cause* of death."

"Okay. I think I can tie them both up for you in a minute. If we're going to cover the waterfront—go over all the possibilities simply because they *are* possibilities—then let's say that froth in the right ventricle was due to air in the veins. Because someone was horsing around with the I.V. And the stabbing was an extra, a means of screwing Sam."

"And if we're going to be ruthlessly logical," Charlotte said, her anxious eyes on Kristin, "and we've eliminated Kathy and Sam, then what's left is Myra Barstow."

"Oh, nonsense!" Kristin said. "We've been through that before! Are you suggesting that Myra, who loved him so much, did some hanky-panky with that flask and then rammed that knife in him and then went out for *coffee?*"

"Remember what we found, Kris. It could very well be," Matt said gently.

"What's that? What's that?" Vernon said as Steve bent over the chart again.

"Never mind that now, Doc. Let's just explore the *modus operandi*," Matt said. "Go ahead, Steve. I think you're getting warm."

"Wellthen," Steve said, putting his thick glasses up on his forehead and rubbing his eyes. "Kathy connects a new flask at"—referring to the chart—"eight-fifteen. That's when she's done. Eight-fifteen. She says she's coming back at eight forty-five, and no matter how busy *she* is—or how tired—she'll be on time because she's very careful with that guy, as Charl and I found out.

"Now. A full flask, the one she hooked up anyway, holds five hundred milliliters. A touch more than a pint. Okay? Now. The normal rate of flow is—how much, Charl?"

She swallowed another piece of Danish and washed it down with coffee. "Fifty drops a minute. That's more or less normal. That's three teaspoons a minute, roughly."

"Yeah. And three teaspoons is a tablespoon. And there are sixteen tablespoons in a cup and thirty-two in a pint, right?"

The old doctor dosed himself liberally again and nodded impatiently. "So what?"

"Just wait a minute." Steve adjusted his glasses, copied some figures from Graham Barstow's chart, did some swift calculating, and nodded in grim satisfaction. "Yeah. It looks possible. Doesn't even matter when Silva marked the death on the chart. Stupid of me. He was certainly dead at eight forty-five . . . It just might be. Of course it's very rough, it wouldn't necessarily hold up in a court but—"

"Crissake, Steve, what're you up to?" Vernon said.

"Just this. Whether Myra killed her husband between eight-fifteen and eight-thirty, or if someone else did between eight-thirty and eight forty-five, there's still a discrepancy between the amount of juice that was left in that I.V. and what ought to have been left in it. But there'd be *less* if Myra *didn't* kill him. *If*, in other words, it flowed uninterruptedly for fifteen minutes and she left at eight-thirty without touching it.

"*But*—if *she* horsed around with it and left him *dead* at eight-thirty, then it wasn't flowing for part of *that* fifteen minutes or for *any* of the next fifteen minutes when she and Kathy got back. There'd be too much left."

"And?" Matt said tensely.

"And, to put it simply, Matt, according to what Nora Silva wrote down when she disconnected that tube—it's an automatic thing, has to be done—there was just too damn much juice left in that flask!"

"Oh god!" Kristin whispered. "Oh no!"

"I'm afraid so, Kris," Steve said sympathetically. "As I say, my figures are rough, but they're too damn close to be disregarded. We didn't have any of this in mind after the autopsy or when we saw you Tuesday night—or any other time this week. All we'd been circling around was logical possibilities. And there just wasn't anyone else in the picture *but* Myra. Naturally we didn't want to upset you but— Well, the last question is, how did she do it? Did she know how to do it?"

"Well," Charlotte said, "we know she watched Kathy disconnect the old flask and connect the new one to the catheter in his vein. It isn't so hard to do."

"Myra was in New Hampshire twenty years ago. She must have heard all about that Sandler or whoever he was. Maybe she just took the tube out of the catheter and the air flowed in," Kristin suggested miserably.

Steve shook his head. "No, Kris, it wouldn't work that way. The blood would come out of the catheter in his arm."

"But he didn't bleed to death. Besides, I thought you said when a venous channel was open, air got sucked in and caused a fatal embolus."

"Yes. But that's a rare situation—hardly a dependable murder weapon. If you want to zap your enemy, you can't rely on some natural phenomenon. Sure, that death I told you about when I was interning—it's true that an appreciable amount of air sucked in by negative pressure from a defective tube and an empty flask could kill. Or an accident case, as I mentioned before, might lie around untended for several hours or be attended to but an open vein overlooked, and death—from vascular embolism—would occur hours or days later. Sometimes a patient's ready to leave the hospital ten days after surgery, and he goes into the john for a bowel movement and—bingo!—he keels over dead, because the embolism finally got to the right place. But a murderer has to take more positive steps to ensure death from air embolism, because air has to be injected very rapidly and in enough volume to do the job. It isn't the most dependable murder weapon either, I'd say, but when it works—which is also very rare, obviously, though I don't know the statistics on that—it's sure-fire. Provided you have the right size syringe and the right size needle and the right amount of air—and the time. Uninterrupted time."

"How much, Steve?" Matt said. "And how big a needle and syringe?"

"Oh, fifty cc. of air would do it, probably. A hundred or more would be better. Some pathologists might say ten or fifteen, but it would have to be put into the right place right away—heart itself, probably. Take ten or twenty seconds to inject it—half a minute anyway but fast, all at once, if possible, so the air stays together and doesn't disperse into small bubbles the body can tolerate. Death in two, three minutes. Eighteen- or twenty-gauge needle, I'd think. Twenty-gauge at least. And a big syringe. Fifty cc. if possible. Otherwise, if you had even a ten-cc. syringe, you'd have to take the needle out and fill it with air and inject it several times. And the essence of this is a lot, all at once. Plus of course the extra time for the whole works."

"I just thought of something," Kristin said. "Your brother, Matt—when I went there Monday morning for—for Frey's ashes, Joe was complaining about loss of equipment. Syringes and things. I said Dandie was a lot better after her first shot Sunday night, and he said the way his syringes were disappearing it would be all he could do to give her the next one. He said he was reduced to using the big syringes—and that another one of them had disappeared only the day before. I don't remember how big he said it was, though."

"Hold it. I'll call him," Matt said, and dialed rapidly, drumming on the desk while the phone rang and rang. "Dammit, I know he's there—! Joe? Listen, were you missing a big syringe last Sunday night? Monday morning? . . . Yeah. Go ahead and look." He covered the receiver. "He's checking his book to see who came in for what on Sunday." He drummed on the desk again as they watched him tensely. "Yeah? Yeah. I think so. . . . Yes, she had another flash. Do that. Nothing like closing the barn door. Okay, thanks." He put the phone down and nodded. "A fifty-cc. syringe with a twenty-gauge needle on it was gone Sunday night, Kristin. Joe noticed when he was cleaning up. He said to tell you he's ordering that robot you suggested."

She smiled faintly. "But what about that flint knife? Myra said she never found it."

He shrugged. "She said she didn't."

"Here's something else that may fit," Steve said, looking at his notes again. "Remember, Doc, we wrote down everything—"

"Inch by inch we covered that body! Thought we'd be there for a week!"

"Well, don't complain. Your passion for thoroughness turned me on the day I met you. Maybe it's paying off."

"Finally!" Vernon grunted.

"Remember the blood around the catheter? It shouldn't have been there."

"Why?" Kristin said.

"Because when you take off the adhesive and disconnect the hub of the catheter from the needle adapter on the tubing, to hook up a new flask or a new tube—or to inject a syringe of air or anything else—extra medication—a couple of drops of blood come out. Then another couple when you replace the needle adapter. Any good nurse—and Kathy is an excellent one—always wipes that little bit of blood away before replacing fresh tape over the catheter. To a nurse it's as automatic as breathing. And when Silva unhooked that I.V., the blood had stopped flowing, because the venous blood was coagulated by then. And the I.V. had also stopped flowing because the needle point was in the clot. Theoretically clotting occurs in eight to twelve minutes in a test tube. In a body conditions vary, of course, but if it clotted in eight to twelve minutes in Barstow, it must've begun to do so before Myra left that room. That blood on his arm is one more thing against her. She didn't wipe it off—she probably didn't even look at it, didn't even notice."

"What does time of clotting have to do with that extra blood on his arm?" Vernon said crankily.

"I don't know. I'm all mixed up. But did you think of it?"

"No."

"Well then! All I know is, that extra drop or two of blood under the tape is another thing against Myra."

"And there's another one," Kristin said sadly. "That grimace she talked about. You said death from air embolism—anoxic shock—is very painful, Steve. Like the bends. I guess we've all seen it in the movies. Kathy told me Graham wasn't unconscious anymore. Not way under."

"That we didn't know! But in that case he felt it all right. Of course a grimace doesn't last long from that cause. The muscles go limp after death. But that's the way Myra saw him when he was dying, and that's the way she'll always see him. She trapped herself again."

"Reminds me of that old picture with Henry Daniell and Boris Karloff. *The Body-Snatcher*," Vernon said with grisly relish. "Daniell's the doctor who buys bodies for his med students from Karloff—and catches him making quick corpses of healthy human beings. Then he kills Karloff because of the blackmail situation but his undoing comes when he sees Karloff's face on everybody else. He cracks up."

"Yeah, Doc," Matt said. "But the really classic murder method is in that flick, in case you didn't know it. Burke and Hare used it to advantage for a while along with grave-robbing. When a drunk passed out they squeezed his nostrils shut and suffocated him. His alcohol level was so high that he offered no resistance, so his body showed no evidence of violence. A reputable professor desperately in need of cadavers would draw the line at murder but not suspect an unnatural death in a case like this, and pay good money for it. Very neat. I read this way back in school. I almost forgot about it. Very neat."

"Oh, very," Kristin said in a quavery voice as she got up and went to the door.

"Oh, Kris, don't go," Charlotte said.

"I've got to. I have to shape up for what's coming."

She was pale and strained, and Dr. Vernon said anxiously, "Where?"

"To the beach, that's where. I need sun, I need some fresh clean air—" She went out and slammed the door.

Chapter XVIII

She put on a bathing suit under her shirt and jeans, snatched up a towel and her sun hat, and left the house quickly, hoping that Myra and Jonathan would not return and stop her head-on in the middle of the hill. This will be all wound up soon and I'll probably leave tomorrow afternoon, she thought miserably as she reached the county road. I'll just drop in and say good-by to Joe and Capo and then I'll go soak this out of my system. Maybe Polly and I ought to pack up and stay at Grandma Potter's overnight. Grandma wouldn't mind. I don't think I can stay with Myra one more night . . . Poor Myra . . . What a hideous nightmare. Only it isn't a nightmare, it's real . . .

The progress that the dog had made in twenty-four hours was astonishing. He was still alone in the infectious ward but on his feet now, and he greeted her joyfully albeit with the restraint imposed by weakness and the healing wound.

"He's picked up nicely," Dr. Amaral said with pride. "Youth, that's what did it. He's young enough and tough enough to take a lot of punishment. Only thing is, Kristin—if you don't mind me calling you that—every time you leave he cries for an hour or more. He's still a baby after all."

"He'll get over it. I've come to say good-by. Matt has about wrapped things up—he'll tell you about it. I don't feel like going into it now—"

"Myra Barstow?"

"Looks like it. I'll leave tomorrow on the six-o'clock boat, Joe, but I had to see you and Capo again before I go. I didn't know if there'd be time—" She bent to kiss the white muzzle and to hide her tears. "Take it easy, Capo. Just—hang loose, big boy." She managed a smile as she gave the doctor her hand. "You've been—you've been—" she whispered, and rushed out, hearing the dog whine and bark as she closed the door behind her.

The day was flawless. The water danced in the sun, the air was fresh, the sand was almost dried out after the long storm. And the little beach under the headland was empty except for the sandpipers who ran back and forth at the water's edge trying to pin the wavelets to the shore. She took off her shirt and jeans and sat down on the towel to watch them, to let them replace the vision of a monstrous murder which had been delineated so explicitly in Dr. Vernon's office.

Soon the strain began to ease and she leaned back on her elbows, squinting at a pair of sea gulls wheeling gracefully about a little sailboat far out on the sunlit waves. There was nothing else in sight, and the simplicity, the rightness of it—of birds and only birds in the sky, and a small white boat powered only by wind and guided only by hands and eyes—was intensely satisfying. She felt herself begin to smile.

The little craft came steadily on and she sat up again, wondering when the sailor would go about and disappear from view, reducing this little bit of world to its elemental state. But he did not tack. He held his course and presently he hauled down the sail and floated to shore, jumping lightly into the water to haul the boat onto the sand. He took something out of it and walked slowly toward her, a big man in rolled-up jeans and jersey shirt, and she sat staring at him openmouthed.

He dropped the bag he was carrying onto the sand and sat down beside her. "Hi," he said.

"Hi."

"How are you feeling now?"

"Better. Worse. Oh, Matt, why did you come?"

"Because I knew you'd be here. Hungry?"

"Yes. No. Yes. Oh, I don't know!"

"Well, I know you. You haven't eaten anything, have you."

She shook her head.

"Thought so. Here." He took sandwiches out of the bag and put one into her hand. "Eat that. Coffee? Scotch?"

"Both. Thank you. You're very—thoughtful, Lieutenant."

"It's a gift." He leaned over and took her discolored chin in his hand. "Don't give me that lieutenant business. We're way past that, Kristin," he said firmly, and kissed her. "Let's eat. And then I'm going to take you away from all this."

"I don't think I want to go."

"You do. Or I wouldn't be here."

"That's what I'm afraid of, Matt."

"If you were, *you* wouldn't be here."

His matter-of-fact tone defused the tension and made her laugh, and she began to eat. They did not speak until they were finished, and the gentleness of the day at once surrounded them and freed them, so that they were wholly at peace with themselves and each other.

"Want to talk now?" he said, lying back on a pillow of sand.

"Yes. It's strange, but I don't mind now. It isn't any further away, it isn't less real and dreadful, but—I don't mind. What are you going to do about Myra?"

"I don't know yet. Oh, I'll have to go through the procedures, of course. The warrant, the D.A., the whole bit. I told you last night that I was taking time off. Well, this is it. I don't have to do anything till I'm good and ready. She's not going anywhere anyway. Besides, I hate like hell to spoil the weekend for the D.A. and Trueblood and the judge, dragging in one of the Commonwealth's bluebloods. It'll be a bad scene, Kristin. Nobody'll want to believe me—except the press. They'll have a hell of a time."

"Does everything have to come out? Is it going to be smeared all over the place?"

"Bound to be. The Barstows aren't high up enough to buy them off. But nobody should have to go through it on the principle that the public's entitled to know. Pandering to the baser instincts shouldn't be allowed. As a matter of fact—"

"What?"

"Oh, nothing. Just something I'm thinking about. Tell you later."

"Did you tell Doc and Steve and Charlotte all about it?"

"No, but not for that reason. I wanted to get out of there. I wanted to find you, help you through this. Besides, they really weren't all that interested. Barstow loved somebody else and Myra blew the whistle. That was all they needed. They're all back at work again."

"They're lucky, they'll forget it sooner . . . I've been thinking about it, Matt. How she managed . . ."

"Give. You know more about her comings and goings than anybody else."

"I wish I didn't but . . . There's something I forgot to mention back there. About Graham coming to, feeling the pain. He felt Kathy working over him and he said her name, Matt. Twice. And Myra was sitting there . . . And when Myra came back later with her coffee, she said to Kathy at the door, 'What have you done?' Evidently she considered making a case against Kathy, but I guess she just couldn't go through with it."

"Oh. Kathy didn't tell me that. People tell you things, my darling. You have a knack. It's clear from what we know that Myra had had it by Sunday when Barstow left the hospital. He must've told her, on the way back to the fair to get his car, that he was definitely finished, that he was going to meet Kathy. Probably even that he wanted her out of his house and on the boat Sunday night. She wasn't at the judging afterward, when he left. I think she followed him to the beach—when she said she was looking for the flint. She saw his bug parked on the road, and followed him to the cave. She may not have been a swimmer, according to Kathy, but she was an explorer like Barstow and she must know those caves as well as he did. I think she hid in one of the ones behind. She could probably hear a lot of what they said—acoustics are pretty weird in there. And when Kathy went out, she went in and bashed him. Maybe they talked first, who knows? Then she went home and took Dandie for a walk. All of which made her miss the calls from the people here and from the ones at the fair. How she'd have killed him without Joe's syringe is anybody's guess. Maybe with the flint and nothing else. Maybe with a pillow if he'd been unconscious. But something—maybe that old case in New Hampshire—gave her the idea of an air injection and she took the syringe. And if the flint did fall off the pegboard as she said it did, she'd obviously found it and put it in her purse. She must've known we couldn't hold Sam or that sooner or later he'd be acquitted. *Maybe!* Hindsight's great. But I'm telling you, Kristin, I wouldn't have given two cents for his being acquitted on reasonable doubt, and if he had been, I wouldn't have wanted him to walk around with *that* over his head for the rest of his life. Anyway, I guess we know the rest."

"And we know why she wouldn't divorce Graham, let alone accept his offer to be—to keep on being—a wife in name only, while he lived here with Kathy. It was that family. The charisma of the name. If it hadn't meant what it did to her, she could have divorced him years ago. She had grounds. It would have been easy. Remember where we found that letter?"

"Yes, but I'm not so sure about the sex bit. Impotency doesn't void a marriage in this Commonwealth. It only makes it voidable. They'd've had to go through a dirty business even so, to get a divorce." He sighed. "God, what a case. What else have you got?"

"There's one other thing that's been lurking around the edges. The poison ivy she got, Matt. Steve would say it's one more thing against her. I got mine here—it's about gone now—the only place I could have gotten it was here, on Sunday, when my feet were killing me and I staggered and stumbled up the path to go to the hospital. It's all over the place, that stuff."

"Well, it's another thing I'm glad about. It keeps a lot of people away." He spilled sand on her arm and brushed it off carefully. "Go on."

"Well, on Sunday night, before I went to get Polly, Myra said she had it too. She said she gets it every year no matter how careful she is. But later she said she'd only done some gardening on Monday just before you and Trueblood arrived. She hadn't done any gardening before, and she hasn't done any since."

"But at home—"

"No. I thought so too. But they don't have a house there, Matt, just a big duplex on the Charles. She has a little greenhouse on the patio."

"Oh. Well, we know she didn't come back out this way or you'd have seen her. It looks as if she tried coming in this way first. I bet she stood up there a little way and saw them—and you too."

"I was lying down with my hat on, reading. Trying to, anyway."

"It's possible she may not have recognized you, but I think she did. Otherwise how would she have gotten the poison ivy? There's none on the beach around the corner. No, I think she saw you and Kathy, and then Barstow, and maybe even Sam, if she got there before he took off. So she went back around the other way, where the Porsche was parked. Lee Williams drove it back, incidentally. Had a hell of a time playing with it for a few minutes." He sprinkled more sand on her. "What else?"

"Well, about those books. And the black lace panties. When I told her Monday about the robbery, she was very unconcerned about it, as I told you. All things considered, it wasn't surprising that she would be. Anyway, she had offered to drive me to the ferry to get Polly, because of my feet, but she was anxious to take Dandie to Joe and then go to see Graham. So I said no, she'd be delayed too long. I was out on the sun deck brushing Frey when she got herself together and left, and then I turned off the lights as I went through the house, so I didn't notice the bookshelves. I wasn't planning to read, I was too tired. Then when Polly and I brought her back, she was all doped up and we put her to bed. And I know she wasn't up during the night, because I *was*. And it wasn't till we were getting ready for bed that I realized the robber had come back. I looked around and took stock and saw that some books were missing along with a few other things. So the only time she could have taken those books and the panties was just before she left, when I was outside with Frey. She must have done it very quietly and very fast."

"Which proves, maybe, that she had it in her mind all along, killing him. They weren't in her car?"

"No. I'm sure we'd have seen them if they were. She probably hid them in her closet before she left. We didn't use any of the closets or drawers, as I told you, Matt. I've been living out of my suitcase for a week. Then on Tuesday when I was out, she went out too, trying to get Graham's body released, and she must've taken them along and snuck them into the Clothing Exchange. The way those ladies mill around gossiping and chatting, it would be easy enough to do even if she had to make a few trips in and out to do it. Scatter them around on the shelves there so they wouldn't attract attention, and bury the panties among the underwear in back. If she hadn't said on Wednesday that she'd have to buy another *Lassie,* I would have kept on thinking Toby took the books. But I don't know if her mention of it was a slip or whether she'd looked for it and couldn't find it. She's been very careful otherwise."

"It was a bad move, though, stealing them herself. All she had to do was leave them there—the books anyway. The panties she could have burned. Barstow had a hell of a background academically, and it'd be very understandable that he'd have those books and plenty more like them, if anyone had even thought about it. I know I wouldn't have, and I have a few of them myself. The novels and the Wyeth were just extras, a cover. I think she was trying to wipe it all out, forget it, present a picture of a normal elderly couple whose only bad luck was that they never had kids."

"Yes, but she should have gone through his desk while she was at it and finished the job."

"Yeah, but as I said last night, darling, she obviously didn't think anything *that* crucial was there. I don't know about most people, but would you think they'd save what Barstow saved? I don't think I would."

"I wouldn't either. But Myra said he was very possessive about his things. But maybe he would have gone through all that stuff when he was down here for good, and thrown it all out with the rest of his past, when he had time, when he was starting his new life. But it's clear that Toby thought there might be something in there. I bet he spent many happy hours going through that desk. No wonder the plumbing didn't work! Maybe you were right, Matt. If Toby had a spark of decency left where Kathy was concerned, he wouldn't use stuff like that against Graham."

"Maybe. He told me he loved her but always felt she was too good for him. Too straight. And by the way, it's also obvious that Barstow got himself cured—really cured—not too long ago. I came across a pile of bills he'd gotten from a shrink in Cambridge, and just then you gave me that old report of thirty-four years back and I forgot to tell you. He'd been in treatment for four years, starting five years ago. And then a year ago at the fair he got hurt in the hackney show and went to the hospital—and met Kathy."

"And that did it, I guess," she said sadly. "No wonder his passion scared her. All those miserable years . . . unable to see Myra as anything but his mother . . . cracking up over the horror of having intercourse with her—committing incest with the mother figure, the surrogate—fathering a child on her . . . Then years and years of fetishism—those awful black lace panties—and Myra standing there *watch*ing him! Loving him, yearning for him, for his children, seeing his seed spilled on the ground . . . in those vulgar black lace panties . . . And then he's analyzed and after four years he's ready—and he meets Kathy. All that love, all those wasted years. Oh, Matt, no wonder he was so alive, so vital! He couldn't get enough—of anything! By the time Sam was well along in his dissertation Graham must have had the feeling he could walk on the water. Do anything —even plagiarize. I'll never understand that. Unless—could it have had anything to do with his fetishism? A kind of leftover of the bad days?"

"I don't think one thing had anything to do with the other. Lots of fetishists are klepto's, but only to get their fetish or enhance its value. No, I think he'd been trying all his life to impress his big brother Jonathan. That he never could do enough to prove himself. You said Jonathan called him a fool, that he always thought of him that way. I have a feeling he would *never* have backed down to Sam and given away even a piece of the new book. His analysis failed him badly there."

"Oh, Matt, even Sam felt bad for him! Because, as he'd told Kathy, for once in his life he was happy . . . And now it's all gone —*he*'ll be all gone—burned up to ashes like Frey—in a few hours—"

She got up suddenly, sobbing, and ran down into the water.

Chapter XIX

She stayed overnight in the Barstow house because Matt had asked her to. "They won't do anything without telling you, and as long as your things are there, they'll have to. But I'm going to keep you out tonight as long as I can, my darling. Polly can move down to Sam's if she wants to. She might as well, the way things are going between those two. Call Grandma. I'll bet she'll say she's already asked her. But you stay."

So she had stayed there after all, but not for many hours, and when she woke to a beautiful Saturday morning she found herself alone again. She stretched happily, contentedly, forgetting for a little while that she was leaving on a late boat.

Myra had left a note: "Kris dear, Jonathan and I have gone to hire a truck somewhere for my plants and the pegboard. We should be back by one or two o'clock. Lots to do. We'll try to make the nine-o'clock boat."

And so must I, she thought. If I'm going to settle this properly, I've got to get away. Will I be able to come back?

Miserably she drank some coffee, cleaned up the kitchen, went through all the rooms collecting her things and Polly's, avoiding by look or touch the small wooden casket on the mantel that held Graham Barstow's ashes, and loaded the car. Then she stripped the trundle bed, cleaned the little room and the hall bathroom, and put sheets and towels into the washer. I won't do the diplomat's, though! she said, and did them anyway. And then she lay down on the sun deck to wait for the wash to finish. And, to wait.

Matt called at noon. "Are they back yet? What've you been doing?" She told him briefly and sadly. *"No!* Don't go, Kristin, don't go! We've got to talk. I can't now, I'm in the thick of things. Look, call me at my office if anything happens. Otherwise I'll be there at three. Promise?"

"Yes, I will, I promise," she said, and put the phone down and cried for all the losses and all the gains that had been packed into eight days, until she could not cry anymore. But she was out on the sun deck again, washed and somewhat restored, when Myra and Jonathan returned with Dandie, and a pickup truck rattled up the hill and parked behind them. It was one-fifteen.

"Oh, what a job we had!" Myra said. Jonathan sat on the couch watching from behind his newspaper in icy silence while a dusty young farmer went in and out carrying plants and setting them down at her direction. With the return of each one the odor of damp decay increased moment by moment on this fine dry day until Kristin's stomach twisted with nausea. "The Grange is a madhouse, Kris, simply packed with people. It took us all morning to help Mr. Leary load up his truck. We could hardly get in and out through the crowds. Everyone was moving their exhibits out. They were all supposed to be taken away two hours ago for the dance tonight, but if that place is cleaned and ready by seven it'll be a wonder! The barbecue is going to be such fun. They've dug the trenches and started the fires and the lambs are all set to go. I wish we could be there. It'd be—such fun."

"How did you manage to get the truck? That couldn't be one of Perley's, could it?"

"Good heavens, no. I told you I'd never speak to that wretched man again. He and his son deserve everything they get. No, Jonathan and I left here very early and simply drove from one farm to another until we found Mr. Leary. He and his wife will look over the house for me from now on. I'm so lucky I found them."

"Have you had lunch yet?" It was something else to say.

"We didn't have time, dear. I'm starved. Jonathan, you must be too. What would you like?"

"I'll leave it to your good judgment, my dear," he said indifferently as the farmer banged through the hall with the big pegboard.

"I'll just settle with that nice young man and then I'll fix lunch," Myra said, and Kristin went with her into Graham's study to help

Leary put the pegboard back on the wall. The empty space of honor in the middle of it, where the flint had been, was horribly emphasized by the little description on the card below.

She doesn't act any different, Kristin thought as they went into the kitchen, but she's prattling somehow. No, I think she *is* different . . . More assertive, stronger. *Some*thing. I can't put my finger on it. Oh god, what am I going to do with this! She glanced nervously at the clock and pleaded silently with Matt to come quickly.

"You're very quiet, Kris. What's the matter? And where's Polly? I couldn't bear to leave without seeing her."

"Oh, she's gadding about with friends, I guess. She'll be back soon."

"She hasn't been around much these past few days. I've missed her. But of course we'll see her at the memorial service. We've settled on Monday afternoon."

"Oh? I was wondering."

"Kris, are you all right?"

"I'm—all right, I guess. Just feeling rather down, is all. Frey—and —and Graham. Oh Myra, I'm so sorry, so very sorry!"

"I know, dear. You didn't have to say it. I know. What my life will be like now . . . But without you with me, I couldn't have come this far. Just knowing you were here was a great comfort. It's been almost like having a daughter."

"I'm glad. I wish—I wish I could have done more."

"No one could have done more. Now. Is there any more lettuce?"

Kristin poked about in the refrigerator. "No. But there's an awful lot of food left. What are you going to do with it?"

"Let's divide it and take it home, what's worth taking. We'll finish what we can today, though. There's a lovely thick steak we can broil for supper."

She hung onto the refrigerator door, racked by a violent spasm, and when it passed she closed the door and took the scotch bottle out of the cabinet. "Myra, how about a drink. I don't know about you but it isn't too early for me."

"A little sherry would be nice, I think. Jonathan might like some. Why don't you ask him."

The diplomat declined stiffly, and Kristin asked herself again, as she sipped the whiskey, what it was about him that had made him Myra's favorite for so many years.

"I noticed your car's all packed, dear. When are you planning to go?"

"I'm not sure. I thought at six. But the police are coming. At three." She held her breath.

"They're coming? Again? What for?"

"I don't know, Myra. They didn't say."

"Oh, how annoying! Really! Well, Jonathan will deal with them. They won't be allowed to bother you anymore, dear, with their endless questions and statements. Graham used to say that Jonathan had clout."

That desiccated ungracious old man? Oh god! she thought wildly. Oh Matt, come soon, come soon. I can't stand much more of this. Her hand shook uncontrollably as she poured more whiskey into her glass. It was now only two-fifteen.

"Oh dear. Oh damn," Myra said mildly some minutes later. "I forgot something. I had the list right with me and never even looked at it. I'll have to go out again, Kris. Will you finish shelling this crab for me? And start the water for the corn. I'll get some lettuce while I'm about it. One can*not* serve a proper salad without lettuce. How silly of me!"

She washed and dried her hands carefully and poured lotion into a pink smooth palm. Rubbing it into her strong beautiful hands, she went up the steps into the living room. As Kristin continued shelling the crab she heard Myra say, "I'll be back shortly, Jonathan. With all that fuss at the Grange I forgot to pick up a few things that I must have before we leave. I'll just take this out of here, it's upsetting Kristin. No, stay, Dandie, I'll be right back."

A few minutes later she drove down the hill and Kristin began to breathe more easily as she clipped shells and heaped crab meat into the bowl. Two twenty-five.

Let's see, she said ten minutes later, when should I put up the water for corn? Down to the village and back, at least twenty minutes. Shopping, at least—But I don't know what she needs and where she's going. Pharmacy as well as the market, probably. Twenty minutes at least. She ought to be there by now, but if she isn't back when Matt comes, I'm just going to walk out. I'll go down to Grandma's and relax in peace and quiet until I have to leave. Not this kind of quiet.

The kettle was boiling rapidly at three o'clock. At three-ten she turned the light down. At three-twenty she turned it off. She put the crab meat into the refrigerator, took a final dose of scotch, and went somewhat dizzily into the living room.

"I'm sorry you're having to wait so long, Mr. Barstow, but everything's almost ready. You'll have lunch as soon as Myra gets back. It must be quite crowded in the village this late in the afternoon. I'll just take a turn around the driveway until she comes."

He nodded dismissively, and she put on her sunglasses and went outside and looked at the garden. It was filled with leaves and bits of branches, and the tallest flowers, bent and broken from the hurricane, still lay untidily over the others. Hours of work would be needed to renew the splendor she had seen here a week ago. She turned away and went slowly around the dusty circle, wondering if anyone would come to do it now. The blue jay squawked at her from the pine tree in the middle of the wild garden but she was lost in thought and did not hear him.

She was circling the garden for the third time when a car came up the hill, and then another. Sergeant Williams appeared first in the cruiser. Behind him was the neat dark red Mercedes two-seater she had been in the night before. She waved to the sergeant and walked over to Matt.

"Sorry I'm late, darling. I was up to my eyeballs in this and that. Where's Myra?"

"She went to the village for a few things. I expected her back by now."

He got out and closed the door. "When? When did she go?"

"Two-twenty. I've been watching the clock since they got back at one-fifteen. What time is it now?"

"Twenty of four."

"I don't understand it. She only had a few things to get, she said, and she told me to boil water for corn, she'd be right back. It must be very crowded."

"No, it's slack now, I just came through. What else did she say? What did you say?"

"She didn't say anything else. I said you were coming at three and she took it that you were coming to see me again. She said Jonathan would deal with you. Then a few minutes later she said she'd forgotten to get some things she'd need before the trip home, and she left. Why? What's the matter? Do you think she isn't coming back? Did I say the wrong thing? Did I make a mistake?"

"I don't know. Don't look so stricken, it isn't your fault, darling." He took her by the shoulders and looked at her critically. "My darling. Have you been crying?"

" 'Fraid so." She began to shake. "Shocking bad taste, I know, but—"

"Stop it, Kristin! Look, this is what I want you to do. Go in and get your things. I'll help you—"

"Everything's in the car. Even my purse."

"Good. Don't even bother saying good-by to Barstow. I'll take care of that. Go down to Grandma's and wait for me. Okay? Will you do that?"

"Yes." But she stood there feeling the warm urgent pressure of his hands, and neither of them moved. "Matt, do you—is she—coming back?"

"Did she take Dandie?"

"No. She said, 'I'll be right back.' But Matt, she never goes anywhere without her. Except when I took Dandie to the hospital, they're glued together."

"We'll find her. Don't worry. Now go. I'll be down as soon as I can."

He joined her in the white and yellow kitchen less than half an hour later. "Hi, Gram, how's my girl?" he said, kissing the old lady. "Where's everybody? What's for lunch?"

"The children took Faith shopping, Mattie. I've just been telling Kristin how sweet they are together. It's true that good comes out of evil, just as I've always said. Sam goes to jail and comes out engaged to be married to Polly."

Kristin laughed. "Oh, it's definite, then?" She felt much saner in the jonquil lunacy of this huge room and was happily eating cold beef and salad at the table with the white cloth.

"*I* think so," Prudence said, giving Matt a plate of food. "She hasn't said anything yet, but she's a sensible child. This is a—a lead pipe cinch, as Sam says. He says you can't deny the Life Force. Do you mind if I keep her here a while longer, Kristin?"

"I don't think either of us—any of us—has any say, Grandma. Not even Sam. When the Life Force summons we bow and obey."

"Yes," Matt said, looking steadily at her. "That's how it is. That's how it has to be."

"You're pleased, Kristin," Prudence stated as she left them.

"Yes. Very." She blushed as she bent over her plate. "What happened up there, Matt?"

"I told Barstow, of course. But I think he knew. He's hanging on by his teeth now. The murder was bad enough but to have it all in the family—! He's suffering, poor bastard, and there's nothing I can do about it. He'll probably resign."

"What kept you so long?"

"This morning? Flak! I told you there'd be plenty and there was. All kinds. Why the delay? Why the solution just in time to spoil a gala weekend? Why did Doc Vernon take so long? Why this, why that? Where was I last night? I said I was trying to tie things up. Which is literally true—one way and another. And I'm not through yet," he said determinedly. "And anyway, Myra was out, god knows where, with her brother-in-law last night till very late, so that was that. I also spent a lot of time trying to locate one of the state forensic pathologists—best one *I* know—Nolton Bigelow, great guy. Finally nailed him over in Harwich Port at the inn his wife runs. I don't know why I didn't do it sooner, or why Doc and Steve didn't. But I'm glad we never thought of it, Kristin." He touched her hand briefly. "Then I called Doc and Steve and we had a four-way conference call with Big—thank god it's Saturday, we didn't have any trouble setting it up—and we went over the whole thing. And I asked Big what the D.A. had asked me. Why didn't Doc and Steve figure out air embolism by injection last Sunday night." He stopped to eat some more, chewing impatiently and shaking his head in disgust.

"What did he say?"

"He said—and I gave it to the D.A. later right between the eyes—he said you'd have to be a profoundly paranoid type to suspect such a thing right from the beginning. That in twenty years of practice he'd found air embolism only *ten* times in *ten thousand* autopsies—and that only *one* of them was foul play! It's an exotic means of killing, it just doesn't happen very often, and it doesn't exactly spur guys like Doc and Steve, who have little or no forensic experience to begin with, to beat odds of ten thousand to *one* on the first shot. Anyway it shut the D.A. up. He knows Big, naturally, so he allowed as how we'd done pretty well after all in only five days. But he was still grousing about the weekend being spoiled when I hung up on him."

"What are you going to do now?"

"What are *we* going to do now. *We* are going out—to look for Myra. Plenty of others are too, and there's someone at the ferry just in case she goes there, which I doubt. I'll be in touch with them by radio. And Lee is staying with Barstow. So *we* can take our time. All day and all night. And I hope we don't find her for a thousand years."

"But I can't!"

"Oh yes you *can*. You're a witness, and if it's necessary I'll have the D.A. tie you up with so many subpoenas and warrants and everything else, you won't be able to see straight. Look, Kristin, I have a strong feeling Myra's going to call you. Not Barstow but you. I didn't tell him which was which, or where, but I gave him my car phone number—and my apartment phone if she calls after ten. I told Lee not to interfere, not to touch the phone up there, and Barstow isn't to say Lee's there. He doesn't want to frighten her off either."

"Are you going to put a tracer on the phones?"

"No."

"Why, Matt? If she—"

"I'll go into that later. If and when the time comes. It's a long chance but I think she's going to try to talk to you. In fact I'm sure she will, sooner or later, and you've got to be here. So my conscience is clear. On all counts. Is yours?"

Her clear gray eyes met his honestly. "I told you, yes, only I've tried—"

"I love you, Kristin. Do you love me?"

Her eyes did not waver. "Yes. Yes, I love you. I can say it, finally. In this crazy house I can say it. But—I have to go."

He looked at her bleakly. "And maybe take the chance that out of mistaken loyalty you'll never come back? This is to be just a brief encounter? And that's all? That's not enough for me, Kristin. I want what Kathy and Graham wanted. What Polly and Sam want. A life. Life! *No,*" he said firmly, getting up and putting the dishes into the white sink. "I told you, Kristin. I'm going to fight for you—fight to keep you, and that's that. Now come on. We're going back to my place so I can change. Between the Mercedes and a pair of jeans I won't look like a cop on duty. And I don't plan to feel like one, either. One way and another we're going to bite a piece out of this gala weekend. Take your suit out of your bag. It's a great day for a swim. We'd better hurry, though, it's four-thirty."

"But, Matt—"

"Perks of my rank and job, Kristin, so don't argue. Let's go." He took her hands and pulled her out of the chair.

"But if Myra calls—"

"She'll try the car number first. Then my apartment. If she goes home Lee will call me. And if we're otherwise occupied, my dearest," he said, taking her into his arms, "he'll call Trueblood to make it up to him for losing Sam."

"You have all the answers, Matt."

"All the answers but one," he said, and kissed her.

"Let's drop in on Joe and see how Capo's doing," he said, sometime after seven. "I've got to pick up Joe's report on those dogs, so it's all kosher."

The white shepherd was still in the infectious ward next to the cot. "He's doing fine now," Joe said as he opened the door. "By tomorrow he'll be able to walk up a wall. But I want to be sure, so I'm keeping an eye on him all day and a hand on him all night. He's still a pup, you know."

She laughed. "You'll never be able to get rid of him now."

"Oh, I won't have any trouble," he said as the dog lunged at her, barked her into a corner, and leaned, pinning her to the wall, his tail twirling like a whirligig. She laughed and put her arms around him. "You know, Capo, you remind me of someone though I don't think you'll have quite his heft. Even so, you're mashing my foot, big boy. Back off."

"Joe's turning himself inside out for that pup, Kristin," he said as they drove away. "But Capo knows who he loves best. I think you'll have to take him."

"No."

"Why not?"

"I don't know. Maybe I haven't finished grieving yet. Maybe I'm just tired. Everything's happened so fast, Matt, so fast. I feel I've lived a second life, almost, since last Saturday. It's almost too much, too intense. I don't think I'm capable of giving anymore for a while. Even to a dog."

"You can when you're getting at the same time."

"Maybe. I've certainly been getting back more than I bargained for."

"Are you sorry?"

"No. That's why it's so hard."

The road along West Beach was almost deserted and only a few cars were parked on the shoulder. He stopped at a spot far from any of the others and opened the door for her. "The beach is narrow here, we'll hear the phone. Let's walk. Do you know something? I'm forty-six and I've never taken anyone I loved for a walk on the beach at night. Until last night. Anne didn't like the island. And there was never anyone else. Until you. Kristin, you're a part of this place. It's where you belong. You fit."

"Oh, Matt, you're tearing me apart."

"I'm trying my damndest."

They went down to the water and watched it advance and recede in rhythmic gentle ripples, the last a fraction more distant from them than the one before. There was a soft glow on the horizon of pink and green and gold that narrowed and darkened instant by instant as the sky deepened and the stars winked on.

"Tide's fallen," he said. "It'll be all the way out and gone soon."

"It has to go, Matt."

There was a broken note in her voice and he gripped her shoulders and shook her. "But it comes back again, Kristin, it comes back! It always comes back!" He pulled her roughly to him.

They reached the Grange at eight-thirty, a few minutes after the winning ticket for the car raffle had been drawn. The number was posted outside and she smiled wryly as she tore up her tickets and the two that Polly had bought. Then they pushed through the beery crowd at the door and went inside. It was very hot, airless, and sweaty, and the old floor trembled under several hundred feet as the caller yodeled and sang over the music on a record player.

"Everybody seems to be having a great time," he said.

"You don't really think she'd come here, do you, Matt?"

"I doubt it, but maybe I should've had men here right away, just in case. Maybe I shouldn't have waited till eight. Thompson's around someplace—ought to be at the door—and Hedges is out back. Stay right in this spot, I'll be back in a minute."

The dancers were forming new squares when he took her hand and led her through the crowd. "Let's go out back," he said when they were outside again in the cool sweet air. "Thompson swears he saw her but he isn't sure. I don't see how he could unless he stood right next to her in that mob."

"Are you worried?"

"Only that we'll find her too soon," he said, putting an arm about her shoulders. "Cold?"

"No, Matt."

She slipped an arm around his waist and they walked slowly back to the big field until they came to several long tables lit by kerosene lanterns and piled with corn, watermelon, and tubs of soda pop. Beyond these were eight trenches, each with a long serving table near it, well spaced and filled with glowing coals that hissed and crackled as eight spitted lambs, crusty brown and fragrant, revolved over them dripping blood and fat. Children clamored for a chance at the heavy wooden cranks but gave up quickly and watched, their eyes big, their mouths watering, as the cooks turned the spits slowly and evenly.

"Want some?"

"Oh, Matt, I'd love some! I haven't seen a sight like this since I was sixteen. It's a real country do."

"It's supposed to be ready at nine. I've timed things very nicely, don't you think? Wait, let me talk to Hedges first. There he is, tackling a hunk of watermelon. I'm going through the motions, you understand. If he'd seen Myra, he wouldn't be gorging himself now."

He was wrong, for the trooper was looking right at her as he ate watermelon and the juice dripped off his chin. She was in his line of vision turning a spit at the farthest trench.

But her back was to them and it was dark, and in navy blue slacks, with her hair covered by a floppy chef's hat and her broad body bundled into an oversized apron and distorted even more by the glow of the coals and no other light, she was unrecognizable. The two organizers of the feast knew her, of course, having been her neighbors at the exhibits. They had welcomed her offer to help and promised to respect her need for anonymity, telling her how wonderful it was that she was keeping so busy. They did not know that she was widely sought, and the arrival of a state trooper after full dark was accepted by them and by everyone else as part of the price a democratic people pays to assemble freely. So she turned the spit, keeping her back to the man in the blue and gray uniform, and fed the children and told them to call her Grandma, and Matt and Kristin ate lamb and corn and watermelon with Trooper Hedges not sixty feet away, warned him to keep his eyes open and his mouth shut, and then went back to the car.

"Tired?"

"Exhausted."

"Happy?"

"Yes," she whispered. "Very happy."

"That's good," he said against her lips, and kissed her.

The phone rang at eleven.

"Oh, Matt, must I?"

"Answer it, Kristin."

"But what do I say?"

"You'll know, my darling, my love. Answer it."

She walked unsteadily across the room and picked up the phone, and he put his robe over her bare thin shoulders and pressed her gently down onto the chair.

"Hello?" she said, grasping his hand. "Hello?"

There was a little breathy silence, and then Myra said, "Hello, Kris dear. I hope I haven't called too late. I had to talk to you."

"No, no, of course not. I've been waiting. Where are you?"

"In a booth. It doesn't matter."

"Myra, when are you coming home? It's been a long day for you. Come home and let me help you. You must be so tired."

"Not yet, dear. Not yet . . . I wanted to tell you first . . ."

"Yes? Go on. Tell me what?"

"I wanted to tell you—how it was. Why I had to do it. I couldn't bear it anymore . . ."

"Tell me, Myra. On the phone. Where nobody can see you. It's easier that way. You'll feel better and then you can come home and all of us—we'll all help you. All the way. You'll see. Go ahead, Myra, tell me." She tugged at Matt's hand to have him kneel beside her and listen. He put his cheek to hers and held his breath.

"Yes, I'll tell you. I want to tell you so you'll understand . . . He killed me, Kris. In a way. A long time ago. The only way a woman can be destroyed . . . someone like me, anyway. He couldn't help it, I suppose. He'd been hurt in some way, and he hurt me . . . by depriving me of being all that I was meant to be. I could have left him, I guess. It isn't that I had no choice. But I loved him in spite of it, and the family—the outward part of my life—that meant so much. Too much, perhaps. And I never stopped hoping that someday . . . someday . . . he'd be able to treat me as a woman, a wife . . . a lover . . .

"I had a baby, you know. I didn't tell you that, dear. It was conceived in misery and horror—for both of us—and maybe it was better that it died. If it had been crippled, or deformed in its little soul by the way it started . . . So I was glad. I thought, When Graham comes home from the hospital he'll be cured, he'll be all right, we'll begin again.

"But he wasn't all right. They never helped him there. They didn't know what to do. They didn't understand, all those doctors . . . Drugs and rest. Rest, they said, was what he needed. He'd been working too hard at the university, they said. They *said!*" She laughed bitterly.

"When he came home it was worse. He bought some black underpanties that a—a whore would wear, and I had to put my hand on them and hold them while he—while he—and afterward—afterward I hoped—I hoped there'd be something living on them that would—that would—"

She cried softly and Kristin's hand closed on the receiver until it was numb.

"I thought," Myra continued brokenly, "I thought that if I could somehow have a baby . . . that way . . . it would make a difference. That in the family's eyes at least we'd seem to be a happy couple. They'd think—they'd know he was really better and I was normal, a healthy normal woman, a Barstow . . . And it wouldn't have hurt so much to go on doing—the other. So I kept on washing those horrible black panties . . . and hoping . . . But it didn't happen, it couldn't that way.

"And then about five years ago he went to a psychiatrist. Without telling me. I never knew until it was all over and we'd built this house. He'd stopped using those lace panties . . . I kept them but—I thought he was just getting older and he didn't care anymore . . . about sex . . . But it happened because of the fair last year. He was hurt at the horse show, very much the way he was this time, and I took him to the hospital . . . And he met Katherine Field . . .

"He began coming down here by himself a lot after that. He said he could work better here where he was undisturbed. And I believed him . . . And then at Christmas he told me everything . . . that he'd been psychoanalyzed, that he was normal and healthy as a man should be with a woman . . . and that he loved somebody else. A young woman, young enough to be his daughter . . . young enough to bear his children. He was sorry, he said, to have to leave me after all these years, but he'd lost half his life, more than half, and he had to live while he could. He was going to live here and commute to Hollybrook, and he had it all planned out. He said I was wonderful, that he loved and respected me. He said a lot of things! That I was part of his past, that it was over and done with, that the doctor and he had agreed that he must leave me. *They* agreed! They never asked *me*, Kris. *I* never knew.

"I said I'd think it over, and months went by and we were planning to be down for the fair because it was such fun! We were happy together in some things, you know. Traveling, things like that. But he was hurt again. And then he insisted on leaving the hospital Sunday morning. I took him back to the Grange to get his car—he never would let me drive it, and I would have loved to go dashing about in it—and he said he'd come to the end of the line, that he was divorcing me. That I could have a large settlement and everything we owned except this house. He was going to meet Katherine Field shortly and tell her they needn't wait any longer. I was to leave that day and take my plants with me—or throw them away, he didn't care—and she was to move in."

Her voice grew fainter, farther away, and Kristin had to press the receiver to her ear. "Yes," she said, holding onto Matt's hand. "Go on, Myra, I'm here."

"I'd been thinking," Myra said, "and I'd been reading about divorce laws, trying to find out what I could. I was afraid to go to a lawyer and start asking questions. Not yet, anyway. But I said I wouldn't ever divorce him, *ever*, that I refused to lose everything after all those empty years. That I had to live too! I said I'd bring everything out into the open if he tried divorcing me. And I made him an offer. The most I'd consent to, I said, was that Katherine Field be his mistress, that he spend a certain amount of time here and no more, and that we maintain our residence in Cambridge as man and wife.

"He laughed. He said it was very handsome of me but it couldn't be done. He said he'd stay here with her all the time and commute to Hollybrook, and that sooner or later the scandal would force the issue if that was the risk I wanted to take. He said the family would think less of me when they found that I was the kind of person who would put them through such a dreadful mess and that when they knew about it they would dump me. Dump me!

"I knew where he was going to meet her so I followed him. But

I didn't want to leave my car at West Beach in case, just in case, he'd see it. But I couldn't go into the cave by way of the little beach because you were there. I had the binoculars with me that I always use for bird-watching, and I saw you and Frey with *her,* so I went back the other way again. There was such a crowd, nobody noticed me. And I parked my car way behind his so he'd drive away from it, not past it. I hid in one of the little caves behind where he was until I thought she'd joined him, and then I went out and heard a little of what they were saying. The sound in there is funny, I could hear them from the passageway. He was upset because she'd kept him waiting so long, he said. And she said that Sam Potter had been with her, that she'd been talking with him."

"Myra, did he tell her the new plan was your idea, or his?"

"I don't know, dear. I'm not sure. His, I think, because she grew quite angry with him. It sounded as if he'd given it as his, as if he were actually considering how to spare me *and* keep her. He *was* afraid of the scandal, you see. He was afraid—he was always afraid—of what Jonathan would say. But she was crying and she left him . . . And I went in . . .

"He was sitting down near the opening at the water then, staring out and thinking. And suddenly I got so angry, so angry, Kris! I hit him as hard as I could with those big binoculars—I didn't even realize I'd still been holding them! Even after I'd gone back to West Beach, the strap was still over my shoulder and when I went into the cave I held them in my hand so they wouldn't fall off. I hit him and he fell over . . . And then I thought how simple it would be if he died, if he drowned there. Then no one would know, and there'd never be any scandal, and I'd at least have the family if I'd never had anything else. So I straightened him out with his head down, and I left him as the tide was rising higher and higher . . . And I went home . . .

"But you found him, of course . . . I was glad—and I was sorry. And then I took a syringe from Dr. Amaral—I knew about that doctor in New Hampshire because *I'd* gone to him once when we spent summers there. I thought, Katherine Field's at the hospital, she'll see him again, she'll take care of him, and I couldn't bear it,

Kris! Not anymore . . . And when he came to, and said her name, and she was standing there—

"So I put the air in his vein, in the catheter. I did it three times . . . to be sure . . . It hurt him so terribly, he suffered so! His face was so twisted in agony! But at that moment I was glad because that's how *I*'d felt inside, for thirty-five years . . .

"It was hard to put the flint in. *I* found it—it had fallen off when Graham was in the horse show, and I put it in my purse. Everyone was so busy and I couldn't get it back up, it was too high, so I put it in my purse for later. And when he was taken to the hospital I thought it would serve him right if I killed him with it! I didn't know I could be so angry, Kris, so terribly terribly angry that I'd want to kill the man I loved. That I *could* kill him . . . That I *would.* So I began asking everyone to look for it but I had it all the time.

"So, after I was sure he was dead I pushed it into him, hard! I knew they'd let the Potter boy go eventually, but if I kept saying I couldn't find it, they'd think he had, because he said it was his. And he'd had the fight with Graham before the show, and he'd been at the beach . . .

"I had to take the panties away, and those books, the ones he used to read to try and find out what was the matter with him. I didn't want any trace to remind me . . .

"I couldn't even cry . . . until now . . ."

"Oh, Myra, Myra, please come home." The tears were rolling fast down her cheeks, and Matt wiped them away tenderly.

"Then," Myra continued as if she hadn't heard, "then when you said the police were coming again, and you were so quiet and unhappy, I knew you must have figured it all out . . . everything . . . So I took Graham's ashes, I said to Jonathan that the casket upset you, dear, and I left Dandie . . . I left . . ."

"Myra, where did you go? Where have you been all this time?"

"I went to the barbecue. I cooked. I fed the children. It was—so lovely. So much fun . . ."

She paused and they heard a gurgling sound as she swallowed something and coughed.

"Good heavens," she said. "This whiskey's so strong! I bought some because I was cold . . . Oh, Kris dear, I'm so tired. So tired . . ."

"Myra, where are you? Tell me where you are and I'll come and get you and take you home. You have to rest. You've got to rest!"

"Yes, I will. I love you, Kris. You've been such a comfort. You're right. I'll rest now."

A little click, and silence.

Chapter XX

At dawn they took bread and butter, brandy, and a large thermos of coffee from his apartment and went out to continue the search.

"Are you still going through the motions, Matt? Do you really think we'll find her?"

"We'll find her. And yes, I'm going through the motions. But my conscience is still clear—on all counts. Is yours?"

"Yes, damn you! I told you that before. But—I have to go back. I must. Only . . ."

"Only what? Only *what*, Kristin?"

"It's what I've tried and tried to say. It took three years for my marriage to break up. It began long before the accident, I know that. But even if I start only from there, it took twenty-six thousand hours to fall apart completely. And then, forty hours after John left, I met you. Twenty-four hours later I began to think about you. Forty-eight hours later I knew that I loved you. In about three one-thousandths of the time it took for one marriage to break up I was thinking about another one! You made it very clear that you were ready. It scared me—I actually worked out the time, it scared me so much. How good could my judgment be in that short a time? How good could yours be? I've been caught in the middle of a horrible mess. How good would anyone's judgment be in a mess like this? It wouldn't be so hard if I were sure that compromise with John wasn't worth the effort anymore . . . or if I'd met you and loved you long ago and knew now that you'd always been part of me, as I know now you always will be, my dear, my very dear . . . if I could know for certain whether I'm fleeing to you or coming freely to you . . . that's why it's so hard."

"Would it have happened if Weiden had been here?" he said bitterly. "Would I have had even this much?" He had given up. Or very nearly.

"He wasn't here, Matt. And that isn't a cop-out either. I'm not equivocating. It's the way it was. And is. It's all part of a unity—I've been saying it all week. Everything was connected. Everything was part of everything else. There are no ifs. Not that kind, not any kind. Nothing could have been added or left out or changed in any way. Not my loving you. Not even this terrible feeling that I *have* to go back. Not even losing that silly raffle. The only thing that doesn't seem to fit is hurting you . . . and being *so* unsure of leaving you. But if it had meant anything less to you—"

"And you?"

"Yes, and me, I wouldn't be here now, and you wouldn't either."

"And we wouldn't feel the way we do."

"No."

"Then the unity isn't complete yet! It *isn't* over yet! There's still something missing, Kristin."

"Yes. But don't let's talk about it anymore, not now. Let's go have coffee on East Beach and watch the sun come up. And then—go on."

"All right. But one thing, Kristin. About that unity. When Sam and Polly get married, then what? I've been part of that family all my life, my darling. The ties between us will include you. What will you do then?"

"I haven't thought that far ahead. I can't, Matt. Not yet."

"She's going to tell him in six months."

"I know. When I'm sure, when I've been able to decide, I'll tell you."

"Is that a promise?"

"Yes."

"There's a chance?"

"I don't know yet. I'll tell you then. The day they tell us they're going to be married. Give me that much time. And then one way and another the unity will be—completed."

The air was chill and fragrant, the water calm, and the red limb of the sun was just rising over the ocean's edge.

"It's so lovely. So still. Everything's getting ready," she said.

"Tide's slack now." He laced the cups with brandy. "It'll start to make soon."

"I wonder what it'll bring in. Did you ever find any treasures, Matt?"

"You. I checked. You came on a rising tide." He leaned over and kissed her. "And you'll leave on a rising tide, my love. We won't make it easy for you, the island and I."

She smiled sadly. "You're very poetic. But if it were going the other way, it would be even harder for me. I'd be pushing against it all the way. I will be anyhow . . . But what did you check the tides for? That's the second time you've mentioned them. Is there a special reason?"

"Yes. I think so. We'll know soon."

"Why? What's the matter? Is there something you haven't told me?"

"Only a feeling, a hunch. Remember you asked me if I were going to put a tracer on the phones?"

"Yes, and I'm still wondering why you didn't. We could have found Myra hours ago."

"I'm sure we could have."

"Then why—?"

"Because *she* needed time."

"Matt! Time for what? Time to do what?"

He put an arm about her and drew her close. "Time to decide what she wanted to do, darling. Time to choose whether she wanted to live—or die."

"Oh, Matt, no! Why? Why did you?"

"Because it was her right, Kristin. *Her* right. No matter what she did, no matter what anyone does, they have the right to make that choice. I've been a cop for almost twenty years, Kristin, I've seen it all. I've seen what happened to people who went through what she'd have to go through if she were picked up and sent to prison.

I studied theory in college, I've seen it all in real life, not just in the books. Would you have wanted her to suffer even more? You think I'm playing God. It would be true, I *would* be, if I tried to interfere, to take over her life—or what was left of it—if I took the steps I could have taken to put her through the wringer. Well, I did that once, when I was young and innocent and thought I knew better than the poor bastard I ferreted out and brought in, He had a gun to his temple—and everybody thought it was great, how I'd prevented him from committing the crime of self-murder so that the State could kill him legally! In the courts, in prison, in the press—especially in the press!—as well as in the chair! I never forgot that, Kristin. I learned one of the great lessons of my life—as a cop, as a man—from what happened to that guy and his family. And I damn near cracked up learning it. And I promised myself that in similar situations, I'd never do it again. Never.

"I won't pretend that *we* didn't need time. I won't say that had nothing to do with it. But I'd set my precedent a long time ago, and if you hadn't been here I'd have done the same thing. And I'll do it again. Do you understand?"

"Yes . . . I think I do. I always have believed that, really. I even said something like it to Kathy the first time we talked—here. But I didn't apply it to Myra. Will there—will there be any flak?" She hugged him protectively.

"For me? No. Nobody but the press would thank me—*nobody* from Jonathan all the way up—for doing anything else, although they'll never say so. I'm sorry, darling. I didn't want to tell you yet."

"You think she's dead?"

"I think so. Come on. There's something I have to do now. There's something I want to see. It isn't very far away."

They left the car at the end of the old wagon track, went carefully down the steep path between the oily leaves of the poison ivy to the little beach at the foot of the headland, and walked along the shore to the pile of great rocks under the crumbling cliff. The water curled gently and musically about the smaller stones and she stopped for a moment to watch and listen. She shivered.

"Cold?"

"I was just thinking. How different it was last Sunday when Frey called me over here. The water was rougher then . . . It seems a hundred years ago."

"I wish it were. A hundred years of unbroken time." He took her hand and helped her over the stones into the narrow passage.

It was dark and damp, its sandy floor still marked by Myra Barstow's footprints. Silently, sorrowfully, they looked down at them and followed them to one of the caves in which she had spent her last hours resting, preparing to act upon her final choice. On the cool sand lay her handbag, an empty whiskey bottle, and two empty vials bearing the label of the village pharmacy.

"Sleeping pills and alcohol," he said softly. "The scotch alone would have done it. One of these is yours."

"Doc Vernon gave me a prescription so I could sleep when my feet were hurting. I only took two or three. They didn't help, and then I didn't need them. I thought she'd been taking them all week. I guess she did, a few, because she did sleep, I know that. But she must have saved most of them. Oh, Matt, how sad. How terribly sad. She was planning it all along."

"Are you surprised?"

"No, not really. When I think back, I realize she said several things that are very clear now. It wouldn't have been consistent with everything she was if she'd come home. She was a very private person. And if she hadn't done it here, she would have found a way to do it later."

"I think so. Let's look in the other cave." He took her hand again and led the way.

Through the opening they saw the waves dance and sparkle and the water slapping in against the rocks as the tide slowly began to rise. There were a few pieces of wood lying about and she recognized them and picked them up.

"This is part of the casket, Matt. Graham's ashes—"

He took the sodden sticks from her as she shuddered violently, and steered her through the passageway and out into the warmth of the rising sun.

They sat on the sand and talked while they finished the coffee and brandy, but she was still shaking when Lee Williams summoned him to his car telephone to say that a lobsterman had hauled Myra's body aboard and was coming in to harbor.

"Do you think she knew what would happen, Matt?"

"She knew the tides too, darling." He took her into his arms as she began to cry.

Myra had known, of course, and planned her last hours accordingly. She began to take the pills and the whiskey when she called Kristin, and she took the rest in the damp cold cave shortly afterward when she was too groggy and exhausted even to vomit them up. And then, almost unable to stand, she carried Graham's ashes into the cave that faced the ocean and lay down close to the opening to sleep, knowing that the inexorable tide would soon lift her heavy body up and bear it out and batter it relentlessly against the rocks.

The old car was in line for the noon boat and Kristin had twenty minutes to wait. She leaned over the railing to stare at the water and then went down to the strip of beach and walked slowly away from the noisy crowd.

It had not been easy, after seeing Myra's body and returning to Matt's apartment, to prevail upon him to stay away from the ferry. "I can't let you go, my darling," he had said brokenly. "How sure is sure? How sure can anyone be? If you found someone who told you that he was one hundred per cent sure what you ought to do, would you believe him? Would you have to find someone else to tell you *he* was sure the first one was right? Life gives no guarantees of anything, only educated guesses based on observable evidence—yes, and things we *can't* see, things we can only feel, infer—but again, infer from observable evidence. No, Kristin, no! I can't let you go. I won't!"

But he had given up at last. He had even agreed to leave her outside Sam's house, to let her go in alone.

Sam and Polly were delighted to stay home. "We'll be seeing you soon anyway," they had said, unconscious of everything but their own bliss. So she had said good-by to them and the old ladies, and she had called Dr. Vernon and Steve and Charlotte Black and Joe

Amaral to say good-by again, and then she had driven away, grateful to be by herself.

She sat down on the warm dry sand and watched the boat's slow approach. It blew two cheerful blasts as it came nearer, and its passengers began to wave and shout to people waiting ashore. As the movement on the wharf quickened and the air was charged with the familiar tension, she got up and walked back, head down, feet dragging, like a prisoner weighted with chains.

"Kristin!"

She stopped, took a step forward, stopped again.

He was on the sand near the wharf, and the white shepherd stood beside him holding the end of his leash in his mouth, waiting. If the three of them were going to meet once more, she would have to take the next step. The option was hers. They had come as far as they could, and for the last time.

He was still in jeans and jersey shirt, his thick dark hair ruffled by the wind, looking like any holiday-maker yet like no one else in the world. A big man, whose solidity and strength and natural elegance were no more apparent in the bold planes of his face and the architecture of his body than in all he had shown her of the man within. A graceful man. A man of grace, she thought, staring at him across the sand, seeing him entire.

Capo dropped his leash. He barked, once, and his head came up imperiously. Deep-chested, hind legs well back, thick tail tapering gracefully to a little forked tip that touched the ground, he gave promise of a nobility and beauty exceptional in even this finest of breeds. But he was not wagging his tail now or resorting to a puppy's wiles. There was a "Fish or cut bait!" look on his face. He was issuing an order.

Suspended, detached, alone yet in no sense isolate, she stood gazing at them, her ears closed to the noise beyond them, her eyes unblinking in the bright sunlight: seeing in every particular of the man and the dog a mirror image magically reversed of the paltry life she was bent on retrieving; hearing at last in Polly's words the perfect consonance of five other very different voices.

"A compulsive lady like you," the girl had said. And so had the marriage counselor, and John, Matt, Joe, and Charlotte Black. Exasperation, warning, rejection, anguish, acceptance, amusement—different notes on one theme, her overriding quality of stubbornness, her inability to let go. Talk about unity!

How could she have been so deaf, so blind? How fair was she to leave here withholding for someone else a commitment that he clearly did not want? How honestly did she want to make it, when the very thought of it was pulling her apart? Where was the sense of trapping him and herself in a fruitless search for something that had long since withered away, to the bitter acknowledgment of both? And how could she square her anger for him with her conviction that people had the right to make their own choices and the obligation to deal with their own problems in their own way? His way, and his own anger, had made him cruel, but god knows he had been consistent. Why had she kept insisting that he change? Because *she* thought they'd be happier if he did? Well, he did not want to change —never mind what his reasons were, they were *his* reasons—and she could not live with him as he was. Nor he with her—and with her more subtle kind of cruelty. How could she have been so blind!

All at once her anger and despair melted like ice, not in the hot sun but in that blazing moment when many threads fuse into one clear pattern. A moment that comes only when it will come.

She heard the gulls crying overhead, she heard the noise on the wharf. Could she go anywhere else to find what she needed, when all that anyone could want, when all that people need and search for—love, freely given, freely taken—was here? Could she be any more sure after six months than she was now after six days? Must they lose six priceless months, or more, while she examined her heart for a certainty already there?

Released from her great burden, exhilarated, she laughed joyfully through her tears. "Yes, *sir!*" she said, running lightly to them, and he could see in her eyes, in the whole of her, the answer to his last question.

"Capo—I—he has a new tag," he said unsteadily. "I had it made. It'll last a long time, Kristin. As long as we live. The unity's complete now."

On one side of the large thick disc of sterling silver was the name Capo, and on the other *Sempre Constante*.

Her tears mingled with his as she kissed him. "And together. Always, Matt, always," she whispered. "Starting now. Starting with my going on that boat. What I have to do, I can't do here. But it will be my first step on the way back to you, darling, and when I come, I'll come freely. I'll be free."

"You are already. Now. Finally." He kissed her and held her away from him a little, and through his tears came a mischievous gleam. "But it's a shame you have to be so damn legal."

She laughed again. "You remember everything, don't you. But would a detective's wife make it any other way?"

"No," he said. "Not this one's," and hugged her until she gasped for breath.

Capo picked up the end of his leash and nudged her with his cold wet nose. "You're a bossy type," she said, taking the leather loop out of his mouth and slipping it over her left wrist. "I've got my marching orders, Matt. It's time to go. But we'll be back—when it's time to come back."

She kissed him again, and then she and Capo walked away together.